Romancing the Stones

Praise for Catherine Berlin's *Romancing the Stones*

Rating: 4 Stars, Sultry "From the very beginning I was completely hooked on this story. ...The story definitely had suspense and wasn't one the those where you can easily figure out who the bad guy is and with a touch of paranormal that makes you wonder what is really going on here. I loved it."

~ *Karen, Ecataromance.com*

Rating: 5 Angels "...marvelously entertaining romantic suspense with a paranormal twist. ...The whole story beginning to end is very well done and I hope there will be some kind of sequel. ...If you want to read an intriguing romantic suspense with a paranormal twist, you will enjoy this one!"

~ *Stephanie B., Fallen Angel Reviews*

"I had a wonderful time reading this book. ...The book was wonderfully warm and sensual. The sexual tension between the main characters was a palpable thing. The mysteries in the book make you sit there and go hmm, as you try and figure them out. The progression of the story was natural and there is a twist you just don't see coming. All in all, this is a wonderful story."

~ *Dawn Epton, Paranormal Romance*

Rating: 4.5 Nymphs "an unexpected, but happy treasure. Ms. Berlin has done a wonderful job juggling all aspects of this well-written but complicated tale...romance, suspense, history, myth, murder, and enough twists and turns to keep you guessing until the very end. The characters are intriguing, the pace quick and lively, and the overall story entertaining; leaving you with the desire to read more about these people and what happens after the book ends."

~ *Mystical Nymph, Literary Nymph Reviews*

"...I enjoyed the story and its hints of magic, and twist with the bad guys kept me guessing. Overall I enjoyed the book and recommend it as a good read."

~ *Suzi Booth, Erotic Romance Writers*

Romancing the Stones

Catherine Berlin

A Samhain Publishing, Ltd. publication.

Samhain Publishing, Ltd.
577 Mulberry Street, Suite 1520
Macon, GA 31201
www.samhainpublishing.com

Romancing the Stones

Print ISBN: 978-1-60504-308-1
Digital ISBN: 1-60504-137-8

Editing by Deborah Nemeth
Cover by Natalie Winters

First Samhain Publishing, Ltd. electronic publication: August 2008
First Samhain Publishing, Ltd. print publication: June 2009

Dedication

Dedicated to my sweet, handsome husband, Bob.

Chapter One

Detective Vaiden stared at the shattered edges of the weathered oak door on the Blair residence. It hung sideways with the top hinge completely disconnected from the jamb. Split wood fanned out along the lock like plumes. The boards covering the windows kept the inside of the house dim even though it was late morning. Not a sound floated outside on the cool air to give him a clue about the condition of the home's occupant, Charlie Blair.

Rob Vaiden drew his SIG Sauer, holding it to his chest just below his jaw. He exchanged a wary glance with his partner, Jarod Ronan. They had wanted to be in and out of here as fast as possible. The investigation was dragging out. Too many false leads. But by the looks of the door, things had changed. So much for asking the homeowner a few questions.

With a nod directed more to himself than to his partner, Vaiden nudged the door inward, then shoved hard with his shoulder. He held his position and motioned Jarod inside. Jarod entered just ahead of him and crossed the room to check for intruders.

A huge black creature streaked out of the shadows near the staircase, rumbled past Vaiden, and escaped to the front yard. Vaiden blew air out quietly, calming his breathing. Just a dog.

He stared at the disarray. A small mountain of papers and

books littered the center of the room. The drawers of the file cabinet hung open at varying degrees. The desk nearby had been rummaged to the point of destruction.

Jarod stepped into Vaiden's line of vision and shook his blond head. No one on the ground floor then.

Vaiden moved toward the stairs. "Call it in. I'll check the second floor."

As his foot landed on the first step, he heard the sound of running water. A thief who showers in the victim's home, he mused. That was a new one. He'd be surprised if anyone could hear him above the roaring water, but still, as he eased upward, he kept toward the wall-edge of the stairs to avoid telltale squeaks.

The bathroom door stood slightly ajar. A sliver of bright light marked the hallway floor. Vaiden swallowed. Please let this be a simple robbery, rather than more of Orion's handiwork. He didn't want to find another dismembered body.

Ever.

"Mr. Blair? Police officer. Are you all right?" Vaiden pushed open the door and stepped inside with his gun held out shoulder height. Ugly orange and brown tile, floor to ceiling. He could've fit two normal-sized bathrooms into this one.

"Mr. Blair?" He moved to the shower, closed his eyes for only a second, and whipped back the plastic curtain.

An empty bath, with the water running full blast. The musky scent of strawberries, soap, and steam. But no sign of an occupant. It didn't make sense—until he heard the door close.

He made a note to check behind the door next time.

"Throw the gun into the tub and put your hands up."

Vaiden scrunched his brows together. A woman? That

explained the strawberry scent, anyway. He hesitated, then placed his weapon carefully into the shallow end of the tub, switching off the water with his free hand. He wasn't worried. Hell, Jarod was right downstairs if he needed him. Given the right distraction, Vaiden knew he could take her down, with or without the weapon.

He straightened, turned his head, and froze.

She was naked. And wet. And pointing a Glock at his chest.

"There must be some mistake," he said, wondering why his voice had gone thin. "I'm—"

"I don't give a rat's foot who you are. And turn around!" Her cheeks were bright red, and he couldn't help but notice that the flush extended down her graceful neck and across her breasts.

"Now!" Her eyes flashed.

He couldn't tell if she was embarrassed or angry. But he'd take a perp like this any day. He followed her orders and looked away smiling. He might not be able to see her, but her naked image was burned onto a screen inside his head. Average height, medium length brown hair, and curvy. Very curvy. Hell, it might be worth taking a slug just to have another look.

"Ma'am, I'm with the police department. We came here to speak to Mr. Blair, and discovered the front door had been forced open."

"A likely story. Now move around toward that wall."

He shrugged. Jarod had to have heard her shouting. He'd burst in any moment and tackle her. "Maybe you should move away from the door." He peeked at her over his shoulder. She'd slipped into a huge terrycloth robe and moved toward the window.

"Can I at least show you my ID?"

She frowned, staring at his shoes, but when he inched his

upper body forward, she jerked her eyes back to his face.

"I just got here twenty minutes ago. My door was in perfect condition. You're full of it."

"Vaiden? What's going on in there?"

The young woman's attention wavered for a fraction of a second. Vaiden lunged toward her, in a single motion chopping her wrists with one hand and squeezing them together. The Glock clattered to the tile floor.

Jarod swept inside, recovered her gun, and grabbed Vaiden's SIG Sauer from the shower. He looked toward Vaiden, one eyebrow raised as he dried the weapon with a towel.

Vaiden pulled her arms behind her back and cuffed her. "Good timing, partner."

She went from stunned softness to spitfire in three seconds flat. "What do you think you're doing?"

Vaiden pushed her toward the hallway, careful not to tread on the hem of the terry robe that dragged behind her.

They descended the staircase, Jarod walking in front of her. "You broke in here, wrecked the place, and threatened an officer of the law with a gun. You're under arrest, lady."

Vaiden frowned at the newly arrived uniforms milling around in his crime scene. From this side of the room he could see for the first time the coat rack that had been hidden behind the door. On it hung a well-worn black leather jacket—a woman's jacket. And a backpack-style purse.

He stopped the woman on the landing, an uneasy feeling creeping over him. "Ma'am, what's your name?"

Paler now that she had a room full of people staring at her, but still just as angry, she lifted one eyebrow and licked her top lip. "Charlie Blair."

✧

Back upstairs, this time in her bedroom, Charlie fought her growing frustration. A female officer handed Charlie the clothes she'd requested from her backpack. For six months she'd been looking forward to wearing something besides jeans and work shirts. Back in the country less than a day and already her bad luck had caught up to her.

She shoved her way into the pair of dirty jeans and a tee shirt smeared with Peruvian mud, and scowled at the officer. "I still don't see why I can't get my clothes from the closet. I highly doubt any evidence is in my Levi's."

The woman shrugged. "Nobody touches anything until Forensics clears the house."

"Forensics? What the—What do you people think went on here?" Charlie dusted off the legs of her jeans and gave the officer a pointed stare.

"I can't really say, ma'am. It's all part of an ongoing murder investigation." The officer looked anywhere but at Charlie.

"Murder? Here?" Charlie tucked in her shirt, then jerked it back out. "These people are insane. My house has been shut tight for months." A quick glance at the officer told her that the woman was doing her best to ignore her mutterings.

The officer cleared her throat. "We're wasting time. Let's get this over with."

Charlie rolled her eyes. Yet another person questioning her presence in her own house. As much as Charlie had wanted to explain, she hadn't wanted to do it wearing just her bathrobe. It was bad enough that Vaiden character had kept staring at her on the stairs. Maybe some more cotton between his eyes and her skin would help him forget what he'd seen.

Her face heated. She knew she wouldn't forget.

She had stepped out of the first hot shower she'd had in ages, and frozen in place. The house hadn't felt right. First the voices, then the squeaky stair. She'd nearly tried to climb out of the window. But before her trip, she'd left her daddy's gun tucked behind a loose board inside the linen closet. Without thinking further she'd grabbed the Glock and hidden behind the door.

Only, once she saw the man enter and took in his size and power, she'd realized she might have been better off with her first choice.

The officer coughed and Charlie hurried to fasten her dusty jeans. She grimaced at the dirt-encrusted boots she'd retrieved from the hallway. That was where she drew the line. They may want her to leave their supposed crime scene untouched, but for heaven's sakes, it was her house! She had to have real shoes. Before the officer could protest, she opened her closet door and knelt to retrieve her Reeboks. She glanced over her shoulder as she shoved her sockless feet into the cold white leather.

The officer rolled her eyes and waved her over. "Let's get down there and straighten this out."

Charlie nodded and started out of the room. "Absolutely. I want you and your guys out of my—" As they descended the stairs, her gaze centered on him immediately. He had a stylus in one hand and a palm device in the other. But his eyes were focused on her.

She forced herself to ignore Detective Vaiden, instead taking in the devastation that was once her orderly living room. Twenty minutes—thirty now, she corrected herself after glancing at the wall clock—and her comfortable old home had been torn apart. Her frustration changed to anger.

"What the hell did you guys do?"

"This is how we found it," the detective answered, his voice echoing outside of her perception as the enormity of the destruction hit her.

A gasp escaped her. Months of work, in some cases years of work, carefully organized and stored away—destroyed! She reminded herself to breathe.

Her files full of site notes had been torn apart. She bit her bottom lip, wishing she'd put everything on computer.

From her place midway on the stairs she spied her artifact trays, upended near the cabinet that housed them, and started to move toward them, catching herself before her female escort could restrain her. The aged sheen on the banister scraped off beneath the assault of her nails as she gripped it. Next semester's graduate students were going to be busy as hell fixing the disorganization. If it could be fixed at all. Hell, what if whoever had done this had stolen something?

She narrowed her eyes and frowned. This seemed like something that jerk student she'd had to send home two weeks early might have pulled. Erik Walker had been a pain in the ass from day one. He'd known when he signed up for the semester abroad that the site would be run by a woman, but somehow he had it in his head that Charlie would defer to his masculinity. What little there was. She smirked. What a screw up.

It looked like his threats against her might have been real. He had said he'd "mess her shit up". Somehow this wasn't what she thought he'd meant.

He must have figured out he was still going to get an F in the course, no matter how much he threatened her with his rich family. Charlie rolled her eyes. No matter how much money he had, she had more. She just hid it better.

Charlie pushed her still damp hair out of her eyes. Her skin felt stretched thin, more taut than it should be from the soap she'd used. She hadn't even had a chance to use the lotion she'd splurged on at the airport. With an envious glance at the perfectly made-up female officer, she made her way down the rest of steps. She frowned, gauging what she must look like by the disdain she read in Vaiden's gaze when he approached.

He met her as she stepped off the last stair.

"Gonna cuff me again, Officer?" Her voice dripped with sarcasm.

He shifted, not meeting her eyes. "No need. We've verified that this is your place." He leaned an elbow on the banister. "But you say you've only been here"—he checked his watch—"an hour or less. And the door was fine when you arrived?"

She waited, watching his mouth. She'd seen this little game on TV detective shows. No way was she gonna start chattering and end up in trouble for something she may or may not have done. If this were a customs issue, they'd have stopped her at the airport. Nothing else she'd done would be an arrestable offense.

His lips turned down at the corners. "Miss Blair—"

"Dr. Blair." She held back a smirk when his dark lashed eyes squinted at her.

"Medical?"

"Anthropology."

He tilted his head to the side. "Interesting." He tapped the stylus on the screen of his PDA. "So where were you before you came home this morning?"

She backed up the stairs a bit and sat on the third step, since he clearly wasn't going to let her pass. "I've been on airplanes for the last twenty-two hours. I'm exhausted. And some nutcase broke into my house while I was in the shower and wrecked years of research." She took a shaky breath. "Can you just tell me why you were here to start with?"

"Vaiden?" The man she assumed was Vaiden's partner, tall and skinny with a military-style buzzcut, waved at them with a notepad.

She twisted her neck left and right to work out a crick from sleeping sitting up from Houston to Richmond. Vaiden surprised her by pulling her along with him to the other side of the large open room.

When they reached him, Buzzcut spoke to her. "Mind unlocking this?"

She stared past his crossed arms at the door to her basement. Two silver padlocks hung on awkwardly attached hasps, keeping the door firmly closed.

She thought hard. "No, I don't remember those being there." She half-turned, thinking to check the packet of correspondence from the real estate agent. "Maybe something happened while I was gone and they..." She looked at the papers strewn across the floor. "But, no, I can't think of any reason why the real estate company who was in charge in my absence would have put locks on the basement."

Vaiden and Buzzcut shared a look she interpreted as half fear, half anticipation. "I'll get someone to dust. You get the bolt cutters." Vaiden scratched his cheek before pointing to Charlie. "Go sit on the stairs and don't even think about trying to leave."

Charlie sighed. Screw him. Let them figure out on their own that this was simple vandalism by a punk student. It was like being eight years old again in time-out. Of course, the stairs where she'd had to sit and think about her actions as a child had been behind a cabinet, not in view of a crowd of police folk.

Too tired to protest, she obeyed.

She hoped this wouldn't take long. She had people to see.

The dean, for one, would be waiting to hear her news. And he wasn't going to like what she had to report. She'd lost the gold rod of Manco Copac, the single most important find to come out of the university digs in decades. The dean would want her strung up, or at least fired. She still had a few minutes to decide just how she was going to tell him.

And Harold. She planned to surprise him this evening at work. What a sweetheart. He'd managed to write her three whole letters while she was gone these past six months. Why she'd ever accepted his marriage proposal before she left the States was beyond her.

✧

Vaiden rolled his eyes heavenward. The woman was no help at all. If she stayed awake another ten minutes, he would be surprised. He hadn't noticed the circles of exhaustion beneath her eyes when he found her in the bathroom.

But then, he hadn't exactly been focusing on her face.

"Ready?"

Vaiden moved aside to allow an officer access to the locks. Once the hasps were unscrewed from the doorjamb and bagged, Vaiden licked his bottom lip and drew his gun. The room might be locked from his side, but the basement windows were unsecured.

As the wooden door swung open, both he and Jarod turned away in disgust. Air thick with the odor of decay rushed upward. Vaiden scrunched his nose. Shaking his head, he stepped forward onto the landing. His eyes watered and automatically he grabbed a finger full of menthol rub from the small jar in Jarod's outstretched hand. Just a dab below his nose would at least cut the smell. Even if it couldn't hide it.

Jarod shined a flashlight on the wall to find a switch, which he flicked to illuminate the basement. Afraid to open his mouth and let the stench inside, Vaiden signaled with his eyes and moved lower on the stairs, his gun held in front of his body.

The bottom step faced a cinderblock wall. The room lay directly to the right and back beneath the house. He noted the waist-high tables lining the far wall. Tools hung from nails inserted in a sheet of plywood. Someone had carefully outlined each one with black marker.

As Vaiden neared the tables, the rotten copper smell grew stronger and he traded his gun in favor of his handkerchief. The menthol rub didn't help any longer. Whatever was in hidden in the room waiting for discovery reeked of death.

Below the first table were stacked two wooden crates. Under the second table, one more. On the rear wall stood a large white freezer. It hummed loudly, and the smell of the failing coil mixed in with the rot.

Jarod tapped his shoulder and gestured to the concrete floor. The bottom crate sat surrounded by viscous black liquid. Trevor Harrison, from Forensics, swabbed the ooze and added drops from his kit. He frowned and nodded grimly. Blood was definitely present. Damn.

Trevor stood back, took a few photos, and then gestured to two of the officers. The men stepped forward and, after sliding the table out of the way, unstacked the crates. The lid to the top crate wasn't attached and came away easily. Sawdust, tissue paper, and straw lined the bottom, as though someone had used it to ship antiques.

One of the men grunted when they tried to lift the lid of the bottom crate. Vaiden tilted his head and looked at it closely. Nailed shut.

While they waited for someone to bring in a crowbar, lights were brought down and set up, lending the basement a weird feel. While the brightness cleared away the shadows near the crates, it created deeper shadows away from them.

As one of the CSIs positioned himself with a crowbar, waiting for a signal to begin, Vaiden held his breath. That blood oozing from the bottom of the crate could mean anything. Even a rat squashed beneath it by accident. Just because there were crates, and Orion had often left his victims to die inside similar crates, that didn't mean this would be another victim. Orion liked to pierce his victim's blood vessels and allow them to bleed to death from painful incisions. Just because blood had pooled near this crate didn't mean...

Who was he kidding?

He swallowed back foamy bile as the crate lid came away with a screech of resistant nails. The odor of rot increased tenfold and he pressed his handkerchief tighter against his face. He hated the scent of death. Once inhaled, it never left the nostrils.

As one, the group of men hunched shoulders and fought against inhaling. There was a body inside all right. But she'd been there a while.

Trevor shook his head slowly. "Everybody out until Jack gets here." Jack was with the medical examiner's office. He'd probably been called the moment they'd spotted the leaking crate.

Vaiden's brief glance revealed long feminine hair. The victim's eyes were wide, and the corneas had turned milky white. He wasn't interested in seeing the burst blisters of flesh, or the stew of body juice in the bottom of the crate. His focus was drawn to the lid. The interior had deep gouges, stained deep brown with blood.

The woman had been alive when she was put inside.

Frustration made him turn away from the gore. Orion had to be stopped. And Vaiden knew only one way. He had to find him.

He sent two officers to check the rest of the basement and headed upstairs. Better to let Harrison's people get what they needed. The rest would come soon enough.

He exited the basement and continued through to the front yard, glad for a breath of fresh air.

Moments later Jarod came to stand beside him. "That whole place was sealed tight. Rubber strips along the only two windows, and sheets of thick plastic lining the door. The old coal chute looks like it was bricked up years ago."

"Explains why the smell stayed below." He turned back toward the house. Charlie Blair had followed them outside. She stared at him, brows raised, eyes wide. "I can't tell you anything."

Jarod eyed him curiously and Vaiden realized she hadn't spoken.

"What did you find down there?" She'd found a rubber band somewhere and secured her shoulder length hair in a knot at the nape of her neck. She still looked homeless. Especially in the filthy clothes she'd donned. She tapped one foot and he drew his gaze back to her face.

"This is officially a crime scene, Dr. Blair. I'm afraid you'll need to find somewhere else to stay for at least a few days."

"Crime scene? I haven't even had time to take the boards off the windows, and you're telling me I can't stay in my own house? What the hell did he do?"

"He?"

Charlie Blair sighed and waved one hand through the air.

"Before the semester was over I had a student removed from the dig site. He said he'd get even. I'm guessing this was his idea of revenge."

"When did he return?"

"A few weeks ago. Why?"

Vaiden doubted her temperamental student had time to slaughter a victim. Orion had been active in town over the past few months, not just the past few weeks. And given that the killer wasn't new to this, any college student of Dr. Blair's would be too young. "What's his name?"

"Erik Walker. Erik with a *k*. He's just a junior. I never should have approved his application for the trip. His family had made a major donation, and the administration put a little pressure on me to..." She broke off and stared back at the house, then at him. "What exactly did you find down there? What's taking them so long?"

"We need to check the whole place out, top to basement. I'm sorry."

She sighed again, this time running her fingers through her hair. She turned and scanned the front of the house again, as if looking for an explanation.

Vaiden had noticed the boarded windows when he and Jarod had arrived. "You had the windows boarded up. Why?"

"When you're gonna be gone for six months, it's a good idea to make things as secure as you can. Apparently I didn't do such a good job."

She crossed one foot over the other and dropped to the ground, landing in a seated position. One fluid movement, very graceful. She looked tired. And mad. He frowned.

The arrival of a vehicle from the morgue drew her attention and her jaw dropped. She still had no idea what they'd found in her house. No idea that at least one young woman had been tortured and killed in her basement. He wished she could be spared the horror.

"Why did you come here?"

Her voice, a bare whisper, was addressed to Jarod, but Vaiden answered. "We needed your permission to get access to a rental house on Lormar Street. Your name is listed as the owner."

She shrugged. "Why not get a warrant?"

"We were working on a hunch."

She pushed to her feet. "Can I go now? I mean, you know where I've been. You know where I work. I'm too damn tired to go far."

She'd suddenly checked out, he could see it. She was closing off her mind to whatever had happened. It was a safe way for her to deal with her emotions, he knew, but eventually they would catch up with her.

He fell into step behind her as she entered the house. Jarod stayed outside. "We verified your story, so if you've given your statement, and we can reach you, yes. You'll find another place to stay for a few days?"

She scooped up her small purse-sized pack from the coat rack and slid it onto her shoulders. "Great. I don't suppose I can have my gun back?"

Her hopeful smile made him laugh out loud.

"No, hmm? Okay." She rubbed her eyebrows, sighed, and walked away.

He waved to the perimeter officer as she approached the tape. As she was allowed to pass, it occurred to him that she hadn't asked about her dog. His smile faded. The dog could wait. Trevor Harrison would need him downstairs.

Even knowing the futility of such a gesture, he said a small prayer asking for this to be anything but more of Orion's slow rampage.

Whatever Orion did to his victims before they died, he took his time. In the past, they'd been found in abandoned refrigerators or freezers. This time Orion was leaving the bodies inside crates. But the method of murder was the same. An almost medical destruction of veins at precise points, points that assured the victim would bleed to death, followed by chemical torture to the wound sites, and live burial. Actually, more like live entombment, since the bodies were all recovered above ground, in abandoned houses.

Ten years ago Orion had killed four women before they'd arrested anyone for the murders. It had only taken him a few months to rack up that tally. Now it appeared a new round of victims had been lined up.

This woman made three.

✧

Charlie crossed the residential street, picking up her pace as she passed the elementary school. Hardly anyone was out on the sidewalks. Despite the crisp air, the sun still reflected brightly off the cement. She shivered, but not from the chill in the air.

The city at night was not particularly safe to travel by car, much less by foot. Daylight didn't make it any safer, just easier to see the danger. The neighborhood she would have to cross to get to the university housed drug dealers and tough looking characters. She always walked fast and walked strong, and kept her eyes focused ahead while her brain registered what happened around her.

Of the rental houses her parents had left her in their will, she'd chosen to live in the one most convenient to her job. Still, a few houses on the block had been boarded up over the years. An open invitation to crime. She should just move farther away, but she'd never believed anything terrible would happen in her own house.

At first she'd wondered what the cops had found in her basement. Then she'd seen a man with "coroner" printed on his jacket. There was a dead person in her house? That had ended her curiosity. Whatever had happened, it didn't have anything to do with her. She'd been gone for too long. She was happy to work with remains from hundreds or thousands of years past, but present day? Forget it. She couldn't watch a gory horror movie without gagging.

She paused to fish her pocket watch from the purse pack. She was late. The dean would be waiting, if only because she hadn't yet told him her last email had been sent in haste. Dr. Fisher would just have to understand. About being late anyway. As to the missing gold rod, well, maybe he wouldn't fire her.

Five blocks from the university she passed a cellular phone store. She had to remember to get one of those things. Maybe one of the graduate students could program it for her. Her DVD player back at the house still blinked twelve o'clock just like the day she'd brought it home from the university's holiday white elephant party two years ago. Or, she thought, it had last time she'd seen it.

A hand zipped across her face, yanking her from her thoughts. Thick, round fingers closed over her chin and mouth, filling her nostrils with the scent of grease. The abrupt pain to her neck threw her off balance, and she crashed into a solid force.

Charlie twisted, stomped on the attacker's instep, and

jabbed an elbow into his ribs. He released her, giving her a quick glimpse of his face before he grabbed her by both arms and wrestled her into a nearby alley.

The idiot was wearing pantyhose over his head. Charlie held in a chuckle. Must be an amateur. Two hours in the Andes, and he'd be crying like a baby.

"Gimme the bag."

Charlie hesitated, trying to drag her focus from the bizarre things the hose did to the man's lips as he spoke. "I don't have anything you'd want."

"Just gimme the bag!" Hoseman cut his eyes toward the end of the alley.

Charlie removed her bag from her shoulders and swung it gingerly at Hoseman's head. He grabbed it and pulled the top open, stretching the drawstring wide. He lifted a handful of black stones from the bottom of the bag and shook them at her.

"Where is it?"

"I haven't been to the bank. Sorry to inconvenience you."

Hoseman's face pinched together in anger. He slammed the bag to the ground and reached for her.

She slid lower on the wall to avoid his hands. The rough bricks bruised her back and elbows. She sidestepped him, gaining her footing.

He swiped at her a second time. She seized his forearm in her hand, using his own force to propel him past her into the wall.

During the moment of opportunity she rushed toward the street. She had a brief sense of falling and then the air whooshed from her lungs as she hit the cobblestones. She rolled onto her back. Hoseman had one of her ankles in his fat paws. She could only see the top of his head. Black hair?

Brown? It was impossible to tell with his disguise.

Charlie closed her eyes and kicked upward with her other foot. Her toes stung and pain shot through the tendons, but Hoseman dropped.

Breathing heavily through her nose, Charlie scrambled to her feet and found her backpack purse. She gathered the Ica stones, counting to be sure she had all twelve, including the one in her pocket, which she transferred to the bag. Hoseman stirred and she high-tailed it to the street, swinging the bag around behind her.

And then it was gone.

Her jaw dropped. She paused in shock, considering the possibility that she was still asleep on the plane and having the worst dream of her life. She turned to see a skinny youth, this one with no silly head-covering, cruising west on foot with her bag.

Still working on borrowed adrenaline, Charlie narrowed her eyes. "Oh, no you didn't."

Chapter Two

"Thanks, Bill." Charlie smiled across the high counter at the campus policeman.

The boy had been easy to run down. She had the advantage of breathing thin air for the last six months. She could've run for miles. The kid had nearly soiled himself when she'd grabbed his shoulder and spun him around. Even now he was muttering about suing her for attacking him.

Bill LePrade smirked at the boy's mutterings, but grew serious as he escorted the young male to the small holding room to wait for the city cops. He returned to the front shortly, and Charlie slid a sheet of paper toward his meaty fingers.

"Good enough?" She watched him scan her statement rapidly.

"Yup. I'll send an alert about the other guy, but really, with that scanty description..." He tucked the paper into a folder and slapped it onto the lower level of his desk. "I'll call Dean Fisher and let him know you're running behind."

Charlie squinted at the clock over his head. "Understatement." She pressed her lips together to keep from mentioning the happenings at her house. In all likelihood he'd heard the reports over his radio anyway. She wondered why he didn't ask, but she was three hours late as it was. No need to dwell on good fortune.

✧

Dr. Fisher's low-ceilinged office opened toward the corner of the hall. With his door unlatched, he could view human traffic in three different directions, including anyone who emerged from the stairwell. For this reason Charlie wasn't surprised to hear him already in mid-sentence when she finally entered the room.

His lips flapped open and closed from the moment his tirade began. The drone of his voice raised higher and higher, his words becoming more intelligible with each step closer she took.

"...time it is?" He rubbed at the skin near the top of his forehead. All of his features moved as one unit, shoved along with the wrinkles he adjusted.

Charlie ducked her head, both to appear repentant and to hide the smile the sight of his toupee always brought her. She had respect for the man, because of his position of authority, but if she were hiring men for a dig, Dean Fisher would be out of luck. "Sorry, sir. I've had a bit of a rough morning."

Dr. Fisher scowled, giving her filthy clothes a once over. "Looks it." He turned his back on her and arranged himself at his desk, giving Charlie no choice but to walk deeper into his lair.

She'd admired his office for years, all dark wood, covered with artifacts and memorabilia. Dr. Fisher had awed her as an undergrad, until she realized most of his tokens were the result of clever shopping and the hard work of others.

Now, as an associate professor, she found herself uncomfortable with the way her work in Peru brought him more honor within the anthropology department. It was up to her to do the grunt work, and his job was to take the glory. She knew that was how it worked. And when it came down to it, she loved being in the field. But it still stung to see the occasional artifact on display with Dr. Fisher's name attached to it instead of her own.

"Don't keep me in suspense." Dr. Fisher spread his hands wide, as if waiting for her to pass him an Easter basket. Perspiration beaded on his top lip. "Show me the rod."

Charlie exhaled. "I don't have it."

The dean squinted, flattening his palms on his blotter. "Didn't bring it?"

"Good thing, too. Someone tried to steal my pack this morning. Twice actually..." She trailed off, foregoing the lengthy explanation she'd prepared. The dean paled and she was certain he wouldn't have heard her anyway.

She waited while he eased himself back in the squeaky wood chair. He rolled backward until the wheels hit the baseboard, then opened his mouth to speak twice before he managed to utter actual morphemes. "Where is the rod? Somewhere safe?"

Charlie had never mastered the art of the poker face. The dean must know from her expression that she'd managed to lose the single most important artifact to come out of the university dig near Cuzco in three years. Best to 'fess up.

"We left it in the cave for ten, fifteen minutes, max. When I dropped back down with the right equipment, it was gone. In the spot where the rod had been were these." She slipped her purse from her back and placed the Ica stones on Dr. Fisher's desk.

"You left the golden rod of Manco Copac? An artifact from the dawn of Incan civilization. You left it alone?" The dean's color returned rapidly, turning his ears a frightening purple-red.

"Dr. Fisher, I was injured from the fall. I didn't even go for proper stitches—I had the guide field-stitch my arm." She shoved her sleeve up, intending to show the ragged line from the healing cut, but Dean Fisher's disapproving eyes didn't leave her own.

Charlie lifted her shoulders in a gesture of defeat. "I don't know how anyone could have taken it. There weren't any exits or entrances except the one I made when I fell through the ground. Everyone was accounted for."

Dr. Fisher clenched his jaws so tight Charlie feared for his dentures. "You send me an email with a photo of the rod. You tell me what you've found, and now you tell me it's gone? And you brought these—these worthless stones?"

"I wouldn't say worthless. Ica stones are reported to be—"

"A hoax, Dr. Blair. You and I both know the most recent study shows that Ica stones are not worth the rock they are carved from. You may as well have grabbed a handful of stones from someone's driveway."

The dean shoved his window open, grabbed the stones and threw them outside. "That is what I think of your Ica stones, Charlie."

She grimaced and exhaustion draped her shoulders again. She didn't care that a farmer had admitted to faking some of the first Ica stones discovered. She knew these were real.

The stones, each the approximate diameter of a half dollar, bore ancient carvings incised into the black bacteria-created coating. Finding the Ica stones in the cave was a discovery in itself. Unfortunately, it had come at the cost of the golden rod.

Charlie spread her arms. "When we go back next semester, we'll center our search on the area of the cave-in. If there's any truth to be found about the rod and the Inca creation myth, we'll find it."

Charlie had heard the tales since she was a youngster. Her father's journals detailed his research on the creation stories among villagers he'd spoken with in Peru. The Inca believed that their sun god had sent down his son and daughter to the mountain of the rainbow. When the siblings found the ideal spot, they plunged a golden phallus into the fertile ground, and thus the world sprang forth.

As an adult, Charlie had seen the myth as a metaphor for the sexual act—plunging phallus, fertile mound—it had all made sense to her.

Her father, on the other hand, had always believed the myth literally. And now she knew he'd been right. Crazy as it sounded. The golden rod of Manco Copac was real. She'd just lost it. But she'd touched it. She knew she hadn't dreamed it. Next year she would go back. She had the coordinates. With the right equipment, the artifact could be recovered.

"No, Charlie. Next semester we'll let a different member of the faculty have a go. This...just reeks of a recklessness and irresponsibility I cannot condone. I have to wonder if you hadn't been so focused on discrediting a fine student like Mr. Walker, you might have been able to retrieve the artifact. The board doesn't meet again until next month, but if I were you, I would get my résumé in order."

Charlie blinked. Well, she had expected his reaction to be severe. But she damn well knew she shouldn't be fired. That sexist pig of a student had been long gone when she and Hernandez went looking for the rod of Manco Copac.

Searching for the rod hadn't been on the dig schedule. She'd done the university a favor by looking for it. She should be commended for getting the Ica stones out. Going back down into a collapsing hole in the ground while blood seeped out of her forearm and water trickled in from some unknown spring—she could have been killed. She'd barely gotten herself and the stones out before the wet earth caved in and buried the whole cavern.

Résumé indeed.

She exited his office and rounded the building. Once on the side where the dean's office overlooked, she counted windows and crossed the grass. On hands and knees she gathered eleven Ica stones and dropped them into her purse. The twelfth eluded her. She frowned. Next to the one of the wolf-like creature, the one of the jaguar had been her favorite.

She sighed. Perhaps she would be able to find it in the morning after she'd had some decent sleep and a shower. Someone might stumble across the stone in the meantime, but she doubted it. Not likely that anyone would notice a small black stone in the four-inch grass so far off the pathway.

She would prove to Dean Fisher, and to the scientific community, that her father's life research hadn't been the waste everyone considered it.

Checking her watch, she ticked off time in her head. If she hurried, she could get a new outfit, visit the hair salon, and still have time to drop in on Harold at the car dealership. If there was enough time, she'd love an hour-long bubble bath, a pedicure...but she simply couldn't spare herself the luxury. After the police, the muggers, and her angry boss, seeing her fiancé for the first time in six months would be the bright spot in her day. She hoped.

✧

Two hours later, still dog-tired but more than pleased with her lighter, bouncier hair, Charlie stopped to adjust the strap on her new black heels. Hooker heels, her students called them.

She bent carefully, tucking a stray lock of hair behind one ear so she could see what she was doing. She'd never owned a pair of heels with straps that wrapped her ankles, but the saleswoman had assured her that they made her own husband crazy.

Charlie straightened and smoothed the fabric on her skirt. The black scrap of material came to an abrupt end three inches above her knees. The soft shirt she'd matched with it tied in the back. One accidental move and her whole outfit would explode.

She liked a little element of uncertainty.

As a whole, she decided, the outfit was sexy. Not Grace-Street-lady-of-the-evening sexy, but girl-next-door-who-might-just-leave-her-window-shades-up-a-few-inches-for-the-neighbor-boy sexy. She wondered if Harold would be pleased.

He didn't get excited about much. She frowned. He'd taken everything in their relationship slowly, even reacting with complacency when she'd taken her position at the university. One they both knew by its nature meant long periods of separation.

Surely this outfit would wake him up. Start a fire somewhere. Because by the heavens, if kissing him still felt like kissing a mackerel, she was going to have to break it off.

The car dealership Harold had inherited from his father spread across half a block of Broad Street. Lucky for Charlie the city buses made regular stops nearby. She didn't think she'd have made the trek in the new shoes. Appeal or not, they pinched the dickens out of her smallest toes.

The sales force milled in the parking lot eating hot dogs provided by a local radio station doing a promo appearance. She cruised right through the wide glass doors of the dealership. The fan on Harold's receptionist's desk oscillated, whipping paperwork into a frenzy beneath a large paperweight.

Maybe she should turn around now. Call Harold on the phone. Break it off.

No, she might feel something this time when she saw him. Please, God, let her feel something.

Shrugging, Charlie slapped her palm against Harold's office door and turned the knob with her other hand.

Harold was leaning butt-naked over the edge of his desk. No, not totally naked. His pants were around his ankles. What the hell was he doing?

His pants were around his ankles?

With a zing, realization dawned. Harold—cold, easygoing Harold—was having sex. With a woman. On his desk.

After staring a frightening moment too long at his pale rear end, Charlie closed her eyes and quietly stormed back to the showroom floor.

He'd screwed around on her. The man who'd called himself a slave to her love. She wanted to laugh. She wanted to dance. She was free, and damn, it felt good.

She vaguely heard the office door slam. She definitely heard Harold calling her name as he frog-stepped to catch up with her while yanking his trousers closed.

"Charlie? That is you!"

She wiped the laughter from her mouth and cocked her head sideways as he rounded her shoulder and stopped directly in front of her. "You don't even recognize me now?"

Harold glanced toward an older gentleman looking through the front window. The man was frozen in shock. Harold covered his bare chest uncomfortably.

Charlie rolled her eyes. “Do I even want to know what’s going on?”

“You didn’t get my last letter?” Harold reached for a suit jacket left on the back of a chair and slid his sweaty arms into the sleeves, holding the lapels together.

“Last letter? You barely sent me any letters.” Charlie’s face heated. “I guess it’s good I found out about your penchant for workplace rendezvous before I got invested in this—”

“I got married, Charlie.”

She’d expected him to say anything but that. It was one thing to screw around on your fiancée with some floozy, but screwing around on your fiancée with your wife was where Charlie drew the line.

Suddenly wishing she’d kept her dig clothes on, instead of splurging on the sexy outfit that was beginning to feel quite slutty, Charlie restrained the bubble of laughter wanting to burst forth from her throat. Instead, she wiggled off the diamond ring Harold had given her before she’d boarded the plane for Peru.

She reached out, took hold of his flailing belt and yanked his pants forward. Not daring a downward glance, she dropped the ring down to be with the rest of his family jewels. “Next time, Harold, lock the door.”

✧

Vaiden checked his watch for the third time in ten minutes. He tapped the top of his shoe with his fingers. The seats in the waiting area were entirely too deep.

The real estate office handling Charlie Blair’s rental houses took up the middle floor of a tri-level building in downtown

Richmond. From the outside, the structure resembled a castle. Inside it needed a hell of a lot of work. He hoped they kept the rentals in better shape than their office space.

The wooden floor sloped gently upward toward an area rug near the far wall where a receptionist fanned herself with his warrant. She looked up, caught him staring, and winked. He might have smiled back, but then she used two red nails to remove a cherry pit from her mouth. It was the second cherry she'd eaten since he'd arrived. Rather than throw the vile thing in the trashcan, she opened a drawer of her desk and plunked it inside. Maybe she was growing trees in there.

Vaiden exhaled. She'd told him her boss had gone home early. He would wait a few minutes out of courtesy, but frankly he was losing patience. He needed those records now, and he didn't need to get the man's approval.

A rhythmic ca-lomp noise from the stairwell distracted him and he leaned his hands on his knees to peer toward the entrance. From his position behind the ficus he was hidden from the woman who entered the room and swayed to the desk.

Vaiden angled his head slightly sideways. Nice body. Skirt short enough to make him want her to drop a pencil. He wondered what would happen if someone untied the little bow in the back of the skin-tight shirt hugging her small waist.

Papers shuffled and something small fell to the floor with a tap.

Thank you.

The babe in the skirt bent her knees and scooped up the fallen item, then handed it to the receptionist. The skirt rode up just enough to give him a healthy glance of her thighs. He smoothed his sweating palms on his knees. She probably had a face like a dog.

He slammed a hand through his hair and rubbed his

forehead. He needed sleep. He was getting punchy.

When he opened his eyes, the woman had turned. She waited expectantly, one hand on a hip, the other dangling a familiar backpack purse.

He squinted. "Dr. Blair?" Holy cow. Last he'd seen her she'd looked like a homeless woman in those filthy clothes. His eyes widened. She cleaned up nice.

"You looking for me?" The sexy twist of her mouth reminded him of his first encounter with her.

Vaiden blinked away the image of her wet naked body and cleared his throat. For the first time in his decade-long career words wouldn't come.

The receptionist tugged at Charlie's elbow and handed her the warrant. She spared it a glance, but she didn't read it. "Wanna save me the trouble?"

Vaiden pushed himself up from the sunken leather couch. "We need the records for your rental houses. Alexa here called her boss, but he doesn't seem to be responding."

Charlie licked her full lips and smiled at Alexa. "Burn him a copy onto a CD."

Then she stepped closer to him.

He held his breath. Nice, nothing. The woman was hot.

"Shouldn't be more than five minutes." Her stomach growled and she blushed beautifully.

"Thank you." He put his hands in his pockets. "You eaten?"

She sighed, her chest moving up and down lightly with the effort.

His eyes were drawn to her breasts. He ignored the bolt of desire that shot through his loins and forced himself to focus on her pale green eyes. Had she answered him yet?

"Not since the airline pretzels, no."

She left him, spoke quickly with Alexa, and returned. He blinked. She looked almost as good moving away as she did coming back. "Tell you what, you help me find a place to stay tonight, and I'll cook for you."

His mouth curved in amusement. It had been a long time since a woman had offered to cook for him, and this one barely knew him. Alexa handed a CD to Charlie, which she tapped against his tie. He found the irresistible action endearing, like a kitten pretending to be a tiger.

"What do you say?"

"Shame to waste an outfit like that. Let me take you to dinner. I'll make some calls and find you a place by the time we're done." More time in Charlie Blair's company was probably a bad idea. He hoped she would say yes.

"Sounds like a plan." She winked. "Better than the cold sandwiches I was gonna provide, anyway."

He followed her down the stairs and led the way to his car, a grey Toyota Camry. Brushing against those magnificent breasts, he opened the door for her. "Oh, before I forget again, when we were at your house this morning, your dog got out. I hope he'll be okay. I have the officers there looking out for him in case he comes back."

She shook her head. "Detective, I don't have a dog."

Chapter Three

The absolute only time Charlie ever enjoyed the taste of coffee was when it came disguised as tiramisu. If she ever had to face a firing squad, tiramisu would be her last request.

Her eyes fluttered closed as the first taste hit her tongue and exploded across her taste buds. She didn't bother to contain the audible sigh that hummed out after she swallowed.

Another four bites and she scrabbled together some control of her manners. She wasn't alone, after all.

Vaiden stared at her, his left eyebrow slightly elevated, his lips parted. "Been a long time, hmm?"

She slid the fork from her mouth upside down, then unable to resist, allowed her tongue to trace the center tine. "You have no idea."

Vaiden coughed and shifted restlessly in his chair.

Charlie glanced over his shoulder. "I think they must be waiting for us." When he turned to see who she was referring to, she scraped the small plate with the tip of her index finger and slipped it into her mouth. The only three people left in the restaurant, their waiter and two kitchen employees, straightened. The waiter tossed his hands upward in relief.

Vaiden turned just as Charlie slid the digit from her mouth. The instant heat in his gaze made her laugh nervously.

She buried the offending hand in her cloth napkin and smiled. “Sorry.” She indicated his own untouched dessert. “Aren’t you going to eat yours?”

“I think if we take any longer, these guys are going to kick us out.” While there were advantages to eating in restaurants that welcomed cops, he couldn’t expect their tolerance to last beyond closing time.

Vaiden rose, dragged three bills from his wallet, and left them in a perfectly aligned pile in the center of the table. “Let’s get out of here. Midnight’s probably their limit.”

How had it gotten so late, so fast? Charlie grabbed her purse and followed him to the lobby, bumping into his back when he stopped short at the door.

She peeked around his frame. Rain. Buckets of it. When she moved to his side, the waiter appeared at her elbow, jangling keys.

“Wait here. I’ll get the car.” Vaiden spoke toward her high-heeled shoes. She lifted one foot and chuckled as his eyes followed the line of her leg. Definitely hooker shoes.

“Nonsense. It’s just two blocks. I won’t melt.” She reached for the door, scrunching her face as first the mist, then the pelting drops, cooled her skin.

Vaiden grunted and took her hand and elbow, propelling her down the sidewalk toward the car. Ten feet from the vehicle he beeped the locks open and they both scrambled inside.

A drip of rain ran down her forehead and off her nose. She turned toward Vaiden, who stared at her again, the keys suspended over the ignition. He squinted and his mouth worked to keep from speaking.

Charlie tilted her head to the side. She still didn’t know where she was staying tonight. “Where are we going?” The sentence echoed, despite the pounding rain on the roof of the car.

"There's a hotel a few blocks away. Their rooms are—"

"Hold it, Detective."

He looked up sharply at the hand she'd placed on his forearm.

Removing her hand, she licked a raindrop from her lips, and laughed softly. "Look at me."

He smiled at her sideways, his face dissolving momentarily from serious cop to rakish schoolboy.

Her stomach did a little flip-flop.

She crossed her arms over her midriff and clenched her fingers. What the heck was that? She focused her eyes on the dashboard, then back at Vaiden. Wild butterflies stirred in her belly.

"If I walk into a hotel dressed like this, no luggage, and soaking wet to boot, they're gonna think I'm turning tricks."

"So what do you suggest?"

With a quick exhale, Charlie answered him, embarrassed by the words before they formed. "I could come to your place, wash my clothes, and then get out of your hair."

She coughed and hurried to explain. "Hell, I could even sleep on your couch. I'll be gone first thing in the morning. You'll hardly know I'm there." She could see him considering the idea. Perhaps she needed to give him an extra assurance. "And I won't even try to seduce you." She grinned awkwardly, thinking maybe she'd gone too far. The seduction comment had just slipped out.

Vaiden blinked once, then inserted the key and started the engine. "You sure that's what you want to do?" His hand paused on the gearshift. "Sleep on the couch?"

She nodded, wondering what had made her say something

so brazen. He was a hunk, true, and there seemed to be a little chemistry going on, but no way in hell would he go for someone like her. And she didn't have time for someone like him. It was too stupid to contemplate. She'd just wash her clothes, get some sleep, and get on with her life.

"Absolutely."

✧

Vaiden listened, trying to discern what had jolted him from his sleep. His sheets draped across his abdomen, and a sheen of perspiration coated his skin. He closed one eye and moved his head from side to side, trying to determine if he'd turned the ceiling fan on before he got into bed.

He stopped. There it was. That noise again. Faint enough to be vague.

He swung his legs over the side of the mattress and yanked on a pair of sweatpants. He considered whether to take his weapon from the nightstand. He shut his fist. Most likely it was just Charlie watching TV. He swept a hand through his hair and headed down anyway.

The carpeted stairs hid the sound of his footfalls. The wall where light from the TV should have been reflected was bathed in darkness. He moved the blinds on the front window apart—his motion detector light hadn't been triggered. Maybe the noise was just a dream. He crept toward the back of the couch.

Charlie lay stretched out, one smooth leg bent at the knee for balance. She wore one of his old college football jerseys. It dwarfed her, the neckline bagging open to show him more skin than he had permission to view.

Careful not to graze her with his fingers, he tugged the

sheet high on her shoulders. She snuggled into the cushion and sighed.

Vaiden wavered. She was here because she believed she would be safe.

He pushed himself away from the couch, back toward the kitchen, so he could no longer see her. Remove the temptress from vision, remove the temptation.

Charlie's first day back in the States topped his worst day easy. She never asked about the body in her house. But he hadn't had time to consider why not. Not that he could have enlightened her if she had asked.

He'd had a hard time maintaining his cool in the restaurant when she, laughing, told him about her two assailants. No one had that much bad luck without there being something more to it. If keeping her close meant he might just solve Orion's reappearance after an absence of ten years, then he would do it, whether she accepted his company or not.

Of course, that was half the problem. How was he supposed to maintain a professional distance when she was so damn pretty?

He opened the refrigerator, sniffed the milk, then took a long drink. He hadn't heard anything but his own breathing for minutes. Satisfied that he'd only been awakened by a dream, he started back toward the stairs. He adjusted the thermostat as he passed. And then he heard it again. The noise of the vent blowing open almost hid the scratching sound. Claws to metal.

Vaiden marched directly to the front door and, after turning the lock, opened it.

Other than a slight fog from the remnants of the earlier rain, his yard was vacant. He knelt and ran his hand over the kickplate. Nothing. It was clean.

As he stood, he caught sight of a depression in the mud

next to the stoop. With a cautious glance toward the still empty lawn in front of the house, he placed one foot on the cool cement. The motion sensor finally activated the light over the door. He leaned closer, placing his fingers gently over the smooth wet dirt.

A paw print. And it was warm.

✧

Charlie jerked awake and popped into a sitting position with a gasp. One hand on her chest, she blinked the sleep from her eyes and glanced around the room. Paper-thin sheets of light streamed in from the windows on one side of the dwelling, while blue darkness still hugged the opposite windows.

The faint scent of spice hung in the air. Vaiden. This was his house. She'd slept on his couch. Charlie breathed deeper and exhaled slowly. Today was going to be better.

Or else.

Tentatively, she swung her legs around and touched her bare toes to the Berber carpet. She drew her feet back, disliking the rough snaggy surface. The refrigerator issued a snapping noise from the kitchen, spurring her to remove herself from the warm cozy confines of Vaiden's couch.

Her scandalous clothes lay neatly folded on the beige easy chair. She chuckled. Last night Vaiden had frowned at the way she'd left the outfit crumpled on the floor near her makeshift bed. He'd folded the clothes himself without comment.

She'd fallen asleep before the dryer buzzed to let her know her jeans were dry. She'd be willing to bet Vaiden had them folded somewhere too.

Her freshly chilled skin warmed as she thought of Vaiden.

He lay sleeping somewhere very close. She could almost feel his presence. She smiled, wondering if he'd folded his own clothes as neatly. Before her mind could drift any further toward Vaiden's personal habits, she climbed the stairs.

She found the bathroom just off to the left. Her eyes widened at the size of it. This was a bath for a king. Ceramic tile—or was it real stone?—covered floors and walls. A small chaise decorated one side. The bath and shower occupied a glassed chamber that encompassed half of the space. She deposited her clothes on the double sink counter and crossed the room.

She opened the translucent door and peeked inside. No need for a swimming pool. The huge tub served as a bath and a Jacuzzi. She smiled. It was big enough for a whole family.

Charlie wasted no time. She turned on the hot water and slid into the grey marble tub, backing up to one of the air jets as soon as the water was deep enough.

A set of bottles stood along one edge of the tub. Charlie reached for the larger one, which turned out to be shampoo. She wet her hair, then lathered the mass and rinsed it by submerging her whole body.

A glance at her wrinkling fingers told her she'd been in the water long enough. She found the plug and let the water drain.

She wrapped one of Vaiden's thick Egyptian cotton towels loosely around her torso and squeezed water from her hair with another. When it was as dry as she could get it without a blow dryer, she tossed the towel into the corner hamper and looked around for something to tame her tresses.

No brushes lay on the counter. Charlie didn't want to root through Vaiden's drawers so she turned her head upside down and plunged her fingers into her hair. One of her fingernails tore as she raked them through to comb it.

She stood straight and licked her finger. She'd been unable to keep her nails long in Peru and she'd hoped she could actually grow them out. She squinted at the nail. Couldn't be saved. She had a pair of nail clippers and a file in her purse, but of course she'd left the pack below.

She tugged the towel tighter and whipped open the door to sneak quickly downstairs, but she collided with Vaiden. Trying to grab her towel and right herself at the same time, she landed squarely against his bare chest, clutching at his shoulders. His long fingers nearly spanned her waist as he caught her, surprise showing plainly on his face.

Charlie's mouth hung open as she gazed up at him. Her breath, stolen by shock, prevented her from speaking. She could only stare at his lips, which were just short of too full for a face like his. But damned sexy.

"Oops." She blinked. "I—I need my purse." Her voice had gone husky. She may as well have said I want you here and now. She licked her lips, suddenly at a loss for words as her mouth went dry.

Vaiden looked as if he were going to ask her something, but instead angled his head toward hers and kissed her.

The sudden onslaught of desire floored her.

If she'd thought breathing was difficult before, she now knew what it was truly like to have her breath taken. Her fingers dug into the hot skin on his shoulders and she leaned upward, opening her mouth to deepen the kiss.

Vaiden stepped toward her, propelling her with measured care into the bathroom without breaking contact. Her feet barely met the floor. Cool stone touched the skin on her back and she pulled apart from him, straining for control over her spinning emotions.

She followed his line of vision and realized her towel had all but dropped in front. She pressed closer to hide her breasts from view. The sensation of her nipples against his hard chest made them tighten, sending another wave of need through her body. She drew in a ragged breath and let her eyes close. To hell with modesty.

Vaiden growled low in his throat and twisted her to the side. She gasped as she found the chaise directly behind her legs. He eased her down onto the smooth cushion and kneeled beside her. She wondered if the floor hurt his knees, but the moment of concern flew out of her head as he bent to take one nipple into his mouth. He drew on her breast while his hand kneaded the other, rolling the peak between his fingers.

Charlie's eyes closed and she chewed her bottom lip to keep from making noise. Her back arched and she gave in to the need, unwilling to stop the unbelievable waves of heat sweeping through her. The heavenly sensations rocketing through her body were unlike any she'd felt before. If she cried out, would it ruin the moment? Would he stop? His free hand slipped between her legs then and she shrieked.

But Vaiden didn't stop—rather he stroked her until she moaned without considering his reaction at all. He brought her quickly to a climax, covering her mouth with his lips and swallowing her scream of pleasure.

Charlie wanted him then. All of him. Her body, sated for the first time in her limited experience, needed him. Only him.

She took his arm, drawing his body down toward her again. The weight of him above her was the only thing that would satisfy her.

Instead of accepting her offering, he reached for her cheek and stroked a thumb over her lips. He placed a kiss at the corner of her mouth and closed his eyes.

When he opened them, she could tell that inside he'd

pulled away, despite the proximity of their bodies. Her cheeks flaming with embarrassment at his rejection and her own forwardness, Charlie pushed past him and stood. She abandoned the towel and, without looking back, she left the room, closing the door behind her.

✧

At nine o'clock, Vaiden entered the Selkie's Den, a tiny restaurant Jarod had discovered when he'd first moved to Richmond three years ago. Jarod claimed he liked the place for its name, but Vaiden figured it was more for a particular pencil-thin waitress who always lavished them with attention.

"Usual?" Ruthie swung her ebony ponytail off her shoulder and grinned at Vaiden from the other side of the counter.

He nodded and moved toward the far table by the front window. Sliding into the booth seat opposite Jarod, he shook two packets of sugar. Just as he tore them open, a coffee mug appeared. Ruthie, efficient and predictable, poured only half a cup, leaving a small pitcher of creamer behind.

Jarod pulled his gaze from Ruthie's retreating backside and concentrated on cutting a round sausage pattie into eight perfect triangles. "What did you do with her?"

The cream pitcher slipped from Vaiden's hand and he caught it, righting the container before the liquid spilled. Not what he'd wanted to do with her.

He couldn't believe he'd almost taken Charlie right there in the bathroom. He'd behaved like an animal. One touch of her bare skin against him and his control had snapped. And she'd been so damn responsive; she'd loved everything he'd done to her.

It had been the hardest thing he'd done, maybe ever, stopping himself from climbing between her sweet thighs. She wanted him. Wouldn't have told him to stop. And he wouldn't have until he'd—but she was part of his investigation, and he had to distance himself. If he'd made love to her...

Jarod was staring at him.

He swallowed and then added cream to his mug, bringing the liquid within a half-inch of the rim. He pushed the image of her leaving the room stark naked from his mind. "I put a tail on her."

"You considering her a suspect then?"

"No. Her story checks out. Besides, she was out of the country with her family ten years back."

Ruthie placed a plate of toast on the table, butter and jelly on the side. "You boys been MIA for a few mornings. I was starting to wonder if you'd left me for another woman."

She directed her comment at his partner. Jarod tried hard to busy himself flipping papers in his stack of folders near the salt and pepper shakers.

Vaiden kicked him and turned to Ruthie. "Of course not. Best toast this side of the James."

"Hmm." Ruthie pursed her lips and waited a beat longer for Jarod to look up. When he didn't, she pushed the check to the center of the table.

He would have to have a talk with Jarod when this case got off the front burner. Ruthie clearly shared his unspoken crush. The man was either blind or stupid.

Jarod lifted his head, sending Vaiden a frown. "Ten years back?"

Vaiden sighed. "That's when Orion was active. When I joined the department they were in the midst of the investigation. Four vics, all female—same MO as our guy." He squeezed the tiny paper cup that held the scoop of butter, then spread it across his toast. He jutted his chin toward the files. "It's in there somewhere."

"Yeah, I haven't read through it all yet. Had a big test." Jarod was taking science classes three nights a week to earn credits toward a forensics certification. Vaiden was all for his partner bettering himself, but sometimes he resented having to pull Jarod's weight. Especially when it put people in Orion's path.

The case needed six detectives, not two, and not one covering for his partner. The women who'd fallen victim, or would fall victim, to this guy deserved better.

Vaiden gritted his teeth and then sipped his coffee. When he smeared the jelly on his toast, the knife went through the bread. He dropped it onto the plate. "We never arrested anybody for the murders, but about a year after the case went cold, some whack job in for assault copped to the killings. He knew facts that hadn't been released, so we thought we had our guy."

"Then what, you think this new perp is a copycat?" Jarod reached for his wallet and pulled out two bills, placing them on top of the check.

"Don't know. Our guy, Elwin Kent, got stabbed in a prison fight two days later. His DNA matched on one vic, inconclusive on the others." He chewed his toast, wishing his stomach could handle the eggs and sausage Jarod downed daily. They smelled like heaven, but one plate of that stuff and he'd be hell to deal with the rest of the day. Heavy food tended to stick in his chest like he'd swallowed a tennis ball.

Vaiden cleared his throat and took a sip of water to wash down the toast. "The women were never really connected, not that we found. True, they all lived near the university, but that was it. Different majors, different part-time jobs, different lifestyles." He scratched his ear. "I don't know. And now that these new killings are so damned similar to those others—" He balled his fists. "If it's not the same guy, then it's got to be someone who knows a hell of a lot more than they should."

Jarod pushed the check closer to the edge of the table. "Any ID yet on the body?"

Vaiden shook his head without lifting his face. He fought the nausea that rose at the memory of the rotting body in Charlie's basement. Somewhere there was a family who didn't know yet. Someone's mother was wondering where her daughter was. He hated this. This guy had to be caught.

Jarod leaned sideways in the booth, catching Ruthie's eye before turning back to Vaiden. "This vic yesterday was number three. Last time there were four. You think we've got another one out there we haven't found?"

"I'd hoped not. But there's the Charlie factor now."

"So you're having her followed because?" Jarod pulled his files closer, tapping them into a neater pile.

"Charlie—Charlotte Blair was attacked yesterday. Once by a street thug, a kid, and once by a pro who was after something specific. I think this guy, Orion, or whatever he's calling himself this time, could've been that pro. The first two women we found? Both were mugged a week before their times of death."

Jarod rolled his eyes and stuffed two pieces of sausage into his mouth. "If every woman who got mugged around here turned up dead, the morgues would be overflowing."

"I know." Vaiden balled up his napkin and tossed it on the table. "It's just a hunch. We've gotta work every angle we have."

Jarod shook his head. "I promise, Vaiden, I'm gonna be with you on this. I just have one more big test, and then I'm all yours."

Vaiden sucked down the rest of his coffee and wiped his mouth. “It’s under control, Jay. Don’t sweat it.”

✧

Charlie approached the clerk at Blair Storage with as much dignity as she could muster, given that she was wearing her tight shirt from the night before and had left her panties in Vaiden’s bathroom. She’d been too embarrassed to go back upstairs after their encounter, and her other shirt had come through the wash nearly as muddy as before.

Yesterday in her new outfit she’d felt sexy in a classy sort of way—at least, until the rain. But the second day of wear lent the blouse a certain air of trashiness, especially paired with the loose jeans that she fought to keep from creeping. The lack of underwear didn’t help.

No way was she buying new clothes when she had perfectly good ones locked in her house, and still more here in storage. She was a woman who spent money only after careful planning and thought. Years of lean living on dig sites as a child had taught her what she could live without, and what she needed.

She smiled at the heavyset woman through the security glass and tried not to bend to speak directly into the hole used for transferring. “I need to get to my things please.” Charlie lifted a blank card from the short stack and filled in her name. Most folks kept a key of their own, but she had a knack for losing keys, and besides, she owned the place, so she figured she was entitled.

Taking the card from Charlie’s hand, the woman—her nametag spelled out *April*—grunted and flipped through the B drawer. April lifted one shoulder. “ID.”

Charlie slid her driver's license through the hole. The edges were frayed and the coating scratched almost to the point of obscuring the photo. "All I got on me," she said when April raised a brow in disdain.

She knew the moment the employee realized she was the owner because a pinkish stain grew across April's cheeks, and then spread over her entire face.

Charlie smiled pleasantly. "My key? Thank you."

She clutched the silver key in her palm, tucked her license back into her weather-beaten purse, and chuckled. Poor woman would be nervous about her job now, but she didn't have to be. It wouldn't be wise to work at a place like this and be too personable.

A prickle raced across Charlie's nape. She stopped walking and rubbed her free hand through the back of her hair as she gazed around. Just buildings and sidewalks. Locked doors and chains.

She shrugged and continued to the back of the lot, teetering a bit as she stepped on stray bits of gravel that had found their way into the sidewalk. The largest storage unit belonged to her. When she was younger, no available storage facility could store their belongings reasonably, so her father solved the problem by having this place built.

Charlie opened the cool lock, yanked it free of its chain, and entered the small side door. Amazing that no matter how many times she'd been to the storage facility, she always had trouble finding the damn switch. She fumbled for the meager light, hoping the bulb hadn't failed in her absence.

Cursing her lack of a flashlight, she managed to find the pull and tugged gently, illuminating her Jeep and the stacks of boxes and trunks that surrounded it. She was halfway through a sigh when once again she felt the urge to check outside.

Leaning against the door, she craned her head left and right, still spying no one. The faint odor of cigarette smoke wafted past and she drew back, wrinkling her nose. Tapping her thumb and forefinger together, she began to understand why her colleagues urged her to get a cell phone. If she'd had one she could have simply called April and inquired about the presence of other clients.

Satisfied for the moment that she was quite alone, Charlie closed the door firmly and locked it from the inside. She located four boxes containing her "real clothes," the ones of the non-trashy variety, and arranged them in the rear of the Jeep. As an afterthought, she jammed a canvas bag between the boxes. It might come in handy for carrying her things.

She'd stored most of her clothes during this dig, wanting to avoid another bug incident like last year. As much of a tomboy as she was, the sight of critters crawling through her dresser drawers had definitely been a problem. Hoping her clothes didn't reek too awfully of mustiness, she dug out underpants and a low-necked blouse, and shimmied into the clean clothes.

She crossed to the much larger door on the opposite side of the unit and released the locked handle, lifting with her legs. The grooves on the pulley gave her a fit, but on the third hard pull, the door rolled up and across the ceiling.

Whispering a prayer, she climbed into the driver's seat and cranked the engine.

✧

The heavy green canvas bag landed with a thwack on the floor. Charlie cocked an eyebrow. She'd been expecting a thunk, not a thwack. Bending at the waist to peer closer, she saw a small chip missing from an orange plastic seat, last in a connected row of five. The metal buckle of the army-style bag rested innocently next to the damage. Oops.

She scanned the room. The laundromat, one of the oldest in the area, was filled to capacity with a bizarre variety of customers. From the embarrassed, quiet women whose washers or dryers had broken to the loud-mouthed twice-a-week visitors, the place rolled with action.

True, she could have washed her things at Vaiden's, but she needed to get out of there. After almost begging him to make love to her, she needed distance. It was going to take a while to get her clothes done, so distance would be no problem. She would have to wait like a vulture for a washer to open up so she could try to rescue the clothes she'd taken from the storage area. They had seemed the best of the lot at the time, but now they reeked of mold.

The smell was augmented by the heavy humidity of the laundromat.

The plate glass front was completely fogged, rivulets of water streaking down, creating a small pool of condensation on the floor at that wall. The few seats that were empty of people held baskets and bags of laundry or small children, some sleeping, some playing. One such child was beating his feet against the bucket baby carrier filled with a screaming sibling on the wet floor below him. The baby had a torn tissue in one hand and a dust-bunny-covered sock in the other.

Charlie fished the tiny orange flake from the floor, thinking as she did so that one tiny bit of trash in the filthy laundromat wouldn't make a difference, but she didn't want the one thing *she* left there to be what a child found and choked on.

Once she wrangled a washer and got her clothes started, Charlie planted herself on a table next to her washer and tugged her notebook from her backpack purse. She held the dog stone in her left palm and sketched with her right. She didn't know why this stone fascinated her more than the others. Maybe because it was the most normal?

She used the small ruler on her keychain to measure the stone and the size of the markings, so that she could draw it to scale. She'd just finished her sketch when the washer stopped and she tossed everything into a dryer.

A screech from the front of the laundromat caught her attention. A woman with curlers in her hair covered by a wild blue-flowered headscarf came high-stepping into the room, hollering and swatting her kids inside. It was hard to hear over the loud noise from the machines, but Charlie got the impression that something outside had frightened her into coming in. None of the other people up front seemed bothered, so she shrugged and turned the page in her sketchbook.

She dropped down into the chipped chair and braced her ankle on the knee of her other leg to give herself somewhere to put the sketchbook. After chewing on the eraser, she realized she was being watched.

Warm, slightly grape breath blew down from her right shoulder. On all fours on the table behind her crouched a child of about four years, grape lollipop drool covering her chin. Two thick, very tight braids stood out on each side of her head, tied off with red rubber bands.

A grin spread on Charlie's face. "Hey, cutie."

The child's eyes widened and she froze like the wild guinea pigs Charlie often found in Peru. They had that naiveté that made them think if they stayed still, they were suddenly granted the power of invisibility. Charlie chuckled.

"Whatchu gwanna drawr?"

A snort escaped Charlie. "Could you take the lollipop out? I didn't get what you said."

Just the purple-stained stick emerged from the kid's mouth. "I said, 'Whatchu gwanna drawr?'"

"Not sure yet." But as she said it, Charlie knew what she wanted to draw. The dog from the stone. This time, though, she'd draw him from memory, not by staring at the stone that nestled in her pocket.

The sketch seemed to come quickly, but then pictures Charlie drew from her imagination always came easier than ones she drew from something she had in front of her. *Real* objects called for precision, but no one was going to crawl into her head and tell her that her imagination was wrong.

The grape breath faded away, and Charlie assumed the girl had gone back to help her mother. Just as she finished the sketch, the dryer buzzed and Charlie looked up. The crowd of other customers were gone. One dryer besides hers still spun, and another dryer hung open, a rag doll perched inside.

Charlie tossed the sketchbook on the folding table and stood. After a long stretch, she opened her dryer and started folding her clothes. They didn't smell much better. She wrinkled her nose. She was gonna have to buy some new ones, nothing else to be done.

She looked at the three items she'd folded and rolled her eyes. Way too messy. She grabbed the shirt from the top of the stack and refolded it, taking time to make the folds crisp.

She sighed. She was so different from the other archaeologists she met in the field. They wouldn't know it though; she hid her problem well. Her innate messiness.

It wasn't her fault she was this way. Archaeology and the deep need she had to uncover the secrets of the past were in her blood. But somehow she'd become a mix of both parents. Her father was the academic, the dreamer, who spent all his free time researching that one elusive find. Always a discovery that one had to stumble across after following clues.

Her mother, on the other hand, liked the digs. Liked the precision, the surveying, measuring, taking the earth away a fraction at a time. She had patience.

Once when Charlie was eight, she'd found the lip of a pot in the small square of earth her parents had assigned her, thinking it was well out of range of the main part of the dig. It took two days of her mother measuring, photographing, and researching before the pot could be touched again. Finally it was unearthed, but Charlie wasn't allowed to do it.

The grad student who took over the spot brought the whole floor of the quad down bit by bit, so that the pot could emerge along with anything else near it in situ. Even then, Charlie wasn't allowed to touch it. No one was. Her mother had too many tests to perform. On the surface of the pot, on the dirt inside it, near it, beneath it.

At the time Charlie had suspected that her mother didn't want her to work the square because she was afraid Charlie would break the pot, or that it was just a potsherd and she might lose any other bits of pottery in her excitement.

It was probably true, she admitted, but all the precision and exactness her mother had forced on her turned to rebellion once Charlie and her father had been separated from her.

Charlie still obeyed her mother's wishes for crisp detail and neatness at the dig sites, but at home—whether home was a tent or a brownstone—she was a slob of the worst kind. An on-purpose slob, who secretly tidied after the fact. After her mother saw the mess. And the habit stuck.

"Hey, lady, how'dyu do that?"

Beneath her elbow stood the little grape girl, clutching the rag doll from the other dryer and leaving grape fingerprints on Charlie's sketch of the dog.

"It's just a scribble." But it wasn't really. The dog looked half-Chow, half-lion, with matted fur and chipped teeth.

"That's the dawg that wuz barkin' at me and my momma outside."

✧

With her new phone in her left hand, Charlie plunked a quarter into the parking meter. Lunchtime had snuck up on her while she haggled with the cell phone salesman over rates. She didn't need three thousand minutes, for heaven's sake. She continued past the row of parallel-parked cars and entered a small sandwich shop.

Tucked into a space between empty retailers, the small shop had done a booming business for as long as she could remember. A cheap, fast lunch restaurant near a university. Not a big stretch.

Just inside the door, she caught sight of the shadow she'd noticed lurking outside while she was in the cellular store. Her head turned to allow for peeking through her bangs at the front window, she waved to the man behind the counter. "BLT, please?"

"Toasted?"

Charlie's smile warped into a half-grimace. "One side toasted, one side plain?"

The man looked up slowly, his bushy eyebrows colliding with his small white paper hat. "You again. I told you no more special orders. No mayo and ketchup mixed but on the side. No French fries with sugar instead of salt. And no half-toast sandwiches." He shook his head and turned away, sliding her ticket into a spinning order holder. "Five minutes. That's three-o-six."

The man was a grump. But he smiled and winked, and Charlie knew she'd get her order just like she'd asked.

She sat on one of the tall red-topped stools, angled to view the street, and handed the man three one-dollar bills and a dime. He dumped her four cents change into the dingy foam cup next to the register and moved to take another order.

The person who'd been following her had backed out of her peripheral vision. She tapped her nails on the counter, then remembered the phone she still held in her hand. She pushed the number for her voicemail box at the university.

After deleting fourteen messages left in the past month, she began to listen to recent bits of news. There was a message from Leonard Kedansky, a faculty member, requesting a debriefing of her trip. He led small field school expeditions, but only during the school holidays, and only to high-yield digs run by other organizations. She deleted his message. She'd see Leonard around soon enough.

The most current message had been left the previous afternoon shortly, she imagined, after she'd left the dean's office. Dean Fisher reveled in his ability to send voicemail to everyone in his department at once, and he did so at the slightest provocation. She closed one eye, preparing to hear herself disparaged to the entire faculty of the department. Instead, the dean, in a voice reminiscent of a wild boar being pursued by a predator, complained about pets in the building.

She chuckled and played it again, trying to make out more of his garbled ravings.

"...that damn dog...in the building again...stared me right down, the piece of... If I ever see him again I'll have him put to sleep..."

Charlie pressed the save message code and chewed her

bottom lip. Strange that a dog should be roaming the halls without an owner. She wondered if it had come in on its own. Students propped the doors open on a regular basis to access the labs after hours, so it wouldn't have surprised her.

A white paper bag thwacked onto the counter just beneath her nose and she jumped slightly in her seat. She mustered a scowl for the counter-man and started toward the exit. A face near the door drew back quickly and she reversed her steps.

She hurried past the man in his paper hat and into the kitchen. Not one of the three men working in the back paid her more than a quick glance. Tightening her grip on her bag, she plunged out the back door and into the alley.

To the right stood a delivery truck, effectively cutting off her escape with stacked pallets of who knows what for the furniture store on the end of the block.

The quickest path to her vehicle led left. An enormous shadow of a man blocked that end of the alley. And he was coming toward her at a rapid pace.

She jogged to the truck, wanting to get assistance, or at least witnesses, but finding no one, she realized they could be having their lunch break about now. She spared her nearing stalker another glance. He'd stopped ten yards from her. She recognized the lovely pantyhose he now dragged over his head, just as in their other encounter. She cringed. With the sun still at his back, she couldn't make out his face, with or without the disguise.

She twisted the doorknob to get back into the kitchen she'd just fled, but found it locked.

He laughed very close behind her, and the warmth from his ragged hands reached her before they touched her skin.

Chapter Four

Charlie stepped backward into her attacker, her shoulder blades brushing his chest. She reached back, gripped his forearms and thrust her spine and hips back and up, sending the man over her head and toward the brick wall next to the door.

Unfortunately she'd been too close when he grabbed her, and she hadn't had sufficient time to gauge the distance. The close-quarters factor, combined with his weight, sunk in when the man was halfway over. She retreated beneath him and he landed hard on his rear end. Her purse dropped; the contents scattered.

Her eyes flew wide and she resisted the instinct to grab her spilled bag. Her breath came rapidly. When the man's growl vibrated through her flesh, her gut tightened.

She hopped lightly on one foot and poised her other one tentatively, not sure if she should flee or try to get a better look at the creep. He didn't appear to have a weapon, but why take a risk?

She eyed the stones spilled out in the alleyway and made a note to get something better to carry them in. They might be worthless to Dean Fisher, but she knew they had to have a bigger significance. The chance to study them was well worth any hassle some freak in pantyhose was giving her.

The man on the ground groaned and she wondered if her attacker needed an ambulance. Her new cell phone was probably broken in the mud.

Hoseman's face was matted with wet dirt and leaves. She doubted he could see through the pantyhose. He reached for his own face, apparently in agreement with her. Tearing his inconsequential disguise from his head, the man pushed himself upright. His reddish-blond hair stood at odd angles, resembling bed-head.

Charlie drew back, curiosity taking over for common sense. Set deep within a weather-beaten face were two of the saddest eyes she'd seen in quite some time. And bloodshot as hell. The hands he held waist-high trembled. Grease rimmed the nail beds of his fingers; calluses covered his palms.

His mouth rolled into a sneer and his eyes snapped into ice. The moment she thought he would lunge, a shout startled them both.

"Police! Freeze! Don't touch the girl!"

Charlie swiveled her head. The stranger she'd seen near her Jeep waved his gun, almost as a hello gesture. *That* was the man she'd expected to see attacking her in the alley, not Hoseman. And he was a cop?

The man poised to grab her instead turned toward the delivery truck. Seeing no way around it, he took a step she had to admire. He scrambled up the short hood and over the top, his tan work boots leaving smeared prints along the metal. Hoseman was gone before the smaller man reached her side.

Charlie rolled her eyes at the young man, maybe younger than herself. How much could happen to one woman? How many people were following her? "Now who the hell are you?"

"Officer Caine. Just wait here, I've gotta call the detective."

He was either nervous or excited, she couldn't tell which

from his fidgety actions. No wonder she'd spotted him so easily. He'd probably never done this before.

Why would a cop waste his time on her? Charlie narrowed her eyes. "Vaiden had me followed?"

He stopped talking into his phone and looked at her, but didn't respond. A blush crept over his face and he turned his back to finish the conversation.

She knelt and collected her possessions, dropping them into the purse in a jumble. Ten stones. She dug her fingers into the dirt accumulated near the shallow curb, hoping the eleventh stone had somehow rolled farther than the rest.

She shook her bag and the heavier stones tumbled out into her hand. Dog, bird, sun. Dino, monkey. The jaguar she'd already lost. She ticked the list off in her head.

There were four she'd deduced represented constellations, all accounted for. So it was one of the two med stones missing. She turned one in her fingers. A man reaching into the belly of a woman, removing an object. That meant the missing stone showed a man reaching into another man's chest.

Her rough notes in her larger backpack bore drawings of the stones, but the photos taken at the site weren't due to arrive until the end of the week. As long as the pictures weren't damaged, she would still have a record of the intricate drawings, and half a chance of keeping her job. Publishing her find would go a long way toward that end. She swallowed a momentary rush of frustrated tears. Why couldn't she control this?

"Starting a dig here in the alley?"

Charlie almost laughed. Vaiden. "You got here pretty fast." She allowed him to help her to her feet, then stepped back from his grasp.

"You got yourself into trouble pretty fast." He leaned over to pick up a muddy white bag, still folded crisply at the top. "Your lunch?"

She nodded, not trusting herself to speak. She'd taken care of the situation herself, or would have, even if the officer hadn't interrupted. So why did she feel so relieved to see Vaiden?

✧

"I don't need an escort, Vaiden." Charlie quickened her pace, and Vaiden lengthened his stride to keep up.

"I'm not your escort. I just happen to be going to the same place as you." She hadn't insisted he get out of her Jeep when he'd accompanied her from the alley to the parking garage, so he doubted she'd make a serious attempt to lose him now. In fact, this was the first she'd expressed any desire to get rid of him.

"Really." She stopped at the corner, half-watching the traffic. "Don't you have a killer to catch? And where is it, exactly, that *you're* going?"

The light changed and he grasped her elbow in his long fingers, propelling her across the narrow street. "Oh, I'm sure you'll show me."

"So it's not enough that you had me followed, now you gotta do it yourself."

"I told you. That was for your protection." *And mine.* His gut told him that Orion had targeted her. His idiotic actions back at his house had come pretty close to scaring her away from him, and close to jeopardizing his unofficial investigation. Jarod's advice had been to take himself off the case, but he couldn't do that. He'd just have to be more careful around Charlie.

He'd hoped putting some distance between them would help. Instead the incompetence of the officer tailing her showed him that the only way he was going to keep her safe was to do it himself.

"Some protection." She darted across the next intersection and grinned as the traffic delayed him.

Vaiden waved a thanks at the car that slowed to let him pass. They'd entered university property now, and in the academic area traffic would no longer be an issue. He caught up and moved in front of her onto the sidewalk between two tall campus buildings.

"Charlie, about this morning..."

She rolled her eyes and stepped around him. "Forget about it."

Typical. She was angry. He grabbed her arm and she turned toward him. "You don't understand, I can't afford to get involved with you while I'm working on this case."

She stared through him with cold eyes. "Who asked you to become 'involved'? It was just a kiss. Get over it."

Just a kiss? He frowned and followed her inside a tall brownstone. They entered an open elevator and she pushed the number four.

"The sociology and anthropology offices are on this floor. We should be able to find a few people around who you can interview if you need to verify anything about my job. I have to see the dean." She faced the closed doors, her shoulders held stiffly. He'd thought she was mad, but maybe the kiss really *didn't* make a difference to her. What did he really know about this woman, anyway? He'd forget it, like she said.

If he could just stop wanting to do it again.

Charlie exited the elevator and walked down the hall to a

large office. A plain metal desk with an old-fashioned rotary-style phone on it sat empty near the entrance. She passed it and pulled a handful of papers from an office mailbox on the back wall.

She did an excellent job of pretending he didn't exist while she flipped through the envelopes and memos.

"Damn. That was fast." Her green eyes narrowed and her chin dented into a scowl. With a sudden action she crumpled the memo and crammed it into the overflowing garbage can next to the desk.

She rested her fists on her hips, the rest of her mail crunched in one hand. The streaks of red on her cheeks combined with the slight shine to her eyes gave his fingers the urge to dig out the memo and read it for himself. He resisted briefly, but then sneaked the paper after she stomped out of the room. Was she angry, or just upset? A letter from a lover, perhaps? He folded the wrinkled paper and slipped it into the inside pocket of his blazer. He could read it later. Then he'd figure it out.

Vaiden peered into each open door they passed as she moved down the corridor and around the corner. Only three of the offices had occupants. Two of those noticed them; one gave Charlie an unreturned wave as she stormed past.

Charlie had stopped just out of his vision, and he almost knocked her over. "What's the matter? Why'd you stop?"

The metallic stench of blood hit him and he pulled her behind him to shield her.

"That's the dean's office. He never closes that door." He barely heard her thin voice.

The brass plate outside read *Dr. Fisher.* The door wasn't quite shut. Vaiden drew his weapon, knowing from the sickly smell in the air that something wasn't right. Charlie's hands crushed the material of his suit, but he didn't brush her away. Better to know exactly where she was.

In two steps he crossed the hall and pushed the door wide. Only one figure occupied the space. The blood-soaked body of an older man lay collapsed in a chair behind a dark wooden desk, hands clenched tightly, mouth frozen in a silenced scream. His throat had been ripped out.

Vaiden noted the closed window as he turned toward Charlie. All color had drained from her face. He blocked her view of the room with his body and nudged her toward a bench in the hall. She sat, her head in her hands, then leaned to the side and lay back on the slats, bringing her legs up to balance on the armrest. He kept one eye on her as he made a phone call to report the vicious crime. He'd bet money she was going to faint any second.

"You okay, Charlie?"

"I can't handle remains with flesh on them," she whispered cryptically before covering her eyes with the inside of her elbow.

He pressed his lips together. She'd be fine. "You stay right there. I'm just going to check the stairs." He should secure the building. "You got a cell, right?"

Her lips thinned, and he thought she might have nodded.

"Call campus police. Make sure they heard the dispatch. They'll get here faster. Have them lock this building down."

The arm not covering her face flopped down toward her pack and her fingers rummaged through, pulling a dirty phone out and up to her ear. "I'm okay. I just need to stop thinking about it. Go on." He could see one eye peeking at him from beneath her elbow as she pressed buttons on her phone.

Satisfied, Vaiden approached the door to the stairwell.

✧

He'd told her she could go home, but instead Charlie waited for Vaiden on a stone bench outside of the building. A shiver crept up her arms and she wished she'd worn a jacket. At the same time, she welcomed the chill breeze that blew past as she stared transfixed at the black body bag carried out by uniformed men. The cold would keep her on her feet. She hated the smell of blood. She found it difficult to believe that Dean Fisher had been murdered. He wasn't well-liked, but she'd never met anyone who'd want him dead. Not really.

She told Vaiden as much when he joined her thirty minutes later. He turned his back to speak on his cell phone again. When he finished he walked across the narrow cobblestone path in front of her, the antenna nub between his front teeth. She saw deep lines between his brows and tension in the stiff way he held his shoulders. His frown didn't help the picture.

He remained standing and rubbed one side of his face, his fingers pressing hard on his forehead. "There were only a few people in the building when they locked it down."

Charlie waited, not knowing if he planned on telling her more. She'd learned from her students that if she waited long enough, they'd usually crack and tell her more than they ought. Or had she learned it from TV? Didn't matter. He'd tell her or he wouldn't. Nothing she said or did would change that. Just like the body in her house—a mystery until he chose to tell her what happened.

Seconds stretched into minutes and finally she found herself suppressing a grin. Vaiden was using the same technique on her as he had at her house. She sighed. "How was he killed?"

Vaiden moved behind her and sat on a low fieldstone wall,

forcing her to change position to see him. "Coroner said it looks like an animal tore out his throat."

Her gut twisted. The phone call. "Like a dog?"

He shook his head and blinked slowly. "Why?"

She got out her cell and punched the numbers for her voicemail. She'd saved the dean's enraged message for sheer amusement, but now it could be important. If the dog he'd complained about was the one who killed him... Had he confronted the animal? No, he was at his desk. He couldn't have been there long. She shuddered. The blood had still looked wet. It just didn't make sense. She held the phone out. "Listen."

As he listened, his brown eyes narrowed, then widened suddenly.

She reached for the phone, but he kept it close. "Why'd he send this to you?" His swallow was audible, and his stare grew intense as he waited.

She shrugged. "He sent it to everyone in the department."

He seemed to accept this, but he dropped her phone into his pocket and drew a wrinkled sheet of paper from inside. "Charlie, why was Dr. Fisher recommending you for suspension?"

She turned over the question in her head. Who could have known already? Then she focused on the paper in his hand. Her mouth fell open with a gasp. "You pulled that memo from the trash?" It was a copy of a memo Dean Fisher had sent to the board of trustees, outlining why he wanted Charlie suspended from her position at the university. If she'd been teaching longer, his request wouldn't have carried much weight, but she didn't have tenure, and her father's work had faded from the new board's memory.

Vaiden remained as immobile as the stone on which he sat. Eyeing her just as coldly.

The tips of her fingers had numbed from her tight fists. How ridiculous. Did he think *she* had something to do with the murder? She'd been with *him,* for Pete's sake.

Exhaling on a growl, she flung her hands up in exasperation.

"The artifact I lost. It was a gold relic, identical to one described in the Inca creation legend." She tried to read his reaction, but he had none. "I have nothing to prove it exists, that it was really there, other than a picture I emailed to Dean Fisher. Before the damn thing disappeared."

Chapter Five

Peru, two weeks earlier

Charlie pushed back the yucca leaves that blocked her view. Rising on her toes, she waved to Miguel Hernandez, her friend and guide, who stood opposite her on the south end of the valley below Rainbow Mountain. She peered through her binoculars and noted his signal. She'd found the spot they'd surveyed from the south.

After wedging two legs of her tripod into the ground, she squatted to move a bit of earth to balance the third leg.

Without warning, huge drops of rain splattered across the valley, quickly obscuring her view of all but the immediate area. She spat and cursed the deluge. She'd known the rainy season was due to begin, but she'd hoped to get in a few last moments of research before her return to the States. There was always one more artifact waiting to be found, one more turn of the trowel to find it. To her, closing a dig at the end of a semester was like a death.

She sighed, resigning herself to the fact that she would have to mark the site and return in a few months. It would be useless to try to gauge distance with the surveyor now. Even with her binoculars, she couldn't make out Hernandez any longer.

She pushed to her feet, pulled up the tripod, and slid the

telescoping legs together. As she removed her backpack to shove the equipment inside, a slight tremor wiggled beneath her feet. She dropped the tripod and leaned back, catching herself on her fingers.

The tremor passed, but her hands still tingled. Something wasn't right. She pressed against the ground to stand, and the green mounded earth gave way beneath her.

She had the sick feeling of leaving her stomach on the surface while her shell of a body plunged downward into the gaping hole. A second of panic sheathed her and she prayed the pit had a bottom. She landed hard. Pain shot through her forearm as the air whooshed from her lungs.

The struggle for breath lasted only seconds, but left her dizzy and panicked. She closed her eyes and forced herself to breathe normally.

She'd landed on her left side, half on her backpack, so she angled herself to a sitting position and grabbed the pack close. Her right arm throbbed and she touched the thick flesh of her extensor muscles. Wet warmth. The sickly metallic smell of blood. Her fingers curled back—if she got too much dirt in the wound, she'd be in real trouble.

She removed the ragged strip of cloth that held her too-long hair out of her face and wrapped it around her arm. She dug into the pack with her left arm, blindly touching, hoping to find her flashlight undamaged. Her fingertips grazed the metal casing of the light. As she pressed the switch, the walkie on her hip coughed to life.

"Charlie? Did you feel that? Where are you? I'm headed down your way." Hernandez actually liked the rain, but he knew Charlie had a plane to catch in two days. He'd been reminding her all day that they needed to move north if they were going to make Lima in time. Mud from this heavy rain would slow them down more.

"I'm in a hole." The light struck each evenly hewn wall. Manmade. "Make that a chamber of some sort."

"*¿Cómo?* Is it the site you wanted?"

"Hold on. I don't know yet." Charlie rose and looked down on a knee-high idol of an owl-eyed man. Behind the idol, a small oval-shaped hollow in the otherwise square room drew her closer. Crumbled pieces of jade formed a nest on the base of an altar.

Cradled in the jade, half-buried, a gold rod gleamed, its luster undimmed by time. Could it be real? Or had she hit her head in the fall?

Charlie instinctively lifted her hand to touch the artifact, but the sudden burst of pain in her arm brought her back to her senses. She couldn't disturb the find until she recorded its exact position. Instead, she retrieved her digital camera from her bag and captured images of the phallus, the altar, and the snub-nosed idol.

Dr. Fisher was going to lose his mind when he received her news. If this find was what she truly thought, then the golden rod of Manco Copac was real.

A sudden rush of icy water flooded the floor of the chamber, skimming across her boots. The water rose to her knees within half a minute. "Hernandez—Try to hurry," she shouted into the walkie.

Charlie hoisted her backpack, the camera safely tucked inside, onto her shoulders. Her forearm hung all but useless, the field dressing soaked through with blood that trickled down her hand in rivulets.

When Hernandez's head popped into view, Charlie wanted to cheer. "There's water in here and more of it is coming in. Get a rope!"

The water surrounded her waist before Hernandez managed to drop to her the rope he'd spent interminable moments securing to a nearby tree. She coiled the hemp around her good arm and gave a tug. Inch by inch she bounced up as Hernandez pulled her to safety. Good thing the man was strong as an ox.

Completely soaked, by rain, by the water from the chamber, by blood—she had no idea which—she crawled to Hernandez and collapsed.

By the time Hernandez rigged a shelter and stitched her wound, she'd stunned herself into despair. She barely registered the pain when the needle pierced her skin. She'd had no time to collect the rod. Once the water threatened to overcome her, she'd saved herself. She had digital images. And certainly the rod wasn't going anywhere. Still, the sinking horror and fear that she'd lost it hung over her.

"Hernandez—" His frown stopped her.

He placed his hands on his stout hips. "What did you find down there, *mija*?"

Charlie shook her head. "The water will go down. We'll find it." Dig superstitions echoed in her head. If she had to say it out loud, it might disappear.

She scooted the equipment bundle over with her good arm and opened her laptop. While the high-tech modem attempted to link with the satellite, she typed a short message to Dr. Fisher, informing him of her discovery. She plugged her camera into the SCSI port and attached the images to her email. She would be damned if she was leaving without the artifact, and she had to share the news of the discovery now.

Dean Fisher was the one colleague she knew would feel the same thrill as she. He'd been in the department when her father taught there. He knew her father's passionate belief in the existence of the gold rod of Manco Copac. The dean had begged her to send any big news immediately—funding was tight, and discoveries such as this garnered huge contributions.

In the three hours they waited, the water bubbled up from the hole and sloshed down the hillside into the valley below. They rigged a strainer below the wash, to catch any artifacts that floated up and out, but nothing rose.

Charlie considered diving in, but Hernandez advised against it. If the water suddenly stopped and drained back where it came from, she could be sucked into the earth to die.

She knew her guide wanted to get back to his family. Six months in the field was enough. Normally she would agree, but she hated to give up now. She'd almost touched it. Screw procedure. She should have jammed the damned thing into her bag while she had the chance.

The sun punched holes in the still dripping sky, drawing a rainbow across the peak of the mountain. The heat of the day combined with the cold rain to make the valley appear a steaming cauldron. Charlie prodded her newly bandaged arm. The pulsing throb had ceased, but her fingers had begun to ache.

She frowned at the sodden ground and sighed. "Let's get out of here, Hernandez. Life's more precious. There's always next year." She fought the girlish tears that rushed to her eyes and was glad for the rain that hid them.

She reached for the laptop to change her message, but it was too late. The computer program beeped. Her email to Dr. Fisher had gone through, pictures and all. She would have to explain to him upon her return that actual retrieval was simply too dangerous.

"Sí, *mija*." Hernandez flipped open his GPS device and punched their location into its built-in memory. He glanced toward the ground and smiled broadly, his mustache dropping to cover his upper lip. "The gods are pleased with you, *mija.*"

Charlie jerked her gaze back to the hole in the ground. The empty hole. The water had receded. She leaned over the edge, shining her flashlight into the chamber. She could still make out the jade on the altar, but not the gold.

✧

Hernandez clicked his teeth as he tied off the harness.

"This is our last chance." Charlie gripped the braced cross-timbers that held the ropes and dropped down, this time gently, into the chamber. The idol lay prone. She tilted her head. The idol's eyes were closed. She shrugged. Must've had two sides. The owl-eyes were probably pressed into the dirt floor. The solid stone was far too heavy for her to attempt to bring it to the surface on her own. Even with Hernandez's help, it couldn't be done.

She moved quickly to the altar and scraped away the top layer of jade fragments. Black stones, arranged in a perfect circle, rested where the rod had been.

Charlie shined the light on the floor, walked the perimeter, and returned to the altar. There was nothing else in the room. And she couldn't find the place where the water had entered. The walls, smooth and unseamed, were hard, like stone themselves.

Using her machete, she tested the material of the small black pieces. Definitely stone. Where the devil was the rod?

"Charlie! ¡*Mija*! We've got to go. We're losing light. Did you find what you're looking for?"

Charlie bit her knuckles and frowned, then gathered the

black rocks, wrapping each in moleskin and then dropping them one at a time into a small canvas pouch. “No, Hernandez. Let’s go home.”

Chapter Six

"So what you're telling me is, your bad day started way before we met."

She looked up sharply, expecting to see a scowl of disbelief on his face. Vaiden was smiling, his eyes warm again. A shiver raced through her body as his hand shot out and pulled her closer.

He hid his eyes from her, studying something far away. "Do you think Dean Fisher told anyone else about the gold?"

"I assume you're having his computer checked, so *you* can tell *me*."

"No, I mean, what do you *think*?" Vaiden rotated her right hand palm up and ran a finger over the ugly new scar forming on her forearm.

She winced and tugged her arm away. The injury no longer hurt, but it was one more imperfection added to her long list. "Until he had the artifact in his hands, or at least acknowledgement of it through the Peruvian government, he would have kept his mouth shut."

"So, in your opinion, the gold is sitting in that chamber somewhere, waiting for you?"

"Maybe. Maybe it was under that fallen idol. Maybe the water brought a thick coat of mud to the floor, and it's just beneath the surface. I don't know." A sick feeling flew through her. "You don't think I stole the thing?"

"I think that if he was mad enough to fire you over a setback, the dean must have told someone. Maybe even more than one person. Several people in the department claim to know about a big announcement that never came. Maybe one of these people who he may or may not have told, thinks you *did* steal it."

Charlie lowered her eyes. "And you?"

"I need to check with a few sources." He pushed away from the wall and dusted off his backside. "Where are you staying tonight?"

"Why do you want to know?" Was he actually interested in her? Or had she become a suspect? She couldn't bear to ask him, and couldn't bear not to know.

He shrugged, scuffed one shiny black shoe on the ground, and shoved his hands in his pockets. Like a little boy afraid to ask for what he really wanted.

Charlie's heart ached. Why'd she have to meet a man like Vaiden? All man and all adorable boy at the same time. He was perfect for her.

And the last thing she needed.

Figuring Vaiden out was impossible. "I'll let you know." She turned her back on his shocked look and cursed herself for being a fool. If he'd asked her, she'd have gladly stayed with *him.* His pull was too strong, her need for him too great.

No. What she needed was to get away from him and refocus.

This could not happen. *They* could not happen. Damned if she'd let it.

✧

Vaiden emerged from the planetarium at the science museum and stretched out the cramps in his shoulders. Staring upward for an hour had made him stiff. He didn't know why he thought the free class the local astronomy club gave once a month would give him insight into his case. So the killer used to call himself Orion. That didn't mean it actually had more significance than the time period during which he killed his victims.

Bats swooshed past the lights in the parking lot five hundred yards away as they snatched bugs from the air. Still no sign of Jarod. He knew Jarod thought this was a waste of time, but Vaiden was getting desperate.

The star show had been informative, but he'd gleaned more information from simply reading the Orion myths. Two fairly coherent versions existed. In one, the main idea focused on Orion's boastfulness. The mythic Orion, son of an Amazon queen, became a great hunter but a greater braggart. He claimed he could slay any animal, no matter the size. Of course, like in any children's story, the tiniest animal killed Orion. A scorpion.

Vaiden learned from the astronomy show that Scorpius and Orion were always at opposite ends of the sky. Interesting, he thought, that most of Orion's kills occurred during October and November, both in the past and now, the time of the astrological sign Scorpio. He wondered if it was a coincidence, or if their Orion chose those months for a reason. If so, his killing time was nearing its end, and they needed to find him soon.

The second version of the myth held that Orion had no mother at all. He made a play for a princess, whose angry father then had him blinded. Later, his sight was returned to him by the god of the sun. Soon, Orion fell in love with Diana, the huntress, much to the displeasure of her brother, Apollo. Apollo tricked Diana into killing Orion, by asking her to prove her prowess with a spear by hitting an object far out at sea. She only learned later that the object was Orion. Supposedly, Diana then had Orion placed in the stars as a constellation, attacking Taurus the bull.

Vaiden stopped walking near the grand Kugel, a huge black rock sculpture of the planet earth, and observed the small gathering. As he'd expected, it was mostly fathers and sons. A few brought telescopes, but most used the ones provided by the astronomy club. The borrowed telescopes seemed bigger, more powerful perhaps.

He pushed a button on the side of his watch. Where the hell was Jarod? He was supposed to have arrived before the show began, and then afterward help Vaiden wander through the crowd, asking questions.

Truly, Vaiden didn't know why he felt like the informal astronomy group would be a good place to start. Hell, it was probably ridiculous. But he needed something to jar his brain. Orion, the Blair house, Charlie. How did they tie together?

The new murder—the university professor—was a complete deviation. His supervisor had scoffed at the suggestion that there was a connection. Yet, Charlie was in the middle. There had to be something.

He knew his supervisor was right. Orion only killed women, and he did it with slow torture, not by ripping their throats out. Yet, Vaiden had a gut feeling.

He stuck his hands in his pockets. It was too damned cold to wait for Jarod much longer. He backed up a few steps and bumped the leg of a telescope tripod that was standing in the shadow of the Kugel.

The man who'd been using the telescope cursed as he straightened. "Watch where the hell you're going!" He bent down and looked through the eyepiece. "It's all screwed up. Dumb ass."

"Sorry, man." Vaiden was more concerned about the young boys hearing the man's language than about him having to adjust his damn telescope. A blond head visible over the wall separating the lawn from the parking lot drew Vaiden's attention. With a backward glance at the still mumbling man, Vaiden strode forward to meet Jarod.

They met at the smaller Kugel, the one that represented the moon. Vaiden moved closer to the wall to avoid the slight misty spray created by the wind blowing across the wet surface of the stone.

"About time you got here."

"Sorry. My class went long. Did you learn anything useful?"

Vaiden tried to discern whether Jarod was being a smartass. He hadn't wanted to do this in the first place, but he'd agreed to come because Vaiden insisted. "Let's just mingle, okay?"

"You got it."

They broke apart, each walking around a different part of the group. Almost every observer was happy to chat with them, but Vaiden noticed some were reluctant to release their hold on their telescopes. There were more people than eyepieces, and that seemed to create a premium on them.

Twenty minutes later, when Jarod approached him, Vaiden was ready to call it quits. "I'm sorry, man, I don't know why I thought this was a good idea." He stopped explaining when he saw the frown on Jarod's face. "What is it? You got something?"

"Maybe." He turned toward the telescope in the shadow of the earth Kugel. "I was talking to that pair over there"—he waved at the bearded man who saluted when Jarod pointed—"and the guy at that telescope sort of drew in a breath. Real loud. And then he just walked away. He was gone before I could get a good look at him." He scratched his forehead. "It was real weird. And just for the heck of it, I looked in his eyepiece."

Vaiden's stomach tightened, as though a hand were twisting his gut.

Jarod licked his teeth and nodded. "His telescope was focused on Orion."

Chapter Seven

Charlie selected a hotel within sight of Sixth Street Marketplace. Or rather, what had been the marketplace. The mezzanine walkway she remembered from six months ago had been ripped down. She stared out of her window at the construction area. Sometimes the city didn't appear to know what it wanted. A beautiful, fragile blossom that couldn't decide what sort of fruit it would become.

Charlie tugged the curtains across the large glass window and then switched on the television. She hit mute and tossed the remote onto the bed.

She peeled off her tee shirt and dropped it onto her new sweater. After her disappointing conversation with Vaiden, she'd driven west to Regency Square to replenish her wardrobe. Unfortunately, mold had ruined most of her favorite pieces of clothing while they lay in storage. Never mind that they were also out of fashion. Not that they'd been so in fashion when she'd left.

She didn't want for cash when she needed it. She was generally thrifty, but only because the bulk of her salary stayed in one country while she resided in another during digs. Her parents had left her their rental houses in their will as an assurance of income.

She was due for some pampering, and she allowed herself

no guilt for spending five hundred dollars in one afternoon. And, she smiled, now she wanted room service.

Once she'd been certain that a bowl of hot soup, a grilled cheese sandwich, and a double serving of tiramisu would arrive shortly, she stripped off the rest of her attire and climbed into the shower. She craved the heat of the water and allowed it to pinken her skin.

Minutes later, freshly scrubbed and smelling of strawberries thanks to the amenities she'd found earlier at the hotel gift shop, she paraded into the bedroom clothed in a guest robe.

The phone jangled and she sat on the mattress to answer it. Vaiden's voice on the line gave her pause. She'd left the number for the hotel with his answering service, but she hadn't expected him to contact her. Hoped, maybe, but not expected.

"You have the door locked? Chain on?"

"Vaiden, I'm not ten years old." Charlie accidentally placed her free hand on the remote and hit the volume button. A newscaster's voice filled the room and she snorted as she hit mute again.

"What was that?"

"Nothing, Vaiden. The TV. Any news on my house? On Dean Fisher?"

"Nothing I can share." He'd almost sounded sorry, but she was impatient.

"Is there anything else then?"

A knocked sounded on the door and she lifted the hotel phone and crossed the sleeping area to let the room service guy inside.

"Is someone with you, Charlie?"

She handed the employee a five-dollar bill, ignoring

Vaiden's inquiry.

"Charlie?"

She waited until the man muttered his thanks and exited before answering Vaiden. "Everything is fine. Look, if you don't have any information for me, I'm afraid I'll have to go." She grimaced. That came off cooler than she'd planned. She heard him exhale and she closed her eyes.

"I'll see you soon." He hung up without elaborating.

She should be glad he'd put distance between them. She didn't need a real man in her life. Heck, wasn't that why she'd gotten engaged to Harold? He was safe.

As she brushed her hair dry and slipped into a lace nightgown, she couldn't help but wonder what her life might be like if she'd taken a more stable path.

A real man would want her home every night. He'd want her to have children. And though she *did* want children, she just couldn't fathom how they'd fit into her life. She doubted she could bear to be parted from a child of her own.

Her own parents had both been field archaeologists when she was born. By the time she was five years old, she'd been to more countries than most people saw in a lifetime. But when she reached school age, her father took a job teaching at the university during the school year. He thought she should have stability, so he created the illusion for her.

Her mother never settled into such a static existence. She spent less time away than before, certainly, but Charlie and her father never knew when she would appear.

And every school break, every long summer, they spent as a family, "adventuring", as they called it.

The television's flashing lights irritated her, so she lit a lamp and pressed the off button on the remote. Her stomach growled and she seated herself at the small table in the corner. The metal tray cover had kept her food steaming hot. She inhaled the salty air emanating from the chicken noodle soup, tore a piece of crust from her sandwich, and dipped it into the broth.

She didn't remember her parents as unhappy, exactly, during their separations, just different. Incomplete maybe. Her parents had loved each other madly, the sort of love they showed in the movies. And then they'd lost each other. And Charlie lost them.

She'd long given up on finding that sort of love for herself. Hell, she couldn't even find lipstick like they wore in movies—what made her think she could find movie-magic love?

✧

Two dessert dishes, a bowl, and a dinner plate lay haphazardly to the left of room 502. Dinner for two? A quick snack after sex? Either way, she hadn't wasted any time.

Vaiden scowled. He needed to stop thinking about Charlie like she belonged to him. She didn't. She couldn't. Damned if he'd show her it mattered.

He jerked the *Do Not Disturb* sign from the handle and knocked loudly. Hearing nothing, he knocked again, this time with the side of his fist.

So what if it was almost midnight? She'd told him she wanted information, and right now he needed to use that to see what else she knew about his case. She had the answers. He knew it. She knew it. And by God, she would tell him all before someone else got killed.

The door guard clicked against the inside of the wood and

the portal opened. He saw a flash of one green eye before she stepped back to let him in.

He stormed to the bed and took in the tightly tucked comforter. Didn't look slept in. In fact, except for the pillows having been pulled from their cocoon, the blankets looked untouched. He wondered where her company went. He'd seen the lumpy way Charlie folded blankets when she cleaned up after her night on his couch. There was no way *she* could have made the bed so neatly.

She cleared her throat behind him. "Was there something you wanted?"

He glanced toward her, then did so again. She leaned hard against the wall, her eyes clearly fighting to stay open. Her wavy hair was noticeably flat on one side and one shoulder had escaped her tiny black lace gown.

Freckles decorated the top of that shoulder. He wondered if they trailed down her back. He tugged at his tie. The material of the nightgown hung precariously over her breast. Just the barest touch would send it—

"Vaiden?" Her eyes were wider now, and she pulled up the thin strap.

He swallowed. She made him behave like a hormone-raging teenager. He had to control himself. Had to control the situation.

"The preliminary results for Dr. Fisher said that he was probably killed by a large cat." There. That should change the mood in the room.

Charlie walked past him. He resisted the urge to smell her hair as she passed. She bent to turn on a second lamp and he couldn't help watching her. The gown had matching panties.

His groin tightened and his pulse ran rapid. Why'd it have to be *this* woman?

"A cat?" She glanced toward the other side of the room and frowned.

He shoved a hand through his hair. "More like a mountain lion. They won't know exactly what until they do more tests. That could take weeks." A robe was draped over the chair she sank into. Why the hell didn't she put it on?

She braced her elbows on the table, her chin on her knuckles. Her brow furrowed. "You didn't come here just to tell me that."

From his height, he could see straight down the front of her gown. Knowing it was the right thing to do, and maybe the only thing that would keep him sane, he tore his eyes away from her breasts and seated himself across from her. "The case I'm working on... The reason Jarod and I came to your house... We think the man we're trying to nail has killed more than just one woman. He may be linked somehow to some murders from ten years ago. A serial killer they thought was Elwin Kent."

"But it wasn't him?"

"Maybe. And maybe he wasn't working alone. I wish I could figure this out. I know the answer is right in front of me, but I just can't see it." He waited for her to clue him in. Perhaps he should be more forceful. So far she didn't appear intimidated.

She pressed her hands on the armrests and lifted her legs beneath her, cross-legged style. "Who was she?"

"The woman? We don't know yet. Presumably a college student, or someone around that age, but we haven't identified her for certain yet."

For just a second, pain—or was it sorrow?—shone in her eyes. Just as quickly, she hid it from him. "Did the rental records help you any?" She tapped a finger against her lips. His heart began to pound. Thank God her legs were out of his view again.

He focused on her mouth a beat too long. She was blushing. "The place was clean when we got there."

The skin along the top edge of the nightgown flushed pink. He could practically taste her. He pushed his chair back and reached across the table, his hand falling on her arm.

She gazed at his hand intently, but she didn't move. As tan as her skin was, his was a shade darker. She licked her lips and her muscles twitched before she moved.

Unfortunately, she moved *away*, sliding her arms into the robe and closing it. She even tied the damn belt.

She blinked before turning her eyes to his face. Still blushing, she chewed the side of her bottom lip and sighed.

Vaiden waited, unsure what he wanted her to say. If body language was any clue, she certainly didn't want him around. He remembered the dishes outside the room and ground his teeth. "Who was here earlier?"

She chuckled, her lips bending into a half-smile. "Room service. I never got my lunch and I was starving."

Relief swept through him, but he remained cautious. "Who else knows you're staying here?"

"Just you." She scratched at the clear polish on her thumbnail. "When can I have my cell phone back?"

He suddenly recalled her phone in his pocket. "Sorry. Here." He handed the small device to her. Her fingers slid against his. Her skin fired the attraction he'd tried so hard to quell and he drew back quickly. He flexed his digits and tried not to think of the touch of her skin beneath his palm.

She checked the battery level on the cell phone's display. When she spoke, it was as an afterthought. "You checked the storage area records too, right? I mean, if he rented a house from my rental company, he could have easily rented a storage space. There's even a discount plan set up for renters."

"Storage? This is the first I'm hearing about it."

"Alexa should have given you files on all my properties. I own Blair Storage. The real estate folks wouldn't have a list of individual space renters, but there's a hard copy at the facility. Feel free to look around the records in the office all you want. I'll let them know you're coming."

"What time does it open?"

"I could take you there now." One hand rested on the belt to the robe.

"No. I don't want you there. I need to be able to concentrate."

She cocked an eyebrow at him.

"Someone's tried to hurt you twice, Charlie. I'd prefer if you stayed here, with your door locked. I'll see that there's an officer downstairs for your protection." He placed one hand on her shoulder, now that it was safely covered in terrycloth, and squeezed in what he hoped was in no way indicative of lust.

She stared up at him with those clear green eyes of hers.

He kissed her recklessly on the temple and left before his mouth strayed lower.

Chapter Eight

Vaiden enjoyed employing the element of surprise. He and Jarod arrived at Blair Storage the moment the gates opened. Charlie, as promised, called the office at eight-thirty to give her consent for the search. She'd given Vaiden written permission, as well as a copy of the rental contracts for the place. The contracts spelled out clearly that privacy was voided by an illegal activity on site.

His radar would have gone crazy reading a rental contract like that—he wouldn't have signed it. But the rates for the storage spaces were so low, he imagined people were just happy to get them, regardless of privacy.

The skittish office woman, April, hovered as Vaiden extracted the records by hand, cross-referencing against known aliases for his suspect on his laptop.

Jarod attempted to hand April a stack of photos, presumably to see if anyone on their top list of suspects had come through recently.

"I don't never see folks unless they come up to make a payment in person."

Jarod sighed loudly. "Ma'am, amuse me. Just check the pictures."

Vaiden chuckled and continued his search. One name in particular piqued his curiosity. *Earl Kent.* He could find nothing on the name, but the fact that the renter shared a surname with the prior Orion killer set off red flags.

"Jarod. I think we've got something."

His partner looked relieved to have an excuse to leave April's side. He crossed the room and bent over the document. "Kent. Now there's a name I wouldn't pick if I were trying to hide."

Vaiden sat back in the metal chair. "And if you weren't?" He didn't like it. This time around the killer was bolder. The case was way too close to Charlie. If she got hurt because he didn't see something that was right under his nose... Maybe *he* was too close to Charlie. "April, can you see if Mr. Kent has come around lately? Paid bills, anything we can use to check him out?"

She curled her lip and pointed her chin at the ceiling. "Kent. Now, I *do* recognize that name. Paid in full by the drop box and turned in his keys yesterday."

Vaiden's ears rang.

Jarod took a step toward April. "Did you see him?"

"No, honey, I told you, he used the drop box."

Vaiden squeezed the bridge of his nose and pointed in the direction of the photos. "Could you just check, Ma'am?"

She shrugged her shoulders and began flipping through the fifteen-odd images. Seconds later she lifted one. "Oh, hey, y'all, I know her." April grinned as she brought a photograph to Jarod and Vaiden. "She one of the folks you're looking for?" The woman threw her head back and laughed.

A copy of Charlie Blair's passport photo stared back at them from April's cigarette-stained fingers.

Vaiden rolled his eyes. "Of course you know her. She owns the place."

"Well, yeah, but you said anyone I'd seen recently. She was just here yesterday morning. First thing, as I recall."

His stomach dropped. He hadn't read the officer's report on Charlie's whereabouts yesterday. After the attack on her in the alley, nothing else seemed to matter but her safety.

Of course Charlie was mired knee-deep in it again. Too much coincidence. Either she knew more than she was saying, or the killer had closer ties to her than he'd figured. He prayed Orion hadn't selected her as his next victim.

April drew his attention with a shoulder-shake and snatched a key from the pegboard behind her. "It wasn't 'til she left I remembered to check the drop box."

She tossed the key to storage space number seven toward Jarod. "Earl Kent," she said when he caught it. "Go have a look-see. But I checked it. It's empty."

"Did you touch anything?" Vaiden held his breath as he waited for the answer.

"Nope. Just opened and shut."

Vaiden crossed his fingers. *If* this Earl Kent was their guy, and *if* there was any evidence left in the storage space, the CSIs would find it. He and Jarod had been operating on hunches so far. Why stop now?

✧

Charlie arrived at Vaiden's house well before dark. Still, she felt eyes on her. If that man was having her followed again, she'd... A smile crossed her face. If he was, he had his reasons. It was absurd to think some nutso killer would want to do her in. She didn't have enemies.

If her family had made enemies, she'd never heard of it.

Turning around, she planted herself on Vaiden's front step. The chill from the stone seeped upward into her hips and thighs, and she wiggled closer to the edge to avoid as much cold as possible.

In the daylight, she saw that Vaiden's lawn was as immaculate as the inside of his house. His lawn stood lush and green and even. She wondered if he ever walked across the blades. Probably not. He most likely stuck to the sidewalk and driveway. He was a man with goals. Plans. Ideas about how life should be.

Not like her. She wanted to be able to leave on a moment's notice to visit a new archaeological discovery, and often left a mess in her wake. She had no family to work her life around, and she liked it that way.

This was a bad idea. What had she been thinking, coming here uninvited and without any real reasons?

She wrapped the straps of her backpack purse around her fist and prepared to stand. A screech drew her attention to the bushes that bordered Vaiden's yard on the left. The screech repeated. A fan belt? Maybe Vaiden's car needed repairs. She'd ask him when he emerged from the bushes that blocked her view.

If it *was* Vaiden... Charlie suddenly wished she'd driven to his house rather than using public transportation. She didn't like being without a means of escape.

She rose slowly, her hands poised above her knees until she straightened her spine and faced the bushes.

The upper quadrant of the plant shook and she heard a car door slam followed by an oath.

More confirmation that coming to see Vaiden was a bad idea. Trouble didn't follow her, it followed her when she let him take over her thoughts. Nothing to panic over, she thought, even as she backed away from the front stoop.

Her heart rate sped and she flexed her fingers, waiting to see if she should run away. The figure that finally rounded the bushes stunned her. How could it be him, and yet not him?

Thank heaven he walked fast, otherwise she would have called him Vaiden before she realized it was, in fact, someone else. A man who looked remarkably like Vaiden.

On spotting her, his eyebrows rose and after a moment, a grin spread over his face. “Well, hello. You waiting for Rob, too?”

“I—” Vaiden’s first name was Rob? “Yes, I suppose so.” She clasped the hand he held out in greeting. “Who are you?”

“Rob, you devil,” he chuckled. “I’m so sorry, he didn’t tell me he was playing matchmaker. And looks like he didn’t tell you either?”

Charlie opened her mouth, then pursed her lips. “Mm. No. I... I just dropped by. I didn’t know he’d be so late.” He had the kindness to look disappointed, and she felt herself blush.

“No matter. Name’s Nate Vaiden. Rob’s told you about me?” His eyebrows hung high on his forehead in anticipation of her answer. They dropped and knit together when she shook her head. “Figures. Not looking out for his own brother. Let’s sit.” He led her back to the stoop and sat, patting the step next to him.

“You don’t have a key?” She waited where she stood.

Nate laughed. He was handsome, in a not-Vaiden kind of way. She allowed herself to ease closer. He seemed safe enough.

“Rob doesn’t give keys to anything of his to anybody. The man trusts no one.”

Charlie sat next to him, edging over so that a modest amount of space separated their legs. His arms, crossed at her eye level as she sat, showed muscle-tone though he wore a dress shirt. He looked so much like Vaiden...

"I swear. You let a goat loose in a guy's house one time..."

And yet she felt nothing.

"A goat?"

"It was just a joke." Nate chucked her on the chin and she instinctively drew back. He narrowed his eyes and grinned. "So, you got the hots for my brother?"

✧

The sun had set by the time Vaiden returned home, but the motion sensor light over his front steps shined brightly, illuminating two seated figures, one tall, one average height. He switched off the engine of his Camry and groaned. He'd completely forgotten about meeting his brother for dinner. Did he even have anything in his fridge worth fixing?

Male and female laughter sailed toward him over the damp night air as he grabbed his messenger bag and shut the door. He didn't remember his brother saying anything about bringing a date. Lord, he'd better not be trying to set him up with anyone. He was not in the mood.

She giggled again. Vaiden stopped mid-stride. Something about that laugh...

Ten feet from the steps his stomach knotted. The two people stood. His brother Nate, four years his senior, made a show of checking his watch. He tapped on it for good measure.

"I know, I know. I'm sorry." Vaiden turned from Nate and scowled at the woman. Seeing her both pleased him and pissed him off. "Charlie, what are you doing here? I thought you were going to stay put."

To his annoyance, Nate and Charlie burst into laughter a

second time. She poked his brother in the ribs as if to say I-told-you-so. Vaiden used his bag to edge between them on his way to the door. He unlocked it and left it open for them to follow, his ears burning to hear their low-voiced commentary. It bothered him that his brother shared an inside joke with Charlie already.

He draped his jacket on a hanger in the closet and placed his bag on the floor. Charlie's hand touched his back and her fingertips seared him through the cotton fabric of his shirt. He inhaled, assailed by the slight scent of strawberries. They were quickly becoming his favorite fruit.

"I called to find out when I could get back into the house, and they said I had to clear it with you. I figured this was the easiest place to find you." She spared a glance over her shoulder at Nate. And giggled again, damn her. "Found him instead."

"And you couldn't call me because?" Vaiden tried to ignore how closely Nate situated himself behind her. What he wanted to do was shove his smirking brother outside and lock the door.

Charlie's cheeks flushed pink. "I guess I should have." She studied her fingernails. Ragged and short. At least they were clean.

He could read so many things into the way she'd muttered those words. Was she sorry she was here? Come to think of it, was he? Right now he just wanted to kiss that pout from her red lips and make it clear to Nate that he didn't appreciate him chatting her up.

After a brief uncomfortable silence during which he found it impossible to tear his eyes from her downcast face, Nate saved him from embarrassment by stepping around her and leading him into the kitchen. "So, *have* you eaten? Because Charlie and I are starved."

✧

The busy Mexican restaurant was one of Charlie's favorite places. When she saw the lack of food in Vaiden's refrigerator, she'd been the first to suggest it. She liked the noise, she liked the music, and she liked stealth-practicing Spanish when she just listened.

She watched Vaiden and his brother from behind her water glass. Though Nate couldn't be much older than Vaiden, his hairline had receded an extra inch. Even to strangers it would be obvious they were brothers. Both dark, both tall. Same lips. Though she had to admit, Vaiden's lips somehow seemed much more desirable than Nate's despite the fact that she could find no discernable physical difference.

No matter how long she stared at them.

Charlie dug another spoonful of the fried ice cream and slowly licked the spoon. She sucked the bits of granola free and chewed half-heartedly before swallowing. A shoe touched her ankle and her mouth popped open. She moved her feet over, but the shoe pursued, the toe sliding up and down the flesh covering her fibula.

Neither brother spared her a look. Not a wink. Not even an eyebrow.

Though Nate had confessed to her that he was a crime reporter for the newspaper, he never once asked Vaiden about his case during the meal. Neither one deviated from their animated discussion about the local soccer team.

And yet that shoe continued stroking her ankle and edged up her shin, mushing the hem of her jeans upward.

She inhaled sharply and choked on a piece of the crackly

coating of her fried ice cream. She took the opportunity as an excuse to escape the wandering foot and dashed up from the table, waving both men off as they stood.

She walked to the rear of the restaurant and paused in the darkened hallway near the restrooms. From there she could observe them undetected. Their mouths still moved, but neither was smiling now.

Nate's hands spread on the table and Vaiden jabbed the air in front of him with his finger.

She blushed. Which of them had caressed her leg beneath the table? Vaiden would never have flirted with her like that. He'd made it clear that their encounter in the bathroom was a mistake, and he hadn't taken her up on her offer to take it further at the time.

But she couldn't see Nate making a pass at her right under his brother's nose.

Not that Nate thought they were anything more than acquaintances. While they were waiting for Vaiden to come home, he'd asked her point blank if she and his brother were dating. She rubbed her forehead.

Of course she'd said no. Because they weren't. Just because she thought about him constantly meant nothing. She merely needed something to do to get her mind off of him, that was all. If she still had a job, she'd throw herself into her research. Like usual.

The waiter brought the check to the table and Charlie chose to return as he left. "So who won?"

Both men looked at her, then each other, then back at her, eyes darting around in confusion. "The soccer discussion? Did you settle on who was the MVP?"

Nate was the first to cough and then grin. "I won. I always do." He elbowed Vaiden, none too discreetly.

Vaiden glared at empty space. He drew three bills from his wallet and picked up the check. "Let's go pay, and then I'll take you back home." He took her arm. His grip was firm enough that she felt heat through her sweater.

Charlie's heart pounded in her chest. Before the third beat he broke the spell with a stuttered addendum as he let her go.

"To your hotel room."

Nate grunted and laced his arm through hers, then led her away from Vaiden. "We'll wait in the car."

Vaiden's mouth turned down at the edges. He handed the cashier the now crumpled bills, not offering his brother a response.

Nate held the door for her. "So you wanna change your answer from before?"

Once outside, she sent him a blank look, then peered through the glass behind him. "What do you mean?"

"You and my baby brother."

She snorted. "He's not what I need."

"I didn't ask you that. Besides, sometimes we're not smart enough to know what we really need."

Vaiden came through the door then and Nate didn't ask her any more questions. Back at her hotel, he stayed with the car while Vaiden accompanied her to her room.

He couldn't stay, even if she had the nerve to ask him. Not with Nate waiting. Nate the safety net. Saved by the Nate. Still, her palms grew clammy as they neared the room.

Vaiden took her keycard from her and unlocked the door. He did a quick check of the small space, then placed the card back in her hand. "Stay in the room this time. I need to know you're safe."

He moved to the doorway, but he didn't leave. He stood

looking at her. Charlie's stomach tightened.

Her fingers itched to touch his hair. "I came to your house today to see *you*." She couldn't explain why she'd had to see him, at least not without sounding obsessed. She held out hope that he'd been experiencing the same pull.

"Yeah, and?"

She let out her breath.

Her shoulders sank. He hadn't understood. Just as well. "Did you find out anything today?"

He stepped closer. She could touch his hair now if she reached up. He smelled good for a man who'd been working all day. She wanted to taste him. Desire swirled low and lazy in her belly.

She gasped and blinked hard. She could practically feel the heat from his eyes. Was he looking at her lips?

As if she'd spoken, the spell suddenly broke and his face shuttered, revealing nothing. "We're fairly certain the suspect had a storage unit there. But he cleaned it out the day you visited."

The hair on the back of her neck prickled. She'd felt like she was being watched that day.

Her fear must have shown on her face because Vaiden touched her arm. His hand drifted down until he clasped her hand in his. She'd always considered her work-roughened hands too hard and unfeminine, but in his warm, strong hands, hers became almost dainty. She liked that. Holding hands.

"They recovered some fibers and a few hairs, but it's too soon to know if they mean anything." He brought her hand to his chest and eased her against him. "Charlie—"

She leaned upward, then pushed higher onto her toes and kissed him. The contact sent waves of nervous electricity through her middle. Her breath stopped in her throat. She swallowed.

For two endless seconds he remained frozen. Then with a sigh, he crushed her in his arms and kissed her. His hands roamed her back, settling on her behind. He squeezed her closer and she felt the evidence of his desire pressing into her stomach.

Charlie's knees turned to jelly and her feet tingled. Her hands trembled on his shoulders. She let one of her hands wander into his silky hair and smiled against his mouth. He could kiss the pants right off her. God, she wanted him.

Vaiden's hands stilled on the small of her back. He broke the contact of their mouths, and rubbed his chin in her hair near her ear. "I have to go. Nate..."

He backed away, his hands held in the air. Her focus stayed on them. How could he turn on and off so easily?

"It's probably better this way."

Charlie locked the door behind him. Better for whom?

✧

The insistent ringing of the phone brought Charlie from her warm bed, and her even warmer dream. She managed to find the receiver and knock it off the cradle by the seventh ring.

The soreness between her shoulders twinged as she reached for it.

"Hmm?"

"Charlotte Blair?"

"Hmm."

"Sorry to call at this hour, but Detective Vaiden needs you

to meet him over at the morgue. Do you know where that is?"

One eye closed, Charlie tried to read the red glowing numbers on the digital clock. Two-thirty. She licked her dry lips. "Morgue? Yeah. Can you explain—"

"We need you to make an identification. I'm sorry I can't tell you more than that." The gruff voice on the line didn't sound any more thrilled than she was to be on the phone.

Her voice croaked. "I'm on my way."

"We'll send a car for you."

That, she was grateful for. Though the building that housed the morgue was only a few blocks away, downtown Richmond was not the place for any person, let alone a woman, to be on the street in the wee hours. Jeep or not, it just wasn't safe, and definitely not near the morgue.

Charlie stumbled into the bathroom, dragged a comb through her hair, and splashed water on her face. She donned a pair of soft new jeans, a short-sleeved shirt, and a long-sleeved denim shirt. Taking her backpack purse as an afterthought, she headed downstairs.

As promised, an officer was waiting outside to accompany her to the morgue. He directed her to the room where they stored John Does.

A man who looked like he subsisted on caffeine and toast waved her inside. "You're Dr. Blair?"

She nodded, not wanting to speak in the quiet and clean smell of the place. No dirt anywhere. Just metal and flat surfaces. Except for the folks beneath the sheets.

"Detective Vaiden should be here soon, he said we could let you take a peek. Not a loved one, I take it?" He peeled back the sheet from the face of one of the covered forms. "Died of heart failure, though his liver was going to be next given the amount of alcohol in his blood. Found him under the hanging airplane sculpture beneath the overpass."

Hoseman? Bushy strawberry-blond eyebrows. Pale lashes. "This *could* be the guy who tried to mug me. I never got a clear look at him. I'm sorry."

The attendant, probably a pathology student from MCV, grunted and re-covered the face. "Thanks. You can wait out there for the detective if you like."

Charlie gladly left the room. Too much emptiness in there for her. It was bad enough to be deep underground in the dead of night. The utter stillness of the air made every tiny noise or movement seem larger, louder, more frightening.

She backed against the cold wall and rubbed a hand over her face. Maybe if she kept her eyes closed she'd wake up back in her hotel room, safe and far away from the bodies—the shells of the dead.

"Was it him?"

She looked up sharply. Her gasp echoed in the almost empty hallways and her body relaxed in relief. His face bore a thick shadow of stubble, but his eyes were bright.

"The guy who grabbed me in the alley? Maybe."

"Come with me." Vaiden escorted her into a small room containing just a table and a few chairs. On the table he placed a baggie containing an old photo of Charlie, a slip of paper, and a small black stone.

Alarms bells sounded in her head. The missing stone.

"Other than the bottle of whiskey next to him, these were the only things he carried." He slid the plastic bag closer to her.

She focused on the paper. Her stomach dropped. "That's the address of my house." Her blood beat a cadence in her ears, sounding like large feet tramping through crisp leaves. "The second time I was mugged, I kinda figured it was personal, but... Do you think it was him? Do you think this was all his idea?"

Vaiden frowned. "That's what my supervisor thinks. In his opinion it's case closed."

"But you don't think so." The silence around them in the room was an entity wrapping her like a Kevlar cloak. Safe, but heavy to bear.

"The hairs we found in the storage space, and in the basement of your house both match his DNA profile." He sat back, letting his hands rest on his thighs. "Once we ID him and get a handwriting sample, we'll know."

Not wanting to ask how he planned to get a dead man's handwriting, Charlie examined the paper again. "That's a woman's handwriting, Vaiden."

He leaned forward and turned the baggie toward himself. "Why do you say that?"

"The *i* is dotted with a little circle. Look real close."

He smiled and reached across to squeeze her hand. His smile was indulgent and rankled her. "We'll figure this out. Jarod's checking the databases now to see what he can come up with. I'll call you on your cell as soon as I have news."

The officer who'd driven her to the morgue stood waiting at the door. Vaiden's brusque dismissal bothered her. If this mystery tied in to *her* life, then she would have to be responsible for figuring it out. Not him.

A thought struck her. The stone's image... Could it have some sort of dark power? She brushed the thought away as ridiculous.

Still... The cat had gone missing near the dean's office... and the carving of primitive heart surgery—or perhaps it was just ritual sacrifice, the jury was still out—taken by the mugger…"Vaiden, did you notice what stone he took?"

He lifted the bag and turned it in his hands to view the image. She noticed his messy hair then, and the wrinkles in his button-down shirt. He held the stone higher. "What is that?"

"The guy in the alley took one stone when he ran. The one showing a man in a headdress removing a man's heart from his chest. Your dead guy in there, he died of heart failure? And the dean—the one stone I couldn't find after he chucked them out of the window was the one with a jaguar carved on it. We both saw his throat.

"I know that logically makes no sense, but given that these are artifacts from a site where it's quite possible a myth actually happened… These coincidences might not be coincidental at all. Maybe you need to think about that."

His stare, as he rolled the stone over in his hand, was intense. She might as well have not been in the room. The silence hummed.

Charlie got to her feet, passed Vaiden, and succeeded in resisting her urge to touch him.

She knew there was one source where she could find some answers. Her father. May he rest in peace.

She approached the door, planning to ditch the officer and double back to her favorite place to practice breaking and entering. The library.

Chapter Nine

In the center of campus, each edifice lined up to fit like a set of puzzle pieces if viewed on a map. One side of the four-story library faced the rear of the theatre building. The gap between the two brick structures encompassed a mere six feet. Cutting through the small space saved no time, as neither building had a square shape. For this reason, Charlie had rarely encountered another person near her secret entrance to the campus library.

She backed into the narrow *c*-shaped crevice beneath the second-story window. Confident that no one had seen her, she pressed one foot against each side of the indentation and worked her way upward.

As a child, Charlie often snuck out of her house and escaped to the library after hours. No, it hadn't been the smartest thing, but she'd had a bad habit of waking in the night with questions. Asking her father about anything would set him off on an hour-long explanation worthy of a lecture hall. She didn't have the patience for that sort of thing. Not knowing the answers drove her crazy, so she came to the place with the information. The clear, concise information. The research room.

Usually the books Charlie needed weren't in electronic files or microfiche, they were the ones kept under lock and key. No mere child was allowed to peruse the valuable tomes and documents. Not even the daughter of one of the faculty. Now, even though her job gave her carte blanche access to most areas of the campus, she still found the need to enter at the worst possible hours. They should just give her a key.

Charlie winced at the sudden ache in the recently healed wound on her forearm. She made short work of ascending and paused, balancing with outward pressure from her feet and calves.

Careful not to look down, she drew a small knife from her pocket and slid a blade beneath the base of the window frame. She popped the sealed paint and pushed upward on the wood. There were no alarms to worry about. No one but a fool would try to climb to that height just for books.

One foot slipped an inch and she rearranged her legs. A fall from this height would do damage.

Her second shove opened the window. Charlie leaned in and heaved with her arms. She shoulder-rolled to a standing position and froze, listening. Security guards did occasionally prowl the buildings, but they made no secret of their presence since they had no desire to surprise a thief.

She released a breath and moved forward. The rooms were dark, but she knew the layout like it was her own house. Her father's dig journals were housed in the research holdings room. A librarian guarded the door during the day, but rarely was it actually locked, despite the appearance of heavy metallic bolts. Tonight was no exception.

Charlie found the shelf containing the journals and grabbed the volumes she wanted. Rather than remain in the holdings room, she crept out into the main floor and hid in a phone-booth sized reading room. She propped the door open with her knee and dug her penlight from her backpack. She held the light in her teeth and flipped through the first journal.

Her father had donated his research to the university upon his death. She'd used this very journal to calculate the location of the gold rod. Her father had supervised several Peruvian digs, and in his spare time he always added notes leading to his life's dream of finding the rod of Manco Copac.

She wasn't sure her father had believed the Inca creation story, but he'd been sure the rod was out there in the jungle. Too bad he'd never lived to see it with his own eyes. Too bad she'd been careless enough to lose it.

The pages jumbled out and she patted them back into place. She would have to speak to the restoration administrator about rebinding the text.

A list of students working on each dig appeared at the end of that particular season's notes. Those names interested her. If she could decode her father's habit of nicknaming everyone on the dig, maybe she could figure out who might be after the artifact.

In his notes from time to time her father mentioned a student who had disappointed or particularly irritated him. Before her trip, she'd read the section for technical notes, but now she paid special attention to personal ones.

One student, who her father called only Seven-K, had been especially troublesome that season. Because of him, her father had been banned from reentering the country. Seven-K? That could mean anything!

She brightened. There was someone on the university staff who had been around back when her father headed up the South American digs. Maybe he could add some insight into the nicknames.

Somewhere outside the reading room, a door snapped shut. Charlie dropped the penlight into the bag and stuffed her father's journal inside. She crawled out of the small room, where she'd be a sitting duck if the guard did a thorough check.

She scurried behind the stacks, eventually climbing on top of a wide, sturdy wooden bookshelf where she'd hopefully be out of sight. When she saw the sweeping path of the flashlight, she knew she'd be safer if she headed farther up. She eased a ceiling tile over and pulled herself into the framework, leaving herself a tiny viewing space between the tile and the metal rod on which it rested.

The guard strode into the research room and turned on the light. Charlie groaned and slithered along the ceiling with as much stealth as she could muster. The guard had no reason to be in that room unless he'd seen her come up the side of the building. But—she checked her watch—that had been a half-hour ago.

She peered down at the guard. From her angle she could not see his face. She did, however, see that he was knocking her father's journals from the shelves and into a haphazard pile. She had a flashback of the mess in her house that first day back and had to bite her bottom lip to keep from screaming at the man. Could he be the same one who'd trashed her files?

He was obviously not looking for anything; he hadn't read any of the pages. He scrunched down over the mess. Charlie smelled the sulfur before she saw the flames. He'd used a flint lighter to set fire to her father's work!

The flames licked at the edge of the pile, then whooshed into an eager consuming fury. The guard turned as he left and she saw his face for a brief moment. Outrage flew through her veins. How dare he? Her father's work! His life was in these journals. She clenched her jaw. It was like losing her father again.

Her first instinct was to jump down and put the fire out somehow, but in a room full of old dry paper, there was no hope for that. Even now the flames licked at other tomes and zipped upward. Smoke siphoned between the ceiling tiles and Charlie held her breath as she backed away toward another room. If the sprinklers didn't kick on soon, she would be trapped. The fire was already trying to come through the tiles. The shelves in the research room must have caught fire too.

The sharp hiss of water hitting the flames made her sigh. Sprinklers. The fire would be put out. Maybe some of her father's work would be saved. She could only pray.

Her relief lasted only seconds. She had to get out of the building before the firemen arrived and found her. They would be more thorough than a security guard. And she could already hear sirens.

✧

Charlie descended the wall too quickly and scraped the sides of her palms. It was either slow way down, or endure more scrapes. Finally, she dropped the last ten feet to the ground. The lights from the fire trucks spun wildly against the buildings through the tiny vertical view, and she had no idea how close they would come to her location between the buildings.

She'd thrown her backpack down first, before climbing out the window, and now stooped to pick it up. She barely straightened, intent on slipping through the puzzle-pieced walkways to emerge far away from the scene without calling attention to herself.

Then she realized she wasn't alone.

Thick arms circled her waist as she tried to run and someone knocked her to the ground. He angled his shoulder and kept her from hitting too hard, taking her weight as she fell.

His big body landed half on top of her legs and held her still, one hand covering her mouth. A hand that smelled of pencils, not of smoke and sulfur. Not that she would have screamed. Better one witness to lose than a passel of them come to her rescue.

She bit hard on the finger that rested against her lips, then rolled sideways, trying to wriggle away. Who the hell would be back here anyway? Though the sun had yet to peel away the inky darkness, she could see the man's face easily. The black arched brows, thick ebony hair...face full of accusation. Vaiden.

"Ow! What the hell did you do that for?" He shook his hand and then sucked the finger she'd chomped.

He backed up, still on the ground, but she grabbed his arm, pulling him closer to the wall and out of range of the lights. Her determination to get away unseen dissolved into irritation. First he had her tailed, and now this?

"You followed me?" She whispered harshly and pressed him against one wall.

"*Had* you followed. But you managed to ditch your tail when you got on campus. When I saw the fire trucks I figured you had to be in the middle of it. Trouble follows you." His hands rested on her waist, so easily. Too natural. She inched away before her body did what it wanted and leaned in against his strength. She had to fight this damned attraction. She'd end up hurting him if she didn't stop.

He followed, taking a step closer, never taking his hands from her waist. "What are you doing, Charlie?"

"I needed something from my father's journals. They're kept in the records room. And, no, it couldn't wait." She wished she could see him, but when she'd pulled him against the building, she'd lost that advantage. The night filled the passage, and except for his hands, gentle on her hips now, she wouldn't have known where he stood, much less what he was doing with his face.

"So you admit you were breaking and entering?"

"I wouldn't call it 'breaking'. It's not as if I broke any locks."

He sighed. "Charlie you scaled a wall and went in through a window. I think that's pretty classic B and E."

His scent swept past her nostrils and she closed her eyes. His mouth grazed her cheekbone and she held her breath.

"You smell like smoke."

She exhaled. "Yeah, well, I had company. A little firebug." She puffed a bit of air from her nose in anger. When she got a hold of—

"This isn't funny. You could go to jail." His fingers tightened on her side and held the material of her shirt to keep her from getting away.

The jackass thought *she* set the fire?

She placed her palms on his chest and heaved. Like trying to move a wall of stone. "Why would I destroy my own father's materials?" She almost screeched, but was careful to keep her voice down. Most likely the firemen were making enough of their own noise and wouldn't hear them far way between the buildings, but she didn't want to take a chance.

He spoke against her ear. "I don't know, but I assure you I intend to find out."

He actually thought she'd broken in to do harm. She wanted to kick him in the shin, but knew from experience that there were better ways to get a man to release her, and in the process shock him long enough to get away. She closed her eyes, sure that she would regret what she had to do. She opened her mouth and extended her tongue, making contact with Vaiden's neck just below his ear. Then moaned his name.

He stiffened, then clenched her tighter as she kissed his throat. "Charlie, stop."

The pulse that beat erratically beneath her lips reminded her that Vaiden was all man, and he did want her. Power was a heady feeling, but she hated this abuse of it. He'd be angry later when he realized she'd tricked him.

At last she kissed him full on the mouth, feeling empty triumph when he returned the kiss. She had no need to fake her desire for him. He made her smolder with only a look. Maybe the dark did have its advantages after all.

Her hands sought his loosened tie and jerked it from his collar. Her skin sizzled as his hands slid beneath her shirt. She feigned a struggle with the buttons of his oxford to get him to remove his hands from her. When he did, she mouthed an apology he would never see, tightened her hold on her pack, and ran from him. As fast as her feet could carry her.

✧

Vaiden sagged against the wall and grinned at Charlie's fading footsteps. She might think she'd gotten away with something. Two could play that game.

He'd wondered how he'd get the tracking device on her. Her little kissing game had provided the perfect opportunity. Though he'd enjoyed her ruse, and in fact almost forgot to stick the tiny metal disk in her backpack, her sudden assault on his neck had set warning bells clanging louder than the fire truck sirens.

Seeing her shimmying down the side of the building had stopped his heart. If she'd fallen...

But she hadn't. She'd moved like a pro, which meant she'd done this before.

He cursed. She'd kissed him like a pro also. He'd gone hard the instant she clutched him with her treacherous fingers.

Charlie was no debutante screened and approved by his Ivy League parents. She could take care of herself.

She could take care of him too, it seemed.

He cleared his throat, fixed his tie, and headed toward the chaos. He'd give Charlie a head start. Meanwhile, he meant to discover just what havoc she'd wreaked.

Chapter Ten

As usual, the doors of the sociology building had small wedges of wood propping them open, so Charlie had no problem getting inside. It was just about four-thirty in the morning. She didn't expect anyone to be working at the crack of dawn, which was probably better for her.

Dean Fisher's office still had crime scene tape across the door, but the rest of the building had been cleared. She didn't need to get into the dean's office. She had another destination in mind.

Now that the library was off-limits, maybe she could find information elsewhere. At the least she'd find the home phone number of the man in her department who she needed to contact. She wasn't sure she could wait for him to come to work.

Leonard Kedansky's office was locked, but she easily finessed the lock with her pocketknife. She slipped inside, closed the door, and drew the curtains. Like all the offices for adjunct professors, the space was no more than a renovated closet. Somehow Leonard had managed to snag one with a window. She switched on the one tiny light on the desk and took in the décor.

Leonard had only come to work for the university in the past few years as an adjunct professor. He was nice enough, she supposed, but every conversation with him centered on how much he'd learned from her father when he'd taken a Peruvian history class under Dr. Blair. He'd offered once to make electronic files of her father's journals. She'd declined. Maybe she was old-fashioned, but she enjoyed the feel of paper beneath her fingers. Now she wished she'd taken him up on the offer.

A sob rose, unexpected, in her throat. Her father's journals. If they'd been completely destroyed... Her heart ached. She shouldn't think that way. She had to be positive.

Her attention focused on a display shelf. He'd added artifacts to his walls since her last trip. Stone artifacts that—her eyes widened. She removed a thin stone knife from the ledge. The polished stone was smooth to the touch. In the handle, an intricate carving of a monkey with a spiral tail glared at her.

Charlie seethed. This knife had been displayed in her father's office. The monkey's bloodthirsty grin had frightened her as a child. She hated the thing, and was almost glad when it hadn't turned up in his possessions. But for Leonard to just take it?

She considered keeping the knife to show to Leonard and demand an explanation. Instead she returned it to the shelf. She would come back during his office hours and pretend she'd never seen the knife. Maybe her father had given it to him. From Leonard's accounts, he'd been one of her father's best students. It was possible. She tried to relax. Not everyone was out to get her.

She perused the rest of Leonard's artifacts, pausing to examine a broken stone phoenix. The phoenix was one of the representations she liked most. The thought of being able to start over appealed to her.

Leonard, she'd heard, had divorced his wife, then remarried her. He had the perfect family. She glanced at the photos that stood on his blotter. Each person in his family occupied a separate cutout shape in the frame. Smiling wife, smiling son, smiling Leonard. No pictures as a group. She lifted the frame, and tried to read the script along the edge of one picture. A list of numbers and letters. Odd.

She removed the back of the frame and flipped over the backing. With the exception of Leonard's photo, *all* the pictures had similar codes. They'd been cut straight from a stock photo book. Creepy.

The bell in the student union clock chimed. Charlie arranged the frame just as she'd found it and turned to the door. She had a lot of information to think about. If she could find his home number somewhere on his desk, she could get out of there. Breakfast and a quick nap would be just the thing. Then she'd—

"Dr. Blair. Whyever are you in Professor Kedansky's office?"

Him. Did he know that she knew?

"Officer LePrade. I was just trying to find Leonard's home number. You don't happen to have access to that, do you?" She didn't like the way he kept his fingers spread wide at his sides. He edged closer and she circled the other side of the desk, attempting to appear nonchalant.

"Did you hear we had a fire tonight? Over at the library." His pale skin seemed to glow against the black of his uniform.

"'S'that where you got the soot on your hands?"

As the campus security guard put his hands before his face to inspect them, Charlie dashed toward the doorway. LePrade wrenched her arm and pulled her back into the room. "You have something I need, Charlie."

Her heart raced, but she tried to focus. No sense losing a

battle over lack of common sense. She was smarter than he was, even if she was smaller.

Bill LePrade restrained her by twisting her arm behind her back. He yanked her backpack, and Charlie seized the opportunity, knowing he couldn't hold her with just one hand. She bent her knees and turned, reluctantly letting him take her pack as she slipped free.

She scrambled for the door, and he pushed her into the frame. Dazed for a moment, she tasted blood in her mouth. Adrenaline surged through her and she kicked backward as hard as she could. She made contact with his middle. Air whooshed from him and he backed off. She skedaddled from the office and hid around the corner.

Surprise slowly imbued her with fresh energy. He hadn't chased her. Whatever LePrade had wanted, it wasn't her.

Her backpack! She rolled her eyes. She had to go back for the thing. Her lips thinned. He wouldn't expect her to come back. She could get the drop on him. No longer afraid, her anger made her brave.

She stopped just outside the room, her fists high, ready to pounce on him when he exited. But LePrade was speaking to someone, almost whining. She cursed silently and, just to even the odds, backed up and retrieved a broom handle from the custodial closet.

LePrade's yell startled her. She covered the distance back to Leonard's office rapidly and skidded to a halt in the doorway, brandishing the broom handle before her.

At first she couldn't see LePrade, but as she tiptoed inside, she saw him sprawled beneath one of the display shelves. He had a nasty bump on his head, and a thin trickle of blood worked its way toward his ear. The broken phoenix statue lay nearby. Had someone hit him with the artifact? Or had it fallen on him? She'd seen no one in the hall. But then, to whom had he been speaking?

She checked his pulse, thinking all the while of horror movies where the bad guy leaped on the girl as she did just that. The steady beat of the blood in his neck against her fingers made her jump. LePrade was still alive.

No one needed to know she was ever here. LePrade's injuries weren't her fault.

She wrestled her backpack from his still tight grasp and made a split-second decision to leave the scene. But she would arrange for someone to find him.

The ROTC boys would be jogging around campus soon. They'd be sure to notice if she left the window open and the light on.

She'd had enough medical training to know that he'd be fine. And he deserved a smack in the head after setting fire to her father's papers in the library. She'd taken worse blows than that by accident, and in the middle of the jungle. He'd live, but he would have a heck of a headache.

✧

Back in her hotel room, Charlie climbed onto the bed and pulled her sketchbook onto her lap. She rolled the pencil she kept in the spine of the book between her fingers. She'd taken a hot shower to relax herself enough for a nap, and the thick towel she rubbed herself dry with left her skin rosy and her hair barely wet. She should be ready for sleep.

Only, her body wasn't cooperating. She wasn't tired.

Leonard was out of reach until morning when he came in to the office. If he had answers, they would keep until then.

She tugged on a pair of jeans and a tailored button-up shirt, pushed the on button for the TV remote, and lifted her pack from the floor. As the theme song for the morning news blasted her, she palmed the small pouch containing the stones and let them tumble onto the bedspread.

She counted twice. Eight stones, down from ten, down from twelve. “Dean Fisher was right. I should be fired. I can’t keep track of twelve freaking rocks, let alone a priceless artifact.”

Last time she’d checked, she’d had ten. LePrade must have taken two stones.

She bit back a curse. She’d just have to go back and get the stones. LePrade was bound to have woken by now.

And if LePrade didn’t have the stones, they’d be somewhere in Leonard’s office.

She sat on the edge of the bed to tie her shoes. The newscaster said the name of the university and Charlie’s chin jutted forward, bringing her head up. The graphic in the corner of the screen read “homicide”. What the hell?

No names, no details, just a death, possibly a campus policeman.

The air grew thick and Charlie felt as though she’d been slammed in the solar plexus. Dead? They had to mean LePrade, but he hadn’t been hurt that bad. Just a bump. She’d checked him over. Her assessment had been thorough.

What the hell happened?

She fanned the air in front of her face and swallowed back her panic. She had to get over there and find out. If she’d caused LePrade’s death by assessing his injury incorrectly and not calling 911, she’d never forgive herself. At the very least, she could tell them what she knew. She had no other choice.

She shoved the eight stones into the pouch and dropped

them back into her pack. She swiped her damp hair from her eyes and wrenched the door open.

Vaiden stood in the portal, his fist raised to knock.

Charlie backed up and he barged past her.

"Going somewhere?" He removed his suit coat and draped it on the back of a chair.

She smacked her lips together. "Back to campus."

Vaiden gestured at the TV, then switched it off. "You've heard?"

Confess. Tell what you know. They'll find the stones anyway. "I was there, Vaiden. He was the one who—" She stopped. She didn't like the look in his eyes. Accusation. Again. "When I left him, he was fine. A bump on the head, but he was alive."

He wrinkled his upper lip and released a harsh laugh. "Bump on the head? Charlie, his throat was slashed."

Fanning the air did nothing to prevent what came next. Sound swooped through her ears and the carpet rushed up to her. For the first time in her life, she fainted.

✧

Charlie, who gave the impression of being so strong, so in control, was a rag doll in his arms. This was no feigned swoon. He'd seen enough of those. His words had completely taken her by surprise. But that didn't help matters. She'd been in the room with the vic, he'd been injured, and she'd fled the scene.

He should have checked the tracking signal earlier. He'd have been able to stop her. Or save her. Something.

Bending at the waist, he laid her across the bed and then

walked to the sink. He soaked a cloth in cold water, noticing the wet towels on the floor of the bathroom. Later. He'd pick them up later.

He returned to the bed and ran the cloth across her neck and face. Her clothes had no blood spatter on them, but she could have changed.

As he sat beside her, her eyes opened with a jolt, but she stayed prone, her fingers splayed on the coverlet. After a beat she sucked in air and sat up, the clouded look in her eyes clearing as she remembered where she was and what he'd said.

The cloth fell to her lap and she stared at it. "I didn't kill him. Couldn't cut his—" Her hand covered her mouth. Her shoulders sagged and though her head leaned down, her eyes flicked back and forth.

He plucked the cloth from her lap. "Tell me what happened. Start with why you were there." He turned and threw the cloth across the room to land in the empty ice bucket.

"I didn't—you're gonna—"

Vaiden took her fingers into his hand and silenced her with a gentle squeeze. "Don't tell me what you didn't do. Tell me what you did." Her hands had gone cold, but still her touch warmed him inside.

He needed a clear story from her. He needed her words to ring true. He needed *her*. And right now that was the worst thing possible.

While she collected her thoughts, he wondered if she could hear his heartbeat. His heart pounded. No matter what she was about to tell him, he knew he was too far gone. She did something new to him every time he was around her. And he was powerless to save himself from falling.

Charlie recounted her actions that evening, from her trip into the library, to leaving Bill LePrade unconscious on the floor of Leonard Kedansky's office. He kept silent, wanting a clue or a connection to present itself. A reason why his investigation into the Orion murders kept coming back to events in Charlie's life.

When she finished, she was standing near the window, her hand holding the curtains slightly apart as she peered like a cat at the traffic below. "There *was* a knife in the room when I was there. Made of stone, with a monkey carved into the hilt."

The murder weapon. What would she say about it? "Yes, there was a knife."

"Was it the one that was used to kill him?"

"It was on the floor next to him, the blade coated with blood."

"When I left the room, it was on the display shelf. It's my father's, from a South American dig. I know it has to be the same one. I touched it. I considered taking it with me to ask Leonard why he had it. In retrospect, I guess I should have."

He nodded to her back. "Your prints are going to be on the knife then."

"I guess if you can get prints from stone, yeah, they will." She faced him, a plea in her eyes.

"You'd be surprised what we can get prints from these days." He smiled, but the expression fell away quickly. His gut told him to believe her, but the evidence wasn't going to go her way. "What clothes were you wearing when you were there?"

She took a step toward him and stopped, her hands at her sides. "I didn't kill him."

"I don't think you did either, but they're gonna need your clothes." Knowing her, they were in a pile on the floor somewhere. "What I *do* think, is that you're in danger." He closed the distance between them and pushed her hair away from her face. A thin red line down the left side of her face caught his attention. He ran the pad of his thumb down the welt. "This where you hit the doorjamb?"

She nodded. Her lips parted. She glanced at his mouth, then into his eyes and blushed. His heart beat faster and heat rushed through his body. She lifted her hands to his sides and stroked her palms up his back to his shoulder blades. It was as though she were waiting for some signal from him.

He dragged his lips across her forehead and rested his mouth in her hair. He wanted her, but it would break all kinds of rules to actually make love to Charlie Blair. He held her, warring with himself. Was she worth it?

Charlie sighed and settled her cheek against his chest. She fit as if a special spot had been carved out just for her and no other.

He closed his eyes, knew he needed to get out of her hotel room, but was reluctant to actually release her.

It was Charlie who moved first. She tilted her head upward and smiled. She didn't say a word, but something in her eyes spoke to him. And then she kissed him.

He kept his mouth pliant for all of two seconds before the rush of desire swept over him and sent him careening down a path he knew he'd probably regret. But he *had* discovered one thing. She was definitely worth it. Her kiss, like last time, had him instantly hard.

He steered her toward the bed, unbuttoning his shirt as they walked. Her hands worked his belt loose and yanked it free of the loops. They broke contact only long enough for him to pull her shirt over her head, awkwardly yank his own shirt and undershirt from his chest, and throw the rest of their clothing to the floor in a heap.

All control disappeared. He kissed her hard, his pent-up passion sending him over the edge. He wanted no long slow lovemaking from her. He had to possess this woman. Make her *his*. And his alone.

Her level of response inflamed him further. She writhed beneath him, her hands kneading his flesh as though she couldn't get him close enough. She panted at his touch, reacting to his ministrations as no other woman had in the past.

Her body sang to him, told him where to touch, where to put his mouth. A flick of a tongue, or stroke of skin made her stiffen and cry out long before he entered her.

And when he finally plunged deep inside her, he took her mouth with his, echoing the possession. They moved together in perfect synchronicity, riding wave after wave of intensity, until she cried out his name. He allowed himself release, heard himself nearly howl his pleasure as they flew over the edge together.

Minutes later, he rolled sideways, taking her with him and settling her into his arms, one leg thrown across both of hers. Her warm body shuddered and he grinned drowsily. They were good together. Too damn good. He wouldn't be able to let her go. Didn't *want* to let her go.

Sated and overcome by exhaustion and emotions he didn't want to face, Vaiden slept.

Chapter Eleven

Charlie hovered in a haze between dreams and wakefulness. Centered in warmth, safe in a haven of sinew and muscle. Her ears pricked at a noise on the edge of her awareness. Three tones, and a silence. Then a repeat. No, not tones exactly. The sound was too muffled.

Reluctantly she forced one eye to open.

The hotel room came slowly into focus. The sound sharpened. A dog barking? She didn't think the hotel allowed dogs. The animal must be in the hallway, maybe even in front of her door. So loud. Urgent.

The noise wasn't going to cease, and Charlie wasn't going to be able to sleep through it.

She sighed heavily and folded the blankets back. Her skin protested at being separated from Vaiden's warm body. He turned onto his stomach when she crawled from beneath his arm, but he did not wake.

Charlie scratched her head, spied her robe on the floor near the bathroom, and dragged the cozy covering on. The dog's barking cadence plowed through her misted mind.

She wondered how Vaiden could sleep. The clock on the bedside table read five-thirty. They'd been in bed all day, making love between fitful bouts of sleep. She smiled. Well, okay, he *could* be tired.

In the entryway, she wrapped her fingers around the handle and turned it quietly, then winged the door open. The ringing silence told her ears that she hadn't imagined the piercing barks, but her eyes found no dog.

Every door within her sight stood closed. She cocked her head and listened for a full minute. Nothing.

An eerie feeling crept over her and she pushed it away. She'd been painfully aware of the coincidences in the similarity between images on the missing stones and recent events. Again she asked herself if the stones *could* have some sort of power. Could they *kill*? She believed in the existence of otherworldly occurrences. Just not in her life.

She closed the door firmly, locked it, and brought her pack from beneath the bed where she'd kicked it earlier. She breathed deeply and dumped the pouch into her hands. Eight stones. The dog carving was still there. She exhaled in relief, chuckling at her own foolishness. As if the wolf-dog stone could have conjured a barking noise outside her room!

She tucked the stones into their bits of moleskin, and then back inside the pouch. She scribbled a short note to Vaiden on the hotel stationery. She had to find Leonard Kedansky. He had worked with her father, albeit as a student. Maybe he had those relics in his office for a reason. He had to know what was going on, who the student-thief had been. If he didn't know anything, she'd have to believe she was losing her mind.

In five minutes she had her jeans and shirt back on, and her hair pulled into a ponytail. She'd watched Vaiden in the mirror as she dressed. She hadn't meant to let her guard down with him. She'd grown to care for him far more than she'd intended.

Before she left, she leaned over him, resting one knee on the mattress, and kissed his shoulder. As she slid the sheet higher on his back, her fingers ran across a spatter of pockmarks on one side. The ragged appendectomy scar on his belly she'd seen that morning, but the scars on his back were a surprise. Using her fingertips, she traced them. Looked like buckshot. Three circles the diameter of a pencil eraser, ten smaller circles.

Her eyebrows pushed together. She'd seen this scar before. Shock rippled through her and she quieted her gasp with a hand. She knew exactly where she'd seen the pattern.

She moved to the floor and opened her pack with shaking hands. Once more she emptied the pouch of stones. She rolled them on the rug, turning the images, the cool stone surfaces chilling her. Three of the stones had only dot-patterns. She'd assumed since one resembled the constellation Scorpius, and another Orion, that the third was a more obscure sky-picture, one she'd been unable to locate on the Peruvian sky-charts.

But it wasn't a constellation at all. It matched Vaiden's scar perfectly.

Her ears rang and dizziness threatened to overcome her. She gathered the stones as fast as she could, then stood and backed away from Vaiden.

Her life had just crossed into the realm of the bizarre. She needed answers. And she knew where she had to get them.

✧

The computer lab hopped at dinnertime. Many night courses began at seven, so students packed the labs to finish assignments before heading to class. Charlie sat off to the side, in a cubicle next to the window, doing her best to keep her head down. She didn't need the lab monitor noticing what she was up to. This was not work she could do on her department's computers, not if she wanted to remain incognito.

At the front of the room she spied a familiar head of light brown hair. Erik Walker, the student she'd had kicked out of Peru. She seethed. How he'd convinced the university to keep him enrolled was beyond her.

He was bent over a keyboard, typing fast. Maybe he'd do all right if he had only male teachers. Ones he couldn't try to bully sexually to get his way. It had been bad enough that the inexperienced punk thought his meager archaeological training should be superior to her years of study and living on site with her parents. But when he'd entered her tent the night before she'd sent him packing and climbed on top of her to make his point about who was dominant, she'd been furious.

Hernandez, bless his heart, had been alert enough to realize something wasn't right, and burst in just as she punched Erik in the nose. His blood had actually sprayed from his right nostril at first, and for a while they hadn't been sure it would stop flowing.

Charlie stared bullets into the back of his head as he continued working on the computer. Served him right.

She sucked a calming breath in through her nose and released it through her mouth as quietly as she could. Now was not the time to let the kid get to her. He was a jerk. His daddy couldn't rescue him forever. He'd eventually piss off someone who had the power to put him in his place.

She made herself turn away. She had other things to accomplish. She risked a peek at the lab assistant's desk behind her. All she could see were the crisscrossed soles of a pair of large sneakers.

She turned back to the monitor, and rotated her head to work out a slight stiffness from her neck. She'd made it through the firewall into Human Resources. If she couldn't find Leonard on campus, she'd find him at home.

Her pack rested on the floor next to the plastic-backed chair. One strap looped around her right foot, a precaution, given the sudden love every thug and minion had developed for her stones.

No one had to know she no longer carried them. Putting the pouch of stones into the hotel safe before heading to campus had been the first smart thing she'd done since coming back to the States. If those rocks wanted to disappear now, they'd just have to do it all on their own.

She pressed her shoulder blades together, her chest out, and stretched until her spine made a popping noise. With a contained sigh, she flexed her fingers over the keyboard.

The pass code prompt for HR appeared on the screen, a puzzle she welcomed. She held her breath. Most faculty and staff had the same default password pattern: first initial, middle initial, full last name. She knew only one person's full name from Human Resources: Betty Jo Turner. She hoped the woman hadn't had the foresight to change her pass code.

Twenty seconds after the little black and white wheel began spinning on screen, the HR database came online and Charlie allowed herself to breathe. A few attempts at file searches, and she had Leonard Kedansky's records before her. She scrolled to the scanned images of his application, letters of recommendation, transcripts, and résumé.

She didn't want to read the man's life story—though an explanation for his stock-photo family might be interesting—she only wanted to verify that he'd taken a class or two under her father.

She found the listings quickly. He'd taken three classes. In the first two—lecture courses—he'd received an A and a B. For the fieldwork in Peru, a semester's worth of credits, he'd earned an F. He'd retaken the courses under another professor, but the Fs remained on his record.

Charlie hid her shock with a cough. If he'd failed the course... Her eyes returned to his name. Kedansky. Had to be the K in Seven-K. She brought her hand to her face and tapped her forehead. She was slipping. She should have caught that earlier. When this was resolved, she needed a vacation. One where she just slept. And ate tiramisu.

And lounged in bed with Vaiden all day.

Damn. She'd fought to keep him out of her thoughts from the moment she'd left the room. She could smell him on her skin, feel his arms encircling her. He would not approve of her breaking into the university's computer system, that was certain. All the more reason to get out of the lab before he found her. He had a second sense when it came to her location the past few days.

She scribbled Leonard's home address onto a piece of scrap paper left next to the printer. The house was not far from campus. She emerged from the lab and hurried to the location on foot.

A twenty-minute jog from campus, the thin two-story structure sat wedged between two identically designed homes among the row of fourteen or fifteen. They differentiated only by color, choice of railing style, and number. Drapes thick enough to hide whether or not the lights were on blocked her view of the inside.

She opened the small iron gate and entered the yard. A short slate path led to the front steps. She sucked air through her nose and scrambled to find an excuse for ringing Leonard's bell.

She decided to plead for his help. Even if he was behind the mischief with her pack, she couldn't believe him guilty of the dean's death. An animal had killed him. She frowned. Or someone had made it look that way. It was insane. Giant cats didn't roam halls of universities in downtown Richmond, and stone images carved in tiny rocks did not come to life. She needed answers.

The cool, damp night air filled her lungs as she braced herself. She raised her knuckles to knock on Leonard's front door. A hand closed over her mouth, another enclosed her fist. Her eyes went wide as she stumbled backward down the stairs, supported by a hard body. Only at the bottom, safely out of knocking distance, and away from the main line of sight from the house, did the person show his face.

✧

She went from frightened to furious in an instant. Vaiden kept his hold on her arm and escorted her around the corner where his car was parked. He only released her mouth to open the door.

"Get in."

Charlie scowled at him, but she obeyed. Good for her. He didn't want to force her to leave with him, but he would if it became necessary.

When he got in the driver's side, she had her arms crossed, but she'd latched her seatbelt. So she *did* have some self-preservation in there somewhere.

"You wanna tell me what you were doing?" *The truth this time.*

She cut her eyes sideways. "Visiting a colleague."

He started the engine and shifted into drive. "We need to

talk." She wasn't going to like this, and he didn't relish confessing it to her. He frowned. He didn't owe her any apologies. She'd left him sleeping and hadn't bothered to put her research away. So what if he scoured the pages? "I looked at the papers you left on the table in your hotel room."

Contrary to his expectations, she didn't react with more anger. "Why would you? They're notes and drawings."

"I brought your things from the hotel room. You had one sketch in particular that caught my interest. A constellation." *Why*? Once again she'd linked herself to his case. A coincidence? He meant to find out, but she didn't comment during the ride to his house.

The drive to his house passed quickly considering the silence that enveloped the car. By the time he unlocked the front door and carried in her duffle from the hotel, she'd apparently decided to listen.

But he needed her to talk.

He spread her papers on the kitchen table. There had to be a solid connection to his case. Hopefully she could help him find it. Most people were unaware they knew vital information, had no idea that something they considered mundane could be important.

She came to stand next to him and pointed to a sketch of a pattern of dots. "This one?"

Astronomy was never a strong point of his. He dismissed the random design and ignored her smirk. "No." He moved one sketch forward with his fingers. "Orion. Why did you make this?"

She sighed and sat in a wooden chair at the table. "You got anything to eat?" She propped her chin on her fists and rested her elbows on the table. Damn, she was cute. He wanted to take her chin in his hands and kiss her. But he had to focus.

"You talk. I'll make some sandwiches." He opened his refrigerator and took out turkey, cheese, and mayonnaise. He paused by the breadbox and turned toward her. "Well?"

She was staring at him with an odd expression. Her eyes were the same clear green as his grandmother's emerald ring. He had to remember to give it to her. *Concentrate.*

She shrugged and scooted the papers around. "These are sketches of the Ica stones." She arranged them in stacks.

Rather than turn his back to her, he brought the sandwich makings to the far end of the table and nodded for her to continue.

"Orion is one of them. Also Scorpius, which is fascinating considering..." She blushed. "How much detail do you want?"

"Give me the full treatment."

"Orion, in one version of the myth, was killed by a scorpion." She tucked her hair behind her ears and showed him the other dot pattern again. "You sure this one isn't familiar?"

He made lines between the dots in his mind. "Nope. Never seen it."

Again with the smirking.

He handed her a plate of two sandwiches and filled two glasses with water from a jug in the fridge.

"I told you some of the stones have been lost. Well, you have one of them. The one that guy had on him when he was found."

He pulled out the chair next to her and sat, his leg brushing against hers. "Hmm. The one with the feather-headed man reaching into someone's chest."

"Exactly. And you recall the man died of heart failure." She scratched her neck with her short, unpainted nails. Instantly he thought of how that neck tasted. He straightened in his seat, pressing his spine against the chair back.

She inhaled and blew out the air, making her bangs flutter. "You willing to hear things that are gonna sound bizarre?"

He laughed. Everything since he'd met Charlie had been bizarre.

Her smile said she understood. "Bizarre is the new normal this year. For me anyway." Her eyes sparkled. "First stone gone was the jaguar." She slid the appropriate sketch to him. "Dean Fisher threw the whole set out of his window. This was the only one I couldn't find."

He held up a hand. "And the medical examiner said he was killed by something akin to a mountain lion. I think I see where we're going. Charlie—"

"No, listen. There's more. Bill LePrade. He was struck in the head by a statue of a phoenix, and then killed with a knife bearing a monkey carving." She pushed the sketches of two more Ica stones to him before he could protest. "Those stones are gone too. I think LePrade may have taken them when he grabbed my bag."

She took a bite of one of the sandwiches. Her eyes closed and she smiled. "This is good turkey."

He shook his head. She could jump around topics like no one else he knew. It would be endearing if he didn't feel like shaking her right now. Coincidences were not going to help him. Frankly, neither was the bizarre.

"So why the interest in Orion?"

Her question brought his focus back. "A case I'm working—was working—resembles the work of a murderer who called himself Orion." He'd been told to stop investigating, that they had their man and he was dead. But the fact that a victim had been left in Charlie's house bothered him.

The murderer had to know he had plenty of time to kill; he had to know she was out of the country. He didn't buy the mugger as intelligent enough to put it all together.

Charlie wiped her lips with a paper napkin. "The one who left that poor girl in my basement?" The corners of her eyes crinkled and she blinked several times. She was affected more than she let on.

"That's what I'm trying to find out. The man we originally put away for the crimes, ten years ago, he couldn't have committed these new ones."

"Because he's in prison?"

"Because he's dead."

"Oh." She sipped at the water. "Ten years ago. Long time to wait to copycat something."

His own sandwich sat untouched. "Why were you at that house tonight?"

Her eyes narrowed. "You don't know who the house belonged to?"

He sucked in a curse. She'd flip if he knew he'd been tracking her. He sent her a stern look. "Just answer the question."

Charlie chuckled. "Don't turn all detectivish on me, Vaiden." Her hand, cold from holding the glass, caressed his jaw. She leaned toward him and kissed his lips. His eyes drifted shut and he breathed in her strawberry scent.

When he opened his eyes the tiny hint of a smile on her mouth as she drew back set his pulse pounding. He gripped the sides of the chair to keep from touching her.

"Will you tell me?"

She nodded. "You know that when I was in the library, I grabbed some of my father's research papers. In his journal from the last dig he was on in Peru, he mentioned a student, calling him Seven-K, who tried to steal something from a museum. I wanted to see if Leonard knew who it could have been."

"Why Leonard?"

"He was on that dig as a student. But once I saw his failing grade in his records, I knew. My father always had a habit of forgetting names, so he'd associate each student with a type of rock, or an animal, something to help his memory. I'm thinking Leonard Kedansky is the would-be thief."

"And maybe he's the one after your stones?"

She patted the scattered papers into another series of neat piles. Only when she finished did she respond. "I don't know. I don't think he would risk his job over a handful of stones. No one places value on Ica stones. Most scientists consider their origins a hoax."

"But if he thought you'd really brought back the gold…"

Her lips twisted in a frown. "Could Leonard have destroyed my records at the house because he was searching for information on the rod? Maybe. I don't know. Seems really out there. Anyone Dean Fisher told about the gold had to also have heard that it was lost. Certainly nothing to kill for."

"Unless he thought you stole it yourself." Vaiden took their empty plates to the sink and ran water over them. He chose to ignore the fact that she'd apparently hacked into the university's records. If he didn't ask, he didn't know, as far as he was concerned. "So the house belongs to Kedansky?"

"Yup." She'd crept behind him and he felt her head against his back.

He spun slowly and leaned down to kiss her. Just as he'd noticed at the hotel, she fit perfectly into his embrace. As if the place had been designed just for her. It was torture having her this close, so willing and pliant, when he had the overwhelming need to protect her and possess her at once. He couldn't do both.

He rested his forehead against hers. "Then I think we need to pay Leonard Kedansky a visit. Together."

Chapter Twelve

The second time through the gate and up to Leonard's door went much easier. Of course, she had Vaiden at her side. That would make anything easier. The sun had set completely and darkness veiled the yard. The pools of light descending from the street lamps lent a faint brightness to the edge of the property, but the stairs had to be sensed rather than seen. The light next to the front door was off.

Charlie drew strength from the heat emanating from Vaiden's body a fraction of an inch behind her. She knocked on the door. The wide cracks in the paint captured her focus. Could use a paint job.

She rapped her knuckles louder this time and tilted her head toward the door. Not a sound.

"What do you think?" Her whisper shattered the stillness.

"Probably not home." Vaiden leaned sideways and peered through the skinny space between the houses. "Let's try the back."

Charlie emerged from the side of the house first and spied an open window on the second floor. "How about I try this door, and you wait around front. In case he comes out." She gestured toward the window with her eyes, knowing he couldn't officially sanction her plan, but he had to know she planned to climb inside.

He didn't protest, though he exhaled disapprovingly. After a moment he nodded and handed her a flashlight. "Be careful."

As soon as the darkness swallowed him she shimmied up the column supporting the second floor balcony. She pried the window up and moved the drapes aside. Her hands on the window ledge, she stared slack-jawed at the room. Not a stick of furniture. Drapes thick as army blankets, but nothing else.

Surmising that she'd possibly entered through an unfinished guest room, she climbed through the window and headed to the hallway. She walked toe-heel, as quietly as possible.

Every room on the upper level was empty. But there was no dust. She thought of the dust that gathered in her own house on a daily basis. *Someone* had been there. If nothing else, to clean.

A door downstairs slammed hard enough to shake the floor where she stood. A dog barked, repeated bursts of three sounds. The barking echoed inside her head so loudly, he could've been in the room with her. She focused on the noise, ran down the steps to the front door, and flung it wide.

Vaiden lay on the walkway. The biggest black dog she'd ever seen stood over him. He was no longer barking, but she could still hear the sound in her mind.

She paused before the pair, afraid of the dog, and yet desperate to get to Vaiden. He wasn't moving. She fought to control her breathing. If anything had happened to him... She thought of the stones, and their terrible toll.

The dog, resembling something akin to a Chow the size of a Newfoundland, kept his face pointed away from her. She was glad for that. If he'd looked at her with bloodlust in his eyes—

The dog gave a last huff and lumbered toward the street.

She was at Vaiden's side in an instant. Her knees landed

hard on a slate slab in the walkway. She turned him onto his back, and her heart twisted miserably in her chest. *Please be okay.*

She pushed the power button on the flashlight and checked for signs of trauma. No blood. She cradled his head in her lap and reached into his coat for his cell phone. She scanned his saved numbers. She dialed Nate's and listened to the ring while her fingers went over Vaiden's head and torso, still searching for a reason for his unconsciousness.

Before Nate picked up, she discovered a bump on the back of Vaiden's head. She leaned down and kissed him, taking comfort in his warm lips and even breaths.

When Nate answered, she told him there was an emergency, and gave him the address. Since he was still at work, he made it to the house in record time. Vaiden's partner, Jarod, pulled up behind him.

Neither one asked why she hadn't called an ambulance. Nate waved something white beneath Vaiden's nose. Charlie caught the scent of ammonia and felt Vaiden jerk against her.

"How long's he been out?" Nate sat back on his heels as Vaiden stirred.

"Ten minutes. Maybe fifteen." She held Vaiden's hand and smiled into his eyes when he blinked up at her.

Jarod hung back, his eyes downcast. "I should've been here with him. When I saw where you guys had gone, I should've told him—"

Vaiden struggled to sit up. Nate lent him an arm and Vaiden leaned heavily against him.

Charlie stared at Jarod. "Saw? What do you mean? How'd you do that?"

Jarod grimaced. "There's a tracking device in your

backpack. Sorry, man. I blew it." He shrugged at Vaiden.

Charlie's head whipped around to Vaiden and she opened her mouth. She dropped his hand, the absence settling in her stomach like a rock. She could think of nothing to say that would express her feelings—hurt, angry that he'd somehow had her electronically tracked...but wondering why he'd done it. Because he was worried about her, or because he didn't trust her?

"What about this place, Jarod? Why'd it cause you alarm?" She narrowed her eyes at him, wanting him to see her annoyance, hoping to make him uncomfortable.

Jarod glanced at Vaiden, who was still sitting but had drawn one knee beneath himself. He waved his hand downward. Jarod cleared his throat, looking sheepish. "I just figured it out—I finally read all the files. This is one of the houses Orion—Elwin Kent—used ten years ago. Where he murdered one of the women." He rubbed a hand across his blond head.

Charlie wiped a lock of hair from her face. Orion, Elwin Kent, Leonard. How in the hell did this all relate? And why did she suddenly figure into it? All the business with Leonard and her father in Peru had happened ten years ago.

A light bulb went on her in head. Ten years ago. When Vaiden's murderer was on the warpath. And then her father had died.

She circled her temples with her fingers to ease away a headache that threatened her.

Finally she opened her backpack and searched. She wanted to throw the tracking device out, but had no idea what she was looking for. She couldn't find anything that didn't belong. Her nails clicked against her penknife and she pocketed it.

She snatched the flashlight, pushed to her feet, and dropped her backpack on the ground next to Vaiden. He lifted his face toward her, but cringed and touched the back of his head. His shoulders rose as he tightened against the pain.

Charlie sucked in air. She'd take his pain herself if she could, no matter how angry he made her.

Realization clanged like a bell in her skull.

Vaiden was arrogant and pushy, but he watched out for her. He kept secrets, but he was also a man of honor. He was a man who'd keep her safe. A man who could care about her.

A man who'd never let his woman leave him.

She'd fallen in love with him.

Her shoulders sagged. If she didn't walk away now...

He was in good hands. Nate and Jarod would make sure he was okay. She took a stride toward the gate. "I've got some things to take care of, Vaiden."

Jarod stepped forward and clasped her forearm. Charlie raised an eyebrow. "You can't keep me here."

"Let her go." Vaiden's strained voice scratched the wound in her heart further open. "She needs time."

Jarod stretched out his hands and backed off.

Once she got out of sight, Charlie burst into a run. He thought she was scurrying off to pout. Hardly. She blinked back tears. Let Vaiden have his hunches. She had her own.

Why hadn't he told her about the history of that house? She'd thought he trusted her. Now she'd gone and lost her heart to him, only to find he didn't have as much invested in it as she did. He'd tracked her every move, not trusting her to let him inside. Maybe not trusting her to do the right thing.

She slowed, swept the back of her wrist across her eyes and sniffled. With a glance at the waning moon, she gauged how long it would take her to get to the real estate office that handled her rentals. Something wasn't right. Time to stop letting someone else take care of the situation. She needed to see those records for herself.

✧

A soft glow emanated from the window of the real estate office. Charlie cheered silently. She'd lucked out and someone was still working.

She entered the building and took the stairs to the second floor office. The light she'd seen was the work lamp next to Alexa's desk. The receptionist held a phone to one ear with her shoulder while her fingers pounded across the keyboard in front of her.

"Evening," Charlie called.

Alexa gave a little jump in her seat and gasped. The phone fell from her neck, but she didn't make an effort to pick it up. She seemed frozen for the space of three seconds, then stood quickly.

"My God, Charlie, did you see him?"

Charlie shook her head, confused. "See who?"

Alexa's tanning-bed orange skin paled. "That man! He—he came in asking about you. He wanted to know where you were staying." She chewed on a red nail. "He was real scary, Charlie. I—I didn't tell him. I thought he was gonna tear the place apart. But just before you came up he ran back down the stairs."

She saw the phone on the floor and grabbed it. "I was calling the police when you came in and scared me half to death."

Charlie glanced at the furniture and plants. Nothing

seemed out of place, but—

"Oh, God, Charlie. Did you hear that? He's coming back!"

Charlie hadn't heard anything, but there was no mistaking the terror on Alexa's face. Perhaps the sound of the door downstairs had alerted her.

Alexa punched three numbers on the phone. "Quick, shut the door. I'm calling the police back!"

Spurred by the fear in the other woman's voice, Charlie raced to the door and shut it firmly. She twisted the lock and breathed a sigh of relief. There was no sound from the hall. No footsteps on the stairs.

She started at Alexa's sudden appearance directly behind her.

"Thanks, Charlie. Yer a real pal."

She heard a knock and saw sparkles in her vision before she felt the slicing pain in her skull. Her limbs collapsed of their own will, and she could do nothing to prevent the darkness that swept everything away.

Chapter Thirteen

Charlie came out of her fog one sensation at a time. A mouth full of fuzz. Her hair beneath her head. Her hands stuck—no, tied—together. The sound of a computer fan humming, and an occasional click of a mouse.

Careful to keep her lashes down, she opened her eyes a fraction. As she'd suspected, she lay on the floor. Her bottom leaned against the back wall. Alexa's desk and wheeled chair loomed in front of her. Alexa must have dragged her from the door because her arms were fully extended and her shoulder joints ached.

Charlie flexed her fingers and discovered that one arm had gone to sleep. The muscles prickled as she edged her arms closer. She noticed red shoes not too far from her face and stopped.

Alexa removed a CD from the drive and tossed it on the floor near Charlie's head. She stood, then slammed her heel onto the plastic, destroying the disk.

Hoping to preserve her own skin, Charlie closed her eyes. A moment would come, she decided, when she could make a move, but it wasn't now. Not with that spike so near to her head.

Why in the hell had Alexa hit her?

The door to the hall rattled. A key jangled in the handle.

"Alexa! Glad to see you're still here."

Alexa cursed just loud enough for Charlie to hear. The woman's heels rasped away on the carpet toward the male voice.

Charlie opened her eyes. Her position below the bottom edge of the desk afforded her a view of large shiny brown shoes. She wiggled her hands up to her face, hoping Alexa wouldn't notice, and chewed at the knot.

"Georgie. Always nice to see you. How'd the house sale go?"

Georgie. A George Wilson worked at the real estate agency. Would he see her? And if he did, would he help, or was he a part of Alexa's madness?

She debated whether to slide her legs straight out so her feet might be seen. The shoes moved toward the couch on the far side of the room. The vinyl squeaked.

"Sold and signed, baby." George Wilson's muffled laugh ended in a groan. "Whatcha working on so late?"

Alexa's heels lifted into the air and hit the floor again and Charlie quickly put her arms back and closed her eyes. Dust tickled her nose and she swallowed the urge to sneeze.

A drawer slid open above her, the miniscule screech of the metal rollers grating on her eardrums.

"Let's have a drink, hmm? To celebrate?"

Glasses clinked. She hadn't heard anything uncork, but she did hear liquid splash and sizzle. Then a tiny tap.

The drawer closed with a muffled thump and Alexa moved away, her heels twisting as she worked her hips seductively.

Charlie struggled with her bonds again.

"Let's drink to your big...commission." Alexa's giggle was lost in the man's guttural laugh.

A long pause. Charlie hoped they were drinking, rather

than examining his “commission”.

The knot slipped free and she rubbed her wrists. The thin ropes left raised red marks, but hadn’t cut into her flesh enough to make her bleed.

Now that she was untied, she found herself getting furious. She was going to kick Alexa’s butt before this was over. She rolled onto her back, kept out of sight, and gritted her teeth. The spot where she’d taken the blow was tender, but she could handle it. She’d had worse.

She hoped Vaiden had recovered his wits by now. And where the heck was he, anyway? She’d figured he’d be less than an hour behind her. Smart as he was, it wouldn’t take him long to puzzle out where she’d planned to go.

A gurgle brought her thoughts back to the present. Liquid spewed onto the floor. One glass tumbled down with a crash, shattering on the wooden planks. George rose from his seat, one foot off the floor. He gasped for air.

The ficus next to the couch fell and George landed on his knees beside it with a bone-crunching crack.

Charlie could see Alexa’s cherry red heels in front of the wheezing man. The heels stepped gingerly backward.

He struggled to speak, but finally gave up, slapping one palm repeatedly on the floor, each hit coming with less force. His fingers drew into a spider-like contraction.

Charlie’s blood chilled. Alexa wasn’t helping the man. She’d done something to him.

George thrashed backward until he lay prone, his face the color of a tomato, his unseeing eyes angled toward Charlie. She wondered if he saw her, or if his dead eyes had missed her presence.

The hiss of his last breath escaping his body paralyzed her.

She'd never heard someone die before.

"Good riddance." The heels stepped over poor George and stopped in front of the desk. The computer chimed. Alexa, completely calm, rounded the corner of the desk and reached for her mouse. She still held her half-full glass in one hand.

Charlie coiled herself and sprang. Alexa glanced her way, but it was too late. Charlie shoved her hard.

The glass tumbled to the floor and landed on the area rug. Alexa hit the floor with a bump, her legs tangling with George's.

Rather than hang around for a fight she might lose with a crazy woman, Charlie rushed out the door and down the steps. Alexa didn't pursue her.

Charlie bounced on her toes at the street level entrance. She needed to get away, but to where? If Alexa could fool her, anyone could. Who could she trust?

Headlights came around the corner and Charlie waved at the car. Maybe the driver had a cell phone. Maybe she could get them to call Vaiden for her. She squinted as the car pulled over and stopped.

Three doors opened simultaneously and she threw herself at the man who exited the passenger side. "About time you got here!"

✧

He was going to kill her. If someone else didn't do it for him first.

Vaiden had been too dizzy to prevent her leaving the other house, and in his confusion, he'd told them to let her go. At the time it had seemed the right choice. Now that he'd steadied himself and the wave of nausea had passed, he intended to keep her safe. At all costs.

He was tempted to shake some sense into her, but she'd already been through an ordeal this evening. She gave him a half-hearted smile and he shook his head. Like he could stay angry with her when she looked so damned cute.

He checked his weapon and scanned the front of the building. Other than security lights, there was no sign of life or movement. According to Charlie a murderess and her victim were still inside. Thank God Charlie had escaped.

He found it hard to understand what connection petite Alexa Reynolds would have to the case, but he didn't doubt a word that came out of Charlie's mouth.

Still a little dizzy when he moved too fast, he turned toward her. That mouth. He slipped a hand behind her head and pulled her close to kiss her. Her barely audible sigh made him draw up to his full height.

"Stay here." Her lips parted in protest. He knew she wouldn't listen. It was in her nature. "Nate, make sure she doesn't follow."

His brother draped an arm around her shoulders. "You got it."

Charlie rolled her eyes, but she didn't try to wriggle away from Nate.

Vaiden shrugged away the urge to remove Nate's arm from Charlie's person. He was only doing what Vaiden had asked.

Jarod cleared his throat. "Let's get this done. I've got a test tomorrow." He led the way toward the building.

Vaiden winked at Charlie and turned to follow his partner. Before his foot hit the sidewalk, there was a second of shocked silence. His eyes were drawn upward, but he didn't know what slight noise had alerted him.

The sharp crack blurred into a roar. His hands covered his ears and the cold metal of his gun pressed his ear lobe. The middle and top floors of the building exploded outward, the spaces between the bricks expanding like a Lego set gone wild.

The force of the explosion sent Jarod and Vaiden backward onto the ground. Vaiden covered his head and neck with his arms, his gun still clutched tight in one hand. As the debris settled he rolled over and searched for Charlie and Nate. Through the dust he saw them huddled on the ground near the car, Nate's body shielding Charlie's. Good man.

"Jarod?"

His partner waved a hand to let him know he was all right. When Jarod sat up he wiped dirt from the back of his blond hair.

Both men got to their feet and walked to the car. Charlie pulled free of Nate's grasp and wrapped her arms around him. Vaiden held her tightly, a thousand questions flooding his mind.

He was glad the building was in a business district. No gawkers had rushed out to see the commotion. At this hour there shouldn't be many people working.

Jarod, watching the flames, groaned loudly. "Guess we need to call this in." He took a cell phone from his pocket and punched a series of numbers, turning his back to them and plugging one ear with a finger.

Charlie stiffened. "What the..." She lunged forward but Vaiden held onto her. "The car. Vaiden? Did you see it?" She cursed. "That could've been her!" She frowned. "You should've let me go. I might have been able to tell what make it was."

"Let it go, Charlie. Alexa was probably inside the office."

She crossed her arms. "Unless she set the explosion."

Jarod folded his phone and scratched behind his ear with the nubby antenna. "What exactly was Alexa Reynolds doing while you were on the floor?"

"She was using CDs, and then destroying them. George Wilson showed up while she was in the middle of it. I don't think she was expecting him, but she had to be waiting for somebody. I mean, what was she going to do with me? Make me have a drink with her?" Her eyes closed and then opened again. "I wonder what she hit me with?"

"I better get the car away from all this heat." Nate started the car and drove it to the far end of the block. The remaining three walked across the street, all very pensive.

Vaiden rubbed the ends of his fingers together. Sirens from the fire engines screeched in the distance. They would make it in time to save the adjacent buildings, but he'd bet the three-story brick edifice was a goner. They'd have a hell of a time finding evidence now. But they would find something. He would have a lot to answer for, still working a closed case.

A news van screeched to a halt and a cameraman jumped out through the sliding door. Vaiden snorted in disgust. "Nate, these your friends?" His voice dripped with sarcasm.

His brother lifted his arms. "Not my guys. I don't want anyone else getting the story if I can't do it. Besides, you know I'm strictly print. Of course," he added, "I am taking mental notes for my column tomorrow." He re-crossed the street and spoke with the newly arrived firemen.

Charlie pursed her lips. She must want to tell him something, but the way she kept glancing at Jarod, he knew she wanted to tell him in private.

Two police cars arrived then, and all chance of finding out her information was lost for the time being.

Vaiden pressed his keys into Charlie's hand. "Take my car.

Go to my house." He took her face in both hands. "And stay there." He kissed her. "I'll be there as soon as I can."

Jarod's wry laughter floated on the gritty air, breaking the spell her eyes had cast over Vaiden. He looked back at his partner, who had a forefinger to his temple.

His partner grinned. "So do you think we'll *all* get head injuries tonight? Or is this about it?"

✧

Charlie let herself into Vaiden's house and shoved her backpack purse into his front closet. She'd found it on the floorboard of his car. There was no sign of anything inside that she'd call a tracking device and she wondered if he'd removed it.

The warm interior was still strange to her. A stack of magazines on the coffee table in the living room lay neatly arranged. The carpet had vacuum tracks on it.

As she climbed the stairs to his huge bathroom, she saw that the baseboard trim had separated slightly from the sheetrock. She smiled. That must be driving him crazy.

Vaiden didn't strike her as a neat freak, but the fact remained that his home was kept in perfect order. Did he have a maid? How much did detectives make, anyway?

She opened the bathroom door and turned on the water to the tub. She stretched high and pulled her shirt over her head. She folded it half-heartedly and placed it on the chaise. Her jeans and underwear followed.

The steaming water was like a warm hug, and she closed her eyes as she sank in. The sheer ecstasy of the heat seeping into her tired muscles invigorated her.

Charlie didn't lounge around in the bath. Once her hair

was clean, she rose, grabbed a towel, and patted herself dry. She slid her fingertips over the smooth marble countertop. Her hair needed to be combed out. There was no way she was going to be able to do it without a brush or comb this time.

Vaiden wouldn't mind, she told herself, as she opened one of the small drawers. Her lips tightened as she held in a chuckle. His toothpaste, floss, and extra toothbrushes were lined up in formation. Charlie helped herself to a new toothbrush and proceeded to clean her teeth. She looked around for a toothbrush holder, but in the end left it on the edge of one of the sinks.

The next drawer she tried contained several combs and a hairbrush. All very neat and tidy. She selected a black comb and set her hair to rights.

Feeling that she hadn't invaded his space quite enough for one day, Charlie bundled her clothes in one arm and walked to the door she knew was his bedroom. She pushed the door wide and turned on the light, not knowing what she might find. One way or another, she needed something to sleep in. Sure, she could hunt around for her bag—maybe Vaiden left it in the trunk, maybe it was downstairs. But she had something else in mind.

The king-sized bed was positioned on the far side of the room, angled toward the door. No dressers at all occupied the space around the bed, though a large trunk sat against one wall. Above the trunk, on the wall, hung an art sculpture best described as a chaotic mass of twigs, feathers, and arrows. She stared at it a long moment before putting her clothes on the trunk.

She tucked her towel tighter and walked to the headboard. The bed sat against a wall little wider than the bed itself. Each side next to the freestanding wall was open. Charlie placed a hand on the edge and peered around.

A walk-in closet the size of her bedroom was concealed back there. No wonder the man always wore suits. He must have twenty of them! She touched them all. Drawers were stacked on the lower half of two walls, and hanging space and hooks were everywhere. Despite the grand number of items, most of the closet was empty. He'd just spread his things out.

Charlie curled her big toe around a low drawer handle and pulled. Tee shirts. Plain, white, and smelling of fabric softener. She chose one and donned it, placed her towel in a hamper, and stepped back into the sleeping area.

The bed was covered by a thick deep brown comforter and white sheets. She flopped onto the mattress and fluffed a pillow. Once it was tucked behind her head, she encountered a shelf in the headboard. Nestled inside were an alarm clock, a phone, and a remote control.

She laughed nervously. There wasn't a TV anywhere in the room. She was pretty sure it wasn't in the trunk, so she examined the control more closely. What could it be for? One button was for the fan, one for the lights. And yet there were numbered buttons too.

She pressed the small power button and waited. A whirring noise began, followed by the descent of a flat paneled plasma television screen from the ceiling on the far side of the room. She tilted her head in wonder. Vaiden was as neat and progressive as she was messy and rustic-minded. She pressed the button again, sending the television back to its nook. The clock read eleven forty-two. She hoped Vaiden would be home soon. She crushed a second pillow to her chest and inhaled his scent.

She'd fallen asleep for, according to the clock, only an hour when she woke to the sound of the downstairs door closing. She plumped up the pillow she was still holding and returned it to the other side of the bed. The closet near the front door opened with a squeak and she pictured Vaiden hanging his coat neatly.

Soon the bedroom door swung in and Vaiden appeared. Her heart leaped at the sight of him. His eyes found her and he crossed the room to sit on the bed and pull her into his arms. He kissed her and she clung to him. He smelled of smoke and weariness. She wanted to make him a part of her and never let go.

He shrugged out of his suit jacket and allowed it to hit the floor. Charlie worked the buttons on his shirt and tugged the garment up.

She ran her tongue down his neck, then nibbled at the base of his throat. Vaiden groaned and his hand slid up her thigh, over her hip and settled on her waist. He inhaled sharply and moved his hand down again, to where her panties should have been.

He laughed low in his throat and slipped his hand between her legs as he pressed her back onto the sheets. She was slick and ready for him and caught her breath at his intimate touch.

When he eased back to step out of his remaining clothes, she removed the borrowed tee shirt. Her breathing came fast, as did his, and she sought his mouth, unable to get her fill of his kisses.

The world outside of Vaiden's arms disappeared for Charlie. She heard only her heartbeat in her ears, along with his whispered words that caused her passionate torment.

They'd come close to losing each other more than once in the past twenty-four hours, though Charlie didn't want to admit that fact, or that it bothered her. Vaiden made her feel emotions more intensely than she'd ever experienced—anger, confusion, desire, and, she admitted reluctantly, love. A tear slipped down into her hair, and she brushed away the wetness, embarrassed by her weakness.

Vaiden moved over her. Her nipples tightened from the onslaught of his lips and tongue. She reached low and circled his hardness with one hand. Elation surged through her at his hissed, inhaled breath.

His mouth crushed hers in a kiss of possession, one she welcomed and returned. She lifted her hips. The ache building inside her had become an urgent need. Vaiden rolled away for a moment and opened a small drawer in the headboard.

Though the room was cloaked in darkness, she knew he was getting a condom to protect them both. They'd recklessly forgotten to use one at the hotel the first time they'd made love. The lack of protection wasn't a mistake she regretted, but it had been a mistake she didn't want to repeat.

Her thoughts didn't linger long, as Vaiden's strong body encircled hers once again. He pulled her in close to his chest, their legs entwined. When she kissed him, she could feel his smile.

He settled his hands on her hips and lifted her above him, then slid inside her with a groan. Charlie's head tipped back, her hair brushing across her shoulders. He was so huge, he touched every part of her. Instinctively she tightened her muscles on his hardness, then gasped at the sensations that rippled through her.

She experimented with the angle of her pelvis until she found a position that sent waves of euphoria through her center. She rode him, increasing the speed, then maintaining a frenzied rhythm that soon sent them both into rapturous crashes of pleasure.

She collapsed against his chest, holding herself on her elbows. He raised his head and kissed her, long and slow. The sheer joyfulness she received from his kiss rivaled the bliss from his lovemaking.

Words swam in her mind, words she knew were best left unsaid. Words that would tie her to him, or worse, send him running from her. She didn't know which she wanted from him, so she closed her eyes and kept her mouth shut.

He, too, stayed silent. After he settled her next to him, he laced his fingers through hers. The simple action made her heart hurt.

He was so right for her, and yet their lives would never fit together. He was a cop. She was an archaeologist. They would end up like her parents. Sad, separated, and alone.

Chapter Fourteen

"It's a bad idea."

Vaiden couldn't believe what Jarod was suggesting. They'd met at the Selkie's Den for breakfast to regroup and go over their notes. Now his absentee partner wanted him to put Charlie in harm's way.

"You can't tell me you haven't thought about it yourself." Ruthie approached and Jarod wiped the serious look from his face.

Vaiden mumbled a thank you as the brunette put his toast in front of him. She dusted her hands on her apron and walked behind the counter without a glance at Jarod.

A frown creased Jarod's brow.

"Oh, now you notice her." Vaiden rolled his eyes. "Why don't you ask her out already?"

Jarod scowled. "I don't have time to give my *job* one hundred percent, what makes you think I have any time for a woman? I gotta finish my classes, Vaiden. And don't change the subject." He cut his sausage patty into eight small triangles. "If your brother cooperates, we can catch this guy. Or girl," he added.

Vaiden's butter knife pierced his toast and he slammed it loudly on the table. "I don't want Charlie in danger."

"Like you would let anything happen to her. Geez, Vaiden, we've done this on other cases." He scratched the back of his head. "Why don't we let Charlie decide?"

Because she'd agree.

Vaiden bit the bread and chewed, the lack of taste unnoticed. If he went along with Jarod's plan, let his brother hint that Charlie did have the gold artifact, they might just flush Alexa or Leonard out of hiding. Neither of the two had been seen in the week since the real estate office had burned, but no evidence of human remains had been found in the building either.

They hadn't found any link between the two suspects, but they were sure they had worked together. Alexa's convenient forgetfulness when she copied Charlie's rental records should have tipped him off. She'd left off the storage units, allowing whoever had rented under the name Earl Kent time to empty the contents.

He'd also discovered that Earl Kent didn't exist on paper. Not paper that counted. And a decade before, neither had Alexa Reynolds.

He wiped his fingers on a paper napkin and shoved a hand through his hair. He'd never been so frustrated by a case. Jarod, of course, told him it was because he was too closely involved with Charlie. And maybe that was part of it, but mostly it was knowing the answer had to be right in front of him, and yet he couldn't see it.

Jarod shoved the creamer toward him. "Truth is, man, I called her this morning while you were on your way."

His heart went cold. "You what?"

"I called Charlie. And she said yes." Jarod leaned back and Ruthie approached to take his empty plate. He caught her eye and almost smiled.

Vaiden rolled his eyes, annoyed at the interplay between Jarod and the waitress in the midst of his anger. "You shouldn't have done that. You had no right."

Jarod put his palms on the table. "It's the fastest way, man. We've done it before with success."

"We've also done the bait-routine and had it go horribly wrong." Vaiden flexed his shoulder muscles. He still felt stiff in the spot where he'd been shot in that awful attempt to catch a suspect using the same method Jarod wanted to use with Charlie.

That time, the woman had come to his supervisor with the idea. His supervisor had denied her request, but she'd set up a meeting on her own with the man who'd been stalking her. She called the police at the last minute to let them know where it would be going down. Unfortunately, they'd arrived too late.

Vaiden had seen the stalker exit a car with a sawed-off shotgun. He'd run full out toward the woman from the other side of the street. He threw himself at her even as he heard both barrels fire, one right after the other.

They'd both been hit. The woman died on the scene. Vaiden had lived.

And he still partially blamed himself. He'd suspected that she was planning to go after the stalker on her own, and he'd accepted his supervisor's order to leave the case alone. Until the man acted against her, or did something so they could prove he was stalking, legally there was nothing they could do. That woman had been strong, like Charlie—she, too, was proactive, not wanting to sit around and wait to be attacked.

"This is a bad idea," Vaiden repeated, and he pushed his plate forward. His appetite had left and the toast tasted like sawdust in spite of the grape jelly.

"Would you rather worry that she could be attacked when

you can't be there to help her? What if she decided to try to solve the case on her own?"

Vaiden clenched his teeth. Jarod hadn't been a detective on the force when Vaiden was shot. He didn't know the particulars. And he couldn't know how scared he was for Charlie.

He sucked down the last of his coffee. "I'll call Nate and see what he can do."

✧

Shivers streaked across Charlie's shoulders. Two crisp leaves whipped into Vaiden's house as he stepped inside. She pushed them out with her toes and shut the door behind him.

"It's all set," he said when he'd settled at the kitchen table.

Charlie placed a platter of food between their dinner plates and waited, ignoring his opening remark. Her mind was resigned to the plan to smoke out Alexa and her co-conspirators.

She had absolutely no reservations.

There were other things on her mind this evening. First was a test of Vaiden's taste buds.

He scooped a generous helping of the ceviche onto his plate. He tasted the creamed yellow beans first, avoiding the fish. He sipped his ice water, then pierced a piece of fish with his fork.

He sniffed. "Lime?"

"Mm-hmm." She rolled a bite of the fish on her tongue while she observed his cautious nibble.

"Different. Not bad, but different."

She hadn't been sure if he would like the dish. The fish was prepared in tart lime juice and seasoned with red onions, garlic, and raw chilies. It wasn't actually cooked.

Vaiden didn't ask for seconds, but he didn't complain. And he seemed to actually enjoy the churros she'd made for dessert.

She'd been staying at his house for days, and in the absence of work at the university, she'd begun to get comfortable with him. She'd spent much of her time on his computer, researching Ica stone stories. In two, when the villagers had been questioned about magic, they'd sent the scientists away and called the stones a hoax.

When he'd loaded the dishes into the dishwasher and joined her on the couch, Vaiden again brought up the newspaper article. He withdrew a folded paper from his shirt pocket.

"Here's the text of the story. They're running it in tomorrow's paper." His arms rested on the back of the couch, and she settled against his body to read.

The column described the mystery surrounding the recent return of the university contingent from Peru. Because Nate had talked a pal into putting the information into his column, rather than having to do it himself, the paper managed to infer more significance than actually existed.

The author suggested that perhaps a certain professor wanted to keep a certain artifact to herself. He pointed out that when the late Dean Fisher's personal effects were catalogued, several undocumented artifacts were discovered in his home. If the dean was capable of subterfuge, then anyone working for him was capable of the same. And wouldn't the employees of a department follow the example set by their leader?

"Ouch." Charlie knew the school was not going to appreciate such musings. But in the end, they would catch whoever'd killed Dean Fisher and Bill LePrade. Neither she nor

Vaiden believed Alexa could have pulled off those murders. Alexa had killed George Wilson with some sort of poison, Charlie was sure of that, but she just seemed too feminine to rip out a throat, or slash one, for that matter. That's not to say they didn't think she could be involved at all. Vaiden was certain she was—but how?

Unfortunately Vaiden's supervisor had decided that though Dean Fisher's death was undoubtedly the work of the man who'd assaulted Charlie in the alley, Bill LePrade was most likely killed by Alexa Reynolds. Vaiden didn't explain why Charlie's prints weren't found on the knife when he submitted it for evidence. And she didn't press him. She didn't want to know.

The last paragraph of the article hinted that Charlie would be working in the school lab over the Thanksgiving holiday, and perhaps more information on the lost gold would be forthcoming.

She folded the paper and tossed it onto the coffee table. "So it's next Thursday then?"

"No. That's Thanksgiving. I've got plans. We'll do the sting on that Friday. Or Saturday. If the guy shows at all."

Charlie studied her nails. Had plans, did he? Probably she should get off her duff and find a place to stay. She couldn't just move herself in with Vaiden permanently. And she wasn't about to move back into the house where they'd found that girl's body in the basement.

It galled her to have to consider renting a place when she had so many rentals of her own. And given that it was Tuesday of Thanksgiving week, she'd be very unlikely to find a place open any time soon. Maybe Vaiden wouldn't mind her staying a few more days.

"You're thinking pretty seriously over there." Vaiden

touched the spot between her eyebrows.

“Just trying to figure out what I’m doing.”

“If you don’t want to go through with it, just say the word.”

She blinked, then realized he thought she was worried about Friday. “Not that.” She laughed. “I can’t impose on you like this forever, that’s all.”

One of his big hands covered the side of her face and tilted her head toward his. He kissed her softly. “You’re no imposition.” He brushed a thumb over her bottom lip. “I like having you around.”

A laugh bubbled through her. “You do, hmm? I wonder why?” She moved her hand up his thigh and stroked him through his pants.

He chuckled against her mouth. “You better not do that at Mom’s.”

Her hand stopped. “Sorry? What?”

“At my mother’s house. On Thanksgiving. You *are* coming with me, right?”

✧

By the next night, Charlie was ready to pull out her hair in frustration. Instead she took it out on her pencil, rolling it between her fingers and tapping the side against the edge of the kitchen table. She turned it every so often to even out the dents. Symmetry was important, after all.

The starched white sheet of paper in her sketchpad remained blank. Still, she’d made progress on cleaning up her site notes. The details were all there, she just needed to arrange them so that someone besides herself could understand what she’d written. To anyone else, it would appear a jumbled mess.

For Charlie, it was the system that worked for her.

Her personal notes were always made while she was on her feet, usually crisscrossing a larger site. She was too lazy to dictate into a recorder and then transcribe each evening like her mother used to do. She didn't like the risk of a tape failing. She wanted words she could touch and see. Her notes were a jumble of four languages—whichever one had the shortest word for what she needed to say.

Her father's notes were different from both of theirs, and read more like a journal. She chuckled at her own wild mix of handwriting and pictured her father's long flowing script. She missed him. He would have loved knowing the rod of Manco Copac was real. Not that he'd ever doubted it.

She flipped the pages back to her rough drawing of the survey map she and Miguel had completed before they'd found the cavern. Hard to believe a simple math error had kept her father from discovering the rod himself over a decade ago.

Her eyes, which had drifted shut as she fought her melancholy, flew open. A car had just pulled into the driveway. The telltale beep identified the car as Vaiden's. He lived in a low-crime area, but he took every security precaution available, locking his car at all times and bolting his house—even for a short walk around the block. Better safe than sorry, he'd told her. And he was right.

Keys clacked against the door just before she heard it close.

"It's just me."

The muscles in her abdomen tightened. She might be frustrated by his recent overprotectiveness, but damn if just the sound of his voice didn't make her get warm and liquid inside.

If he would just relax.

She wasn't worried—hell, she wasn't even really afraid—though a lot of that was because Vaiden would be close while she served as bait for someone who was a thief, or a murderer, or both.

If she knew nothing else, she knew Vaiden wouldn't let anything happen to her. While it was undeniably very sexy to have a man around who she knew beyond a doubt would protect her, a part of her wondered if he thought she was helpless.

Because she wasn't.

She'd made it through life thus far without death or dismemberment. Well, that toenail incident with the trowel two decades earlier notwithstanding.

The closet closed, and she knew his coat would be hanging neatly. Soon he'd come in and *not* ask her how her day was, because, as she'd suspected, he'd followed her.

It was as if Vaiden was afraid she'd disappear if he didn't watch over her. If she went anywhere, she felt followed. Not that she ever saw anyone. And though he denied it, she knew from his last hands-off episode that he had her tailed.

Charlie put her pencil down.

She agreed with Jarod. The guy behind her trouble was probably planning whatever he was going to do next, not lying in wait for her to skip by with a red hood and basket of projectile points for some fairy tale granny.

Vaiden came into view and Charlie lifted her eyebrows. She was wrong. He still had the jacket on. And his tie was half-loosened, hanging at an odd angle. His hair, always combed back just after his shower—unless she got hold of him—looked like he'd been dragging his hands through it.

She pushed back her chair and walked around the table. He gave her that half-smile that made her heart flutter without fail. She leaned into him, sliding her fingers along his lapel. He lifted one hand to the back of her head and wrapped his fingers in her hair.

There was a moment when the world slipped away and all she could focus on was his mouth, his sexy lips. And then her desire was fulfilled. He kissed her. Lazy heat crept up through her middle and centered between her legs.

Vaiden drew back and chuckled deep in his chest. "Is that all you ever think about?"

She would have been offended if he wasn't close enough for her to tell he wanted her just as badly. She moved back and forth against him. She could tease as much as he could.

"Have you had a...hard day?" She grinned, then laughed. "Sorry, that was bad, I—"

He cut her off with a kiss. His grip tightened, then relaxed and he dropped his hands to the small of her back. The pressure he put there brought her firmly against his arousal.

Charlie opened her mouth to his kiss and groaned as her hips ground against him of their own volition. One of his hands left her back and jerked at his tie, finally sending it across the room. She rose onto her tiptoes and tugged at his shirt buttons. Once she had his shirt parted, she spread her palms across his broad chest.

While he removed his jacket and shirt, Charlie let her tongue glide to the sensitive spot behind his ear, then eased lower to nibble at his neck. She inhaled deeply, every breath filling her with wanting.

His sharp inhale told her she'd found another spot that wanted attention and she made tiny swirls with her tongue against his skin.

Suddenly his hands spanned her waist, and he lifted her onto the cluttered kitchen table while taking her mouth again.

She broke contact to drag her blouse over her head and

shimmy her jeans from her legs. Vaiden's hands were on her, kneading every tender area she revealed, the rough pads of his thumbs sending her nerves dancing. She tried to sit up and release his belt and pants, but he pressed her back, shoving her notebooks to the floor along with a plastic bowl and four placemats.

The noise of the bowl hitting the floor startled her and she drew her knees up, blocking Vaiden with one of them. She wanted to make sure he had protection this time, but her breath came too fast to form the words.

He must have sensed her question, because he grinned and drew a small packet from his jeans. He tossed it onto the table beside her and lowered his head. He tickled one of her knees with the tip of his tongue, then kissed up her thigh. His hands held her legs stiff, forbidding any movement as his kisses crept closer to her center.

When he slid her panties to the side and kissed her, she sagged backward and sighed, giving in to the sweet tortuous sensations.

Too quickly, he brought her to the edge and then over it. She'd barely recovered her senses enough to hear the crackle of the packet, and then he was deep inside her, starting the build toward oblivion yet again.

Charlie raised her legs higher and crossed her ankles against his back, pulling him closer as they collided in passionate rhythm. Her body tightened and as she shattered around him, she heard his cry of triumph as he found his own release.

✧

The grandfather clock downstairs chimed six times. Charlie dragged her fingers across Vaiden's damp, warm chest.

"You know," she began, then blushed when she found his eyes on her, intense and full of renewed hunger. "If we don't get out of here, we're likely to stay in bed through the weekend."

His brows rose as if he thought that might not be such a bad idea. He reached for her.

Charlie laughed. "Rogue. Really, let's go out. Let's do something."

His eyebrows wiggled. "Can't do that in public in Virginia, hon. Hell, right now we're breaking two laws alone." He slid one leg between hers and touched a tendril of her hair, winding it around one finger.

She tried hard not to laugh again. It was true, Virginia had a whole passel of sex laws dictating who could do what to whom, and where. Or rather, Who *couldn't* do what to whom and where. "I wasn't suggesting sex in the park, you big goof. Just dinner and a movie. *Something.*"

There was no doubt that she could starve to death right here in Vaiden's bed and as long as his hands were on her body, she'd die happy. But eventually they'd get tired, and Vaiden would start trying to talk her out of helping the police catch the bad guy.

She wasn't sure if there were even any movies she wanted to see, but an idea came to her. "Ever been to the Byrd Theatre?"

One eyebrow ticked. "Yeah. Mostly when I was a kid. " He leaned on one elbow now, idly stroking her jaw line with his free hand.

The warmth of his skin combined with the lazy satisfaction already humming a sensual lullaby in her veins made her eyes drift shut.

Disjointed flashes of half-dreams called out to her. Frames of places she'd been clicked by. The lush wet greenness of Peru spiraled up on all sides. She strained to get through the branches and vines. As she struggled, the verdant prison opened and she fell forward, down, down—

"Hey."

She jerked awake, a panicked hitch to her breath.

Vaiden frowned and sat up fully. "See, I knew you weren't okay with this. You're even dreaming about it now." He threw back the covers and dressed in jeans, grabbing a tee shirt from his dresser. Clothed and cut off from her, he sat at the bottom of the bed. "It's not too late to back out."

Charlie blinked the dream from her mind. Back to this again. She should have distracted him faster.

She crawled from the sheets and knelt behind him, her arms wrapped around his shoulders. "I'm not worried. Not about that." She wanted to tell him *why* she wasn't worried—because he would be there, he would protect her—but that was too much pressure to put on him. On anyone. And he'd already put enough on himself.

"So you want to go, then?" He angled his head back and she kissed his cheek. He reached back for her and brought her around to his lap.

Charlie rested in his embrace, wanting to stay in that moment forever, even as she knew things had to change. This wasn't a man who could settle for a wanderer.

Even one who always came home.

✧

Standing in the lobby of the Byrd Theatre, memories

flooded back to Charlie. Once, when she was maybe six years old, her parents had both been in Virginia for her birthday at the same time, and they'd given her a birthday party. They had loaded four children she didn't know, though now she supposed they must have been children of her father's colleagues, into the giant bluish white van and driven them all to the Byrd.

They'd piled out and toddled into the already dark theatre to see a Muppet movie. She didn't remember the movie, or much about what the kids looked like. Her parents though, sitting one row behind her, had been happy. She vividly recalled them holding hands as they all left together after the show.

Vaiden nudged her arm and held out a container of buttered popcorn. "Did you come here a lot too?"

"No." She smiled at him and dropped her free hand down into his. "Just once. My parents let me have a movie birthday here."

He squeezed her fingers as the crowd started walking into the theatre. "A movie, huh? How'd they top that the next year?"

She knew what he meant. She'd seen the articles about parents who strived to make every party better and more memorable than the last. But she knew what had mattered. Not the movie or the kids or the presents wrapped in Sunday comics. Seeing her parents' love had mattered. Knowing she was safe in her family.

"Oh, the usual stuff. What was your best birthday?" She moved closer as they descended the inclined walkway toward the seats.

Vaiden laughed. "They were all the same." He stopped to let her cross in front of him and sidle into a row.

Once they were seated, he placed one hand familiarly on her thigh. The warmth curled into her bones and she sighed. This was nice.

"Well, except for one." Vaiden tilted the giant soda he'd bought at her. When she shook her head he shrugged and took a long sip. "One year, the day before my birthday, me and Nate were outside, way farther back on the property than we were allowed to play, and we saw this puppy." He put the cup on the floor next to his leg. "Mangiest thing you ever saw, and skinny as a sack of bones. We started chasing him, because we thought we'd be able to keep him if we could just get him home—Nate always did like to rescue everything—but that dog did not want to be caught. He started running, and we started running, and next thing I knew, the dog was gone, Nate was gone, and I didn't know where the hell I was."

Charlie traced a pattern on his hand as it rested on her leg, but she watched his face. His face looked amused enough, but his voice sounded ragged. She couldn't tell if this story was happy or sad.

"I waited and I listened... Eventually it got dark and I was still standing there, thinking Nate was being funny. Finally I ended up curled next to a tree. My father says I was crying when he found me, but I don't remember that. I just remember how happy I was to see him walking down the ridge toward me."

Her heart ached for him. She could see the scared, lost little boy in her mind, but she couldn't imagine *this* Vaiden ever being afraid. Not *really*.

"I know we got in trouble. But all I remember was that Dad took Nate and me camping the next weekend. Just the three of us. And he taught us all sorts of stuff about what to do if you're lost in the woods. Best damn trip I ever went on."

A whine drew their attention to the front of the theatre. The noise reminded Charlie of the noise a lonely dog might make and she straightened, wondering for a moment if a kids' movie was playing after all.

Then the floor hatch on the stage opened and the great Wurlitzer rose slowly to eye level, the keys already being played by a gray-haired gentleman who smiled and nodded his head at the audience as they clapped. Charlie wondered if the man could be the same one who'd played all those years ago on her birthday.

She leaned her head on Vaiden's shoulder and sighed. Some things should never be allowed to change.

✧

Early Thursday morning, Vaiden took over the kitchen, making what seemed to Charlie an unearthly mess. He prepared enough green bean casserole for a small army.

She would've opted for the easy version, wherein cans were opened and dumped into Pyrex, but Vaiden cooked the beans from scratch. She couldn't help but admire him for that, but she had to wonder why he put himself to the trouble.

As the clock neared lunchtime, he removed the green beans from the oven and produced travel covers for the casserole dishes.

She could resist comment no longer. "I'm impressed."

Vaiden slipped his oven mitt from his right hand and slapped it against the counter with finality. "What do you mean?" He suppressed a grin.

"You didn't strike me as the cooking type."

"No? Wait'll you see what Nate's bringing."

"Something homemade too?"

Vaiden laughed. "Are you kidding? If we walked into Mom's with something from the grocery store's prepared food section, Mom would know in a heartbeat. Then we'd hear about it all day. How we don't make enough time for family, and we need to get our priorities straight." He rolled his eyes and pulled her against his chest.

She stretched onto her toes and kissed him. "Had that happen before, huh?"

"Um-hmm. Only takes once." He smiled at her. Her heart beat faster. "You need to go change. We gotta be there by one."

She backed out of his arms and walked toward the stairs. "So, what exactly is Thanksgiving like with your family?"

He smiled and checked the zipper on the travel covers. "Just family. Everybody brings a dish." Satisfied with the security of the green beans, he turned to her and winked. "Simple."

✧

Simple, my foot, she thought, as seventy minutes later Vaiden parked his car in front of a stately home. A mansion was more like it. The front of the house had pillars. Pillars!

Charlie snorted, then turned to give him a dirty look, but he'd already exited the car. Three young women in patterned day dresses raced down the stairs screeching, and one after another tackled Vaiden in bear hugs.

Charlie bit her bottom lip and opened the door.

One of the women, a slender brunette with huge brown eyes, gasped when she saw Charlie. She was truly startled. The other two females each punched Vaiden in a different arm. "Why didn't you say you were bringing someone?"

He tossed his hands up in surrender. "I told Mom. She was supposed to tell you guys."

You guys. Now there was a misnomer. The two more buxom

girls, twins, now that she got a better look at them, were the farthest things from *guys* she'd ever seen. Soft waves of blond hair tumbled from their heads, ending teasingly above their ample cleavage.

They'd better be relatives.

"Maybe, Rob, if I kept the news to myself, it was because I doubted its verity."

All eyes turned to the elegant woman now towering over them from the top of the stairs. She appeared to be as tall as Vaiden, with his same deep brown, almost black hair. She wore a knee-length, tailored tan skirt and a white blouse with a sweater.

And she wasn't smiling.

Charlie watched in agony as the woman cocked an eyebrow at Vaiden and tilted her head in the direction of the car. Not sure how to interpret the signals, Charlie opened the rear door to retrieve the casseroles.

"Leave them. Genie and my cousins will bring them in."

"Am I about to be skewered?" Charlie tucked her fingers into his hand and faced the house again.

"No, but if we don't hurry up, you might get to see it happen to me," he said with a chuckle. "Mom," he called, "this is Charlie Blair. The girl I told you about."

His mother waited to speak until they'd climbed the steps and Vaiden had kissed her cheek.

"What sort of name is *Charlie*?"

On the aged debutante's lips, her name sounded very base, low class.

Detecting no rancor, Charlie shrugged. "Nickname for Charlotte."

His mother stared at her hard. Charlie held her ground and

stared back, though her eyebrows rose in humor a bit on their own, and she felt her dimple kick in as she held a smile.

Charlie held out her hand. “It’s nice to meet you, ma’am.”

There was an uncomfortable second, then the woman’s face cracked into a grin. She ignored Charlie’s outstretched hand, pulling her into a hug instead. “Call me Margaret, my dear.”

Chapter Fifteen

Thirty-odd relatives milled about inside the huge home, each one wandering over to Vaiden for greetings and introductions. Charlie's head whirled with names and relations—she'd never keep them straight.

When an uncle dragged Vaiden away to examine a horse out back, Genie stuck to Charlie's side and guided her through the masses. Genie, as it turned out, was the little sister of the Vaiden family. She and Charlie entered the wide kitchen and found a corner out of the way of three bustling aunts who were busily reheating food.

"Robbie says you two are an item."

Charlie smiled. Everyone called Vaiden 'Rob' here, except Genie. Charlie had trouble thinking of him as anything but *Vaiden.*

"Well?"

The look in Genie's eyes was more protective than predatory, but still Charlie swallowed and thought out her words carefully. She was Vaiden's sister, after all. "I like him very much."

The brown eyes, so like Vaiden's, squinted. "*Like*, huh? You hurt him and I'll kill you, ya got that?" And with that, Genie hooked her arm through Charlie's and ushered her back into the melée.

Genie stuck to Charlie's side until Vaiden managed to return to her, then she disappeared with the twins. At two o'clock sharp, a bell clanged and the throng moved as one into the dining room.

Vaiden slipped his arm around Charlie's waist as they walked. "You doing okay?"

"Um-hmm. Wish you'd told me I'd be meeting half the state of Virginia today," she joked, still overwhelmed. She had cousins in Colorado and Florida, and a grandfather somewhere in Texas, but she could count on one hand the actual number of times she'd seen any of them in person. When she was growing up, if there'd been traveling to do, it had rarely been to see live people. Centuries-old bones, those were the relatives she was used to—"big picture" relatives.

Vaiden waved to Nate, who entered from a side door looking sheepish and avoiding their mother. He leaned in close to Charlie's ear. "This is nothing. You should see how many of them show up to weddings and funerals."

Charlie didn't comment.

Vaiden's mother said a blessing, everyone applauded, and then they converged on the banquet-set table. Plates were passed over heads and between bodies. The circle of family members rotated about the table, scooping bits of different dishes. They dispersed in a less organized fashion, finding seats where they could.

Charlie and Vaiden were among the last to get to the food. Some of the first had come back for seconds already. She lumped sliced cucumbers and some crab puffs on her plate and followed Vaiden around the corner to a set of sofas. Eating large amounts of messy food wasn't in her plan with the large crowd watching. She was too nervous.

Though everyone was pleasant enough, and the rooms of

the home were of great size, Charlie couldn't get over the way the relatives clumped in groups like mercury spilled from a thermometer, each two or three zipping together, apart from the others, yet close enough to make vocal contact.

Nate, Genie, and the twins glanced up from their seats as one, their chitchat stopped and hanging in the air. The two blonds now looked very different from each other. Something had changed. Charlie distinctly recalled both twins having long hair when they'd greeted Vaiden at the car. Now one had much shorter locks. Odd.

Charlie perched on the edge of one hard-cushioned sofa, despite Vaiden's attempt to put her in the middle. She wasn't used to this many new people all at once. She smiled, thinking of the first day of each semester's field school. Okay, she could deal with people *if* she was in charge of them. Not when she was the object of their curiosity.

She patted her lips with her napkin, and Genie leaned across Vaiden to touch her hand with warm fingertips. "Robbie says you're an archaeologist. Are you a maverick like Indiana Jones, or more along the lines of Schliemann?"

Charlie thought of how she'd fallen into the cave near Cuzco and smiled. "Neither, really. I'm no adventurer, and I am no academic. Maybe somewhere in the middle."

One blond head tilted. Nicole, the shorter-haired twin, tapped her lips with a celery stick. "But Nate's been telling us you've had all sorts of excitement with your last project." She grinned wickedly. "I believe he called it 'the bag of rocks'. Surely any treasure with such an illustrious name, so full of mystery, must have a tale to it?"

Vaiden groaned, but Charlie laughed. "Yeah, 'bag of rocks,' that's about right." She hesitated, knowing that most non-academic audience's eyes glazed over the second she started talking about any sort of research. "Let's just say that most scientists don't consider the find significant."

"Hmm." Nicole nodded with interest, then crunched into her celery. "Fine," she said between chews, "don't share. I'll just wheedle it out of Rob later."

"Oh lord, here comes Aunt Deb." Michele, the long-haired twin, lifted her drink up to block her face, and succeeded only in magnifying her red lips to clown size. "She's been after me all day." A cheery plump woman, about seventy years old, sped in their direction.

Michele put aside her food and stood. Her face a mask of determination, she grabbed Charlie's plate and handed it to Vaiden. "I'll bring her back, I promise," she whispered. Then in a voice much too loud for Charlie's comfort, she said, "The restroom? Certainly, come along Charlie, I'll show you." Michele took her elbow in a death grip and hustled her into the hallway. "Thanks, Charlie, you're a lifesaver," she told her as they raced from the room and from her Aunt Deb.

Wishing she had breadcrumbs to leave as a trail, Charlie tried to memorize the way back to Vaiden. Once they descended a staircase that she was sure they'd ascended only a moment before, she set her feet and forced Michele to stop. "I think we've lost her." The woman had a cane, for Pete's sake.

Michele giggled. "Yeah, you're right. She probably gave up at the stairs." She twisted one ringlet of long blond hair around a finger.

"May I ask why you're avoiding her, your aunt?"

Michele tossed her head and gestured to her hair. "Didn't you see Nicole's hair? Aunt Deb did that to her! Can you imagine? Just walked up behind her, leaned her cane on Nicole's rear end, and started shearing!"

Charlie shrugged. "I thought the style suited her. Helps

keep you two straight in my head."

The other woman frowned, her eyes pitying. "No-o, now she wants to cut mine to match. Not gonna happen. This is the first time in years we've looked different, and I'm not giving in anytime soon. Nicole will grow hers out to match mine soon enough anyway." She moved closer and whispered. "*Prenatal vitamins.*"

"She's pregnant?" Charlie didn't recall a ring on the twin's finger.

Michele's back went rigid and she gave Charlie an overly dramatic look of shock and censure. "Certainly not! She takes them to make her hair grow faster." But then she winked.

These people were crazy. Charlie rubbed her temples. Maybe there was a reason her parents hadn't been close to their own relatives.

"You okay? You look like your head hurts." The blond reached beneath Charlie's arm and opened a door. "Wait in here. I'll tell Vaiden where you are. It'll give you guys a break."

Charlie thanked her and entered an immense library. She blinked. Most of the furnishings in the house seemed new and untouched. Antiques, yet showpieces rather than real family items. In this room, the furniture, while still probably antique, actually looked its age. She ran a hand along the back of a wing chair. The fabric covering the thick padding had once been a vibrant red. Now it was the color of liquid antacid. Her eyes strayed to the shelves. Floor to ceiling, filled with hardcover books. They stretched so high, a sliding ladder stood at each side of the shelves for easier access.

She dreamed of someday having a library of her own, even if it was just a room she could cover with homemade shelves. For the moment, her books were stored in boxes at the house.

The house. Death-house, was more like it. If she spent

more time in this country, she'd buy a real house, but it seemed such a waste to spend all that money on a building that would sit empty so much of the year.

The window on the far side of the room was open a few inches. She walked closer and closed it, then pressed her hands together. She perused the spines of the volumes on the nearest shelf. No dust anywhere. Amazing.

Though she saw several older texts she'd have loved to investigate, she knew the moment she cracked one Vaiden would appear to escort her back into the fray. Once she started a book, she had an obsessive need to finish it as soon as possible. She chuckled to herself. It would probably be rude to read during Thanksgiving. So instead she settled on a stack of travel magazines that sat near a leather loveseat.

Minutes passed and she wondered if Michele's scissors-wielding aunt had waylaid her before she could get to Vaiden. The third travel magazine she flipped through intrigued her more than the first two. It contained recent pictures of Ghana. She could see from the photos why her mother had enjoyed working there.

Charlie had never been to Ghana herself, but both her parents had gone to the West African country, and neither had returned. She braced herself for the wave of guilt. She'd never cried when her mother had died. It hadn't felt real. Still didn't.

Ten years before, during some unfortunate land disputes in Ghana, there'd been mass killings in the area of her mother's dig. Kimberly Blair had been reported dead, and her father had found the first flight out of the U.S. and into the center of the conflict, hoping against hope that there'd been a mistake.

When seven years had passed with no word from either of them, Charlie had to face the truth. A judge declared them both legally dead, and she'd begun to move on with her life. The unexpected demise of both parents left her with a large inheritance. She hadn't wanted to access it, since that would mean accepting the death of her parents as fact.

She drew the glossy magazine closer, staring through it, rather than at it. Her mind elsewhere, she glanced at a picture of a nun working at a small school. The *religieuse* had a tired smile, but deep laugh lines around her facial features. Something about the face, the eyes perhaps?

Charlie bent closer to the page. Her heart beat once, hard, and she held her breath. So weird. That woman looked like her mother.

The door to the library swung open and she crumpled the article into her hand, tearing it from the magazine.

✧

"I've been looking all over for you." Vaiden thought Charlie's skin was unusually pale. He frowned. "You feeling okay?"

Charlie nodded and straightened a stack of magazines on the small table next to his father's favorite leather chair. She shoved something into her pocket.

He raised a brow. "You can borrow those if you like."

She looked up sharply and shook her head.

A quiet Charlie. Not a good sign. He tucked a lock of hair behind her ear. "Too much family?"

She inhaled and exhaled, licked her lips, and put on a pleasant expression. "No, I just needed to collect myself." She turned her face into his hand and rubbed her cheek against his palm. So soft. So pretty.

He tried to read her eyes, but couldn't get past the ivy green wall she'd raised to block him. He settled for a quick kiss, then took her hand in his. "We need to get going soon. Leaving this place takes almost an hour in itself, so we'd better get started."

"Did Michele get a haircut?"

"What? Oh, no. Aunt Deb gave up and decided to see if she could talk my mother into highlights." Vaiden grimaced. Not a holiday went by without someone getting a new look from his aunt. The woman was a menace.

When he and Charlie had finally made their way to the front door forty-five minutes later, his mother was waiting for them. Vaiden hugged her.

"I like her, Rob. She'll keep you on your toes," she whispered before pecking him on the cheek.

He hadn't sought her approval, but now that she'd given it, tension he hadn't known he felt was replaced with a giant veil of relief. His mother hadn't liked any of the girls his brother Nate had brought to the house over the years. She'd predicted the failure of the relationships with astounding accuracy.

If she'd doomed the one good thing he'd found in ages, he'd have pretended to ignore her, but he knew his mother was excellent at reading people. If she liked Charlie, he had only to convince Charlie herself that he was the right man.

His mother embraced Charlie, unbalancing her slightly.

Charlie hesitated, then placed her hands on his mother's back, returning the hug.

"You take care of my Rob. Don't let him get away with anything." His mother winked at him as she squeezed Charlie's hand. "Your father should be home for Christmas this year. Make sure you present yourself."

His dad missed many holidays, but he made a point of being home at Christmas, and on his wife's birthday. Vaiden wasn't surprised that the old man would be showing up this time around. He led a covert outfit, the exact nature of which Vaiden hadn't been told, nor had he ever had the guts to ask. He knew his father helped people, and wouldn't do anything immoral, and Vaiden left it at that. There was such a thing as family loyalty. Everyone should be allowed their secrets, he supposed.

Once Vaiden and Charlie got into the car and started down the driveway, his sister waved from the front door. He honked the horn once and turned onto the highway.

"Long day. How'd you survive? Did they scare you off for good?"

Charlie was still oddly quiet, and Vaiden was concerned. Maybe she was worrying about being bait for the killer. But he had the impression it was something more.

"No. It was very nice. More people than I'd expected. How do you keep all your relatives straight in your head?" She pawed through her backpack purse and soon Vaiden smelled her hand lotion.

"Your extended family isn't that big then?" He already knew the answer to his question, but he wanted to keep her talking while he could. Maybe they could get to whatever was bothering her.

"I guess it's as big as most. But they're spread out all over the place. I haven't met most of them."

Paper crackled and he took his eyes from the road briefly to look over at her. "What's that?"

"A page from one of the magazines." Her voice caught and he waited.

"Did you see something about one of the places you've been? Those travel magazines you were looking through were pretty old. Dad doesn't throw them away, ever." He risked another look. She was smoothing the paper against her pants leg.

"My mother was in an...accident, years ago. She was presumed dead." Charlie pushed the button to open her window and leaned her head toward the wind. "My dad went to the accident site to look for her. *He* never came back either."

He could hear the pain in her voice, and his heart ached for her. He couldn't imagine losing either of his parents, much less both at once. "How long ago was this?"

"Ten years. She was doing fieldwork in Ghana."

"As in Africa?"

She laughed and he was glad to hear a change in the tone of her voice. "You know another Ghana?"

"Hey, don't laugh at me," he joked. "There's a Paris and a Lebanon in Virginia, you know."

"Touché." She was quiet for a moment. "The woman in this picture favors my mother. It's a nun working in Ghana. The photo was taken a few years after the political upheaval that we thought took my mother's life. I shouldn't have torn the magazine—"

"Dad'll understand."

"—but I couldn't bear to leave it, and you came in and I panicked. I've gotta see if I can get someone to check this woman out. See what her story is. I tried everything short of going there myself when my dad disappeared. I was ready to leave grad school and my fieldwork, but there were no leads. Nobody knew anything. My mother had been there on paper, but the authorities didn't remember what happened to her."

Vaiden wondered just how soon his father would be home. He had contacts everywhere. "I'll make a few calls when we get home. I know someone who might just be able to find out something."

Home. His house had never felt so comfortable as it did with Charlie in it. He knew it couldn't last—she was supposed to return to Peru at the end of April, and it was nearly December—but he would take what he could get. Maybe by the time she was ready to leave, she wouldn't want to go. A guy could dream, couldn't he?

Chapter Sixteen

Charlie was making him insane.

Vaiden sat in a wooden chair at the kitchen table while Charlie, with only her feet visible, dug through his pantry. All morning she'd been hurrying around the house, folding socks, rearranging her things in the bathroom, and now this thing with having the food in his pantry in some sort of order. And yet she told him she wasn't nervous about being bait for Orion—if it was Orion—in just a couple of hours.

She sighed loud enough for him to hear it.

"Yes?" He folded his newspaper and half-turned, one arm resting on the back of the chair.

She stepped out of the pantry, a hand on her hip. "You have nothing snacky in here. How is that possible?"

"What?" Vaiden stood, walking around her to peer inside. "There's plenty here. Cereal, chips, granola bars..." He leaned back and caught the scrunched face she was making. "There's no time, anyway. We're meeting with my supervisor before you head to the university." She didn't look worried. How could she not be worried? He tugged her arm, bringing her close, and kissed the top of her head.

Her arms went around his waist. "It's going to be fine, Vaiden."

Damn. She'd read his fear for her safety. He shouldn't be letting her know he was concerned. Confidence was what he needed to give her. "I know that."

Easing back from her, he moved to the closet and grabbed his jacket. "I know a great place on the way where you can get some snacks, okay?" He smiled as she dropped into a chair to pull on her shoes.

The drive to the spot where they were meeting his supervisor wasn't long, and two blocks before they reached their destination, Vaiden turned into the parking lot of a small strip of stores. A convenience store, a dentist, and a health food store. Some smaller shops lay at the end of the row, but he rarely ventured any farther than the health food store.

"Now, this is the place for comfort food." He switched off the engine to his Camry and got out. After holding the door open for Charlie, he followed her inside. One wall of the shop held vitamins, the opposite held herbs. In the center stood four rows of shelves. The place had everything from soy milk to bins of snacks.

Charlie snorted. When he looked at her, she had her fingers to her lips. "Are you serious?"

"What?" She was as bad as Nate, Vaiden thought with a chuckle, for like his brother, she seemed to have an innate dislike for the selections, even though he'd bet money she'd never tried them.

"This stuff is feed, not food." She opened the container of banana chips and stirred them a bit with the small metal shovel provided for scooping.

Vaiden laughed. "Trust me, you'll like it. Here, I'll pick the best stuff for you." He snatched a plastic bag and leaned over the bins to select the least healthy of the choices.

"Okay, well, I'm just gonna look around."

He nodded without looking at her. She'd like this. She didn't know what she was missing.

The smell of the yogurt-covered pretzels had always grossed him out, so he steered clear of them, and the little raisin granolas next to them. It took him five minutes to carefully choose things he thought she might enjoy. Banana and apple chips, even though she'd turned her nose up at the banana. And some dried apricots. They weren't his favorite, but his sister loved them. Maybe they were a woman thing. And just as a concession to her, carob-covered peanuts.

It wasn't as though all he ate was health food. Far from it. He liked a steak and potato as much as the next man. But he liked to keep healthy food around. If the junky stuff was in his house, he'd eat it. Faced with only healthy food as a choice, it was easier. That was his mother's fault. She had the same problem, she claimed, eating the desserts just because they were in the house.

He wasn't trying to change Charlie. She was a knockout. He had no problem with what she ate or did to stay looking the way she did. In fact, he'd love to lick chocolate syrup from her—where the hell was she?

His heart beat hard in his chest. He gripped the plastic bag tight in his fist as he whipped his head left and right, peering over the tops of the shelves in search of her. The store, aside from the Celtic music playing on the overhead speakers, was silent.

The man behind the register cleared his throat. "You lookin' for your wife?"

Not dwelling on the misidentification of her status, Vaiden nodded and set the bag on the counter. The man seemed certain, and calm. Calm was good. He tried to slow his heart rate.

The clerk nodded back and sighed. "She went down t'end of the strip. They all do, you know."

Vaiden handed the man a few bills, then pocketed the change. "Which store?"

"Korzenko's," he said with an eye roll, "all the way down."

Vaiden thanked the man and pushed the door open, turning left. Even though he'd been assured that she'd gone to this Korzenko place, he couldn't help but want to run down the sidewalk and make sure. He bit his lip. She was a grown woman. She could take care of herself.

But damn, he wished she'd let him take care of her a little bit.

Korzenko's. He'd reached the doorway before he knew it. Nothing indicated what kind of store it was. Just a scripty fonted name across the window. And in the display? Couldn't tell.

As he placed a hand on the brass-handled door, it swung open. Charlie looked guilty, and then grinned. She had a white plastic bag under one arm, and a hunk of...fudge? A hunk of fudge in her right hand.

He raised an eyebrow.

She shrugged one shoulder and sent him an impish grin and wink. "I'm ready to go now."

Too cute for her own damned good.

✧

The walk from the parking deck to the department office usually provided Charlie time for reflection and thought. But this morning she hurried. Virginia weather was notoriously fickle. Yesterday for Thanksgiving they'd had sixty-degree temperatures, and today she'd awoken to forty degrees and wind.

She clutched the collar of her jacket together with one hand, her other hand buried in her pocket. She needed to invest in new gloves. Nice ones, not work gloves.

Earlier in the week the cleaners she'd hired to empty the death-house had boxed her clothing and sent it to Vaiden's home. He hadn't said a word when he found half his closet filled with her belongings. Of course, as far as clothes, that didn't entail much. Most, she'd left boxed and donated to the homeless shelter.

Years of fieldwork had narrowed her selections to sturdy materials, her goal being quality rather than fashion. As a woman in charge of a crew of men, she discovered that life at the dig was just easier when she wasn't the sexy thing in heels.

She was glad she'd bought some new things, as she now found she wanted to be pretty for Vaiden. When it came time to teach again, she would reevaluate her wardrobe. Providing she still had a job. The board had been silent on the issue thus far.

She was scheduled to teach a half-semester course in the classroom in January, followed by a few weeks of fieldwork locally. Then it was back to Peru. The prospect of leaving Vaiden left her empty. Somehow the dig, even with the possibility of finding the gold rod again, wasn't high on her list of priorities at the moment.

Charlie climbed one flight of stairs before she realized she'd had time to reflect after all. She needed to pay more attention to her surroundings. She'd walked the route so many times in the past, she could have done it blindfolded.

As it was the Friday after Thanksgiving, not many students were on campus. The student body had been understandably unnerved by the murder of Dean Fisher, and many of those who normally would have stayed for extra study had chosen to visit friends instead. Little did they know how safe they'd have been given that a dozen cops waited in secret for the killer to appear.

Charlie unlocked her office and flicked on the lights. The room was roasting hot. Someone had obviously set the wrong dates in the computer that controlled the heat on campus. Heaven forbid they waste heat on a day no one should be at the school.

She let her jacket fall onto the chair and shoved the office key into her front pocket along with her penknife. Normally she would have closed the door, but didn't this time, knowing Vaiden stood nearby.

The police had told her to pretend to work, and to give the appearance of normalcy. She chuckled. Were they kidding? She did have work. She had yet to enter the grades for the last set of students she'd had at the field school. Her voice mail was probably filled with messages from frantic students waiting for their grades.

She pushed the power button on the computer and watched the start-up screen. The scent of the fudge snuggled in her bag drew her before the start-up screen disappeared. She didn't bother slicing the fudge into delicate sections. The thick rectangle fit nicely into the palm of her hand and she munched while she opened the program. Within minutes she was deep in concentration, plugging in grades, and happy with her chocolate fix. Careful not to get crumbs of fudge on the keyboard, she made short work of the entries.

She checked email and visited some sites on the internet. Each search engine had its own quirks, and it took time to find the right search string. She wanted updates on field work other schools were working on in Peru, and in similar locations. Had any of them encountered Ica Stones?

After the second hour she became bored. There was no way she was going to just hang around the building. She'd never normally do that, so why should she today?

She grabbed her jacket and then took out her cell phone. Vaiden's number was programmed into the phone, so she punched in his code.

"What is it?" His voice conveyed tension, the question bit out almost as one word.

"I'm gonna get out of here. I'll head over to grab some lunch, then I'll get my Jeep and meet you at your place." She listened for his sigh of disappointment, but none came.

He was quiet. Maybe he thought she was speaking in code. They'd set up a signal for her to use if she got in trouble, a motion at the window, so she kept her hands at her sides to avoid confusing him. She could picture him trying to decipher her words. He had to have visual surveillance on her, so he must know she was all right. "Okay. Take your time."

The line dropped and she hit the end button before pushing the phone into her backpack purse. Annoyance crept across her face, wrinkling her lips. She scrunched up her nose and stuck out her tongue as she pulled the blinds closed over the windows. She hadn't thought this plan would work to start with.

The person who'd set the series of crimes into motion probably had a family. He or she was probably home with them right now watching football, eating cold turkey sandwiches and leftover pie. She thought better of leaving her phone in her pack, grabbed it from the bag, and tucked it into her jacket. Draping it over her arm before slipping into the sleeves, she paused in the doorway and wondered if there even was football on TV today.

She inserted the key in the door handle to turn the lock. A

rustling behind her sent tremors up her spine. She half-turned her shoulders toward the noise. A thin man of medium build had emerged from the storage closet, a dark bandana over his mouth like a bank robber from an old western movie.

Abandoning the key in the lock, Charlie dashed for the hallway. Her scream was cut short as the creep smashed his black-gloved palm over her mouth. She sent an elbow into his ribs and smiled under his hand when he grunted in pain.

His other hand rose to trade places with the first, and Charlie gagged at the sickeningly sweet smell of the cloth he held against her face. She resisted inhaling, but failed. Her limbs collapsed like noodles and she lost consciousness. Her last thought was simple. "Crap."

✧

Why the hell had she closed the blinds?

Vaiden clenched his fists. His ears had gone numb in the chill wind, but he'd been determined to stay within sight of Charlie. He folded his binoculars and tucked them into his inside pocket.

He inched away from the tree and dusted bark fragments from the side of his coat. He kept his eyes on the window, willing Charlie to open the damned blinds.

He spoke into his walkie. "Jarod. Can you get a visual on her? She should've been out of the building by now."

"I'll check with Ethan. He's on that floor. Just a minute." Jarod gave a short wave from the window of the building opposite Charlie's location. Vaiden could see his mouth moving.

His walkie crackled. "Get in there now! Everybody, go! Ethan's got our guy."

Vaiden's heart froze, but his feet propelled him forward. By the time he hit the stairwell he'd recovered the power to think. Jarod hadn't said anyone was hurt. Charlie had to be okay.

He arrived in the hallway outside of her office in record time. The acrid smell of blood from the dean's murder in the nearby room lingered, no matter how the cleaning crew tried to cover it with bleach.

Then again, maybe it was just him. He hated that smell.

A piece of furniture clattered to the hard floor and he rushed into the department office. Three officers held onto a wildly kicking young man no older than twenty-five.

Vaiden swung about searching for Charlie. She was slumped on the floor just down the hall and around a corner, with a female officer at her side.

He never knew relief and terror could be combined. On close inspection her color wasn't good, but he didn't see evidence of trauma. "Is she—"

"He chloroformed her. She's fine. Just give her a few minutes." The woman fanned Charlie's face and kept her sitting up.

To the officer's shock, Vaiden kissed the top of Charlie's head. "Watch her."

A second officer joined the first. "We should get her outside. If he used chloroform, she's probably gonna throw up." His deep voice commanded respect, and when he spoke he sounded like he knew exactly what to do. Vaiden was relieved. They would make sure she was protected.

He made himself leave her side. She was okay. She wouldn't want him to see her getting sick, he knew that. She was safe and in the hands of his fellow officers. She couldn't be safer if he locked her in a cell. Although, that wasn't a bad idea, considering her string of luck.

And just maybe, this whole bizarre business was over.

He strode toward the perp, now much calmer and in handcuffs. Vaiden wanted to know who the man was who had dared touch his woman.

He tried counting to ten, made it to five before his rage, barely contained, allowed him to speak in a reasonably normal voice. “What the hell did you think you were doing?”

The younger man paled and looked to the officer who’d cuffed him. That officer lifted one shoulder in mock helplessness.

“I just... I was...”

“Name.” Vaiden shoved him back against the wall.

“Walter. Look I—”

Vaiden didn’t let him finish. He wasn’t ready for explanations. He had rancor to exude. “What made you think you could touch her?”

His anger threatened to take over and he backed away before he ruined the arrest. He glanced to where Charlie had been sitting. She and the officers were gone, most likely downstairs getting air. Or getting sick, he reminded himself. Because of this guy. He clenched his fists.

“Hey, Vaiden. Take a look.” Jarod emerged from the closet with a paper grocery bag clutched in his gloved hands.

Vaiden’s eyes narrowed. “What’s in it?”

“Duct tape. Rope. Knife.” Jarod cut his eyes at the suspect, then handed the bag to another officer and stepped between the two men. “And condoms.”

Had Jarod not blocked him, Vaiden would have ripped the jerk’s head off right there in front of God and everybody. As it was, his breath blew from his nose like dragon fire and he ground his teeth together.

"Let me take over, man." Jarod didn't look at him, but he laid a hand on his arm.

Vaiden nodded and walked away. He needed Charlie. Had to feel her in his arms. This guy was insane. What if he'd taken her? What if he'd gotten his Charlie alone, and—

Vaiden shook his head. Had he heard...? There it was again.

Barking.

What the hell?

He followed the sound to the stairwell door. On the landing below stood a dog with thick black fur, the tips just barely golden. The creature was huge, each paw easily the size of Vaiden's own hands. It barked ceaselessly, staring below. Vaiden approached and the dog skittered down the steps, its claws tapping on the hard black floor.

When Vaiden reached the bottom, he found no sign of the dog. He did see the female officer from upstairs standing in a group of uniformed police in front of the building. She could tell him where Charlie had been taken. He wasn't about to ask if they'd seen the dog. He knew in his heart no one had.

"Excuse me." The officers turned toward him and their conversation trailed off. Vaiden put on a pleasant smile and addressed the female who'd been upstairs with Charlie. "Where's Dr. Blair?"

The woman smiled back and pointed to an empty bench behind a large oak tree. "She's..." She walked in the direction of the bench and turned a full circle. "The other officer took her over here. He..." Her brows knitted together. "Just a minute."

While she spoke to the others in the group, the echo of the black dog's bark sounded in his head like a frantic heartbeat.

The officers rushed around, one back into the building,

another to his car radio. A nervous cadet called for Detective Ronan.

The female officer returned to him. Slowly. "D-Detective Vaiden, nobody knows who that officer was. I just assumed..." She inhaled. "We think... We may have been tricked."

Vaiden tilted his head back and searched the sky as if he'd find an answer there. He closed his eyes and saw Charlie as she'd been upstairs on the floor. Pale, a little green around the gills, and wearing her backpack purse. His heart surged and he prayed she hadn't found and destroyed his tracking device.

Chapter Seventeen

Everything spun.

Black circles with purple edges. Hard cold metal beneath her chin. The echo of that awful sweet smell in the back of her throat.

Bile rose from her stomach and Charlie fought the urge to throw up. She hadn't eaten much, and with great concentration quelled the ill feeling. Still the noxious bubbles burned the back of her throat.

Her eyes opened with effort, but even then darkness surrounded her. She breathed through her mouth as another wave of nausea rolled through her body, causing saliva to pool around her tongue.

She wiggled her fingers and stretched out her arms. Wherever she'd gotten herself stuck, it was small, and reeked of grease. She pressed the back of her hand against the low ceiling, then used her fingertips to trace the metal edges. Worn carpet-covered areas beneath her.

She shrugged her shoulders. Her backpack purse wasn't on her. Maybe it was here in the dark somewhere and she just couldn't find it.

Somewhere nearby a car door slammed. No city sounds. No engines or horns. No snatches of conversations from passersby.

She must be in the trunk of a car, far away from Vaiden. From help.

Vaiden had to have seen him carry her from the building. There was no secret way out—but if so, then why was she here? How had she been taken while the police looked on?

Fear grazed her confidence, leaving it weakened. The last thing she recalled was someone covering her mouth. Vaguely she remembered being carried, and then more of that nasty sweet smell.

Her hand went to her wrist and found her watch. The glowing numbers told her she hadn't been unconscious for long. Thirty minutes at the most.

That dolt who knocked her out had been in the building the whole time. That unnerved her further. He'd had a key, if he was inside before her. And the chloroform he'd used on her meant he'd had a plan. She shuddered.

Two more doors slammed, these belonging to the car that trapped her. The engine turned over and Charlie gritted her teeth. As the car accelerated she rolled into the side wall and cringed.

Somewhere she'd read that if a criminal takes his victim to a secondary location, his plan is murder. She swallowed her panic and made herself think.

She patted the side walls, searching for the cable leading to a trunk release handle, but had no luck. She wished she knew more about cars, and made a promise to herself to take a course in mechanics if she got out of her current predicament alive.

Praying that the car was an older model with an actual spare tire, she yanked the ragged carpet from the floor of the trunk, covering her mouth when the dust made her cough. Bile rose again and she swallowed, twisting her face.

She scrunched back and lifted the thin pressboard that covered the spare. Her hand wrapped around a tire iron that nestled on top of the center hub. She drew her newfound weapon out and replaced the board and carpet so she could once again lie as comfortably as possible.

If her captor planned to kill her, he was going to feel pain before he succeeded.

She waited, nerves tight as springs. A full two minutes later she allowed herself to relax. There was no need to stay on high alert since the slowing of the car would let her know when to prepare.

She adjusted the position of her right leg and remembered her penknife. She probed her pocket and located the blade.

The tail lights. If she could remove them from the inside, maybe someone would see her hands waving and call the police. It was worth a try. She extended the knife toward the area where the light should be, then held herself tightly as the car decelerated, then turned sharply left.

The road they'd traveled previously had been straight and smooth. This one bumped and weaved. They were traveling at a high speed, and as she'd noticed no stops, she deduced that the car must be headed to the countryside. Not good.

She struggled to remove the flat plastic screws from the back of one light. She used the knife to pry off the small panel. The wires pulled easily from the back of the bulb housing, but she couldn't heave the rectangular glass inside. She shifted as far back as she could and kicked at the glass instead, and in two blows the shattered pieces fell onto the road.

A porthole of daylight lit her prison. Outside she saw only fields, trees, and a faded paved road. There was no one for her to wave to for help.

The light did, however, reveal the location of the trunk

release cable that had eluded her. She'd just barely touched the black-coated cords when the car swerved right and stopped.

✧

"Oh, boy, are you not going to believe this."

Jarod's tone didn't inspire joy or relief, and Vaiden turned dead eyes to him.

"Where did they dump it?" Vaiden asked, his voice flat. His one hope of finding Charlie had been in that pill-sized device he'd slipped into her backpack purse. It seemed like years ago. If her belongings had been dropped somewhere, they'd never find her. She'd end up like those other women. Sealed in crates or freezers or boxes, slowly and horribly dying.

Jarod placed a hand on Vaiden's shoulder. "Not that. But they're close. The signal stopped moving about fifteen minutes ago, somewhere near Short Pump, so we should hear from the boys any time now. She's gonna be fine, Vaiden. We'll find her in time." He dropped a manila folder on the desk in front of Vaiden. "Take a look."

Vaiden studied the birth certificate inside the folder. Leonard Kedansky. An illegitimate birth. "So Kedansky wasn't the father's name. So what?"

"I dug up his mother."

Vaiden's mood broke and he twisted his face in disbelief. "You what?"

Jarod frowned, then realization dawned and he grinned. "No, not literally. She lives in Chester." He scrubbed his knuckles against his short blond hair. "You wanna guess who she said Leonard's dear old dad is?"

"Are you going to say that Leonard is Elwin Kent's son?"

Vaiden stood, mentally going over the Orion file, hardly aware of Jarod's presence any longer.

"I think she knows a lot more than she's said so far. But she agreed to a face-to-face." Jarod stuffed his arms through the sleeves of his jacket. "I'll meet with Ms. Kedansky. You get out to Short Pump before you go crazy."

Vaiden nodded. He had to find Charlie. If whoever had her had hurt her, it would be his fault. He'd let her put herself in harm's way. Yes, she'd volunteered to be the bait, but he never should have let her do it.

As he headed toward the exit, he paused outside the interrogation room. Wisely, he'd been banned from the interview with the would-be rapist who'd attacked Charlie in her office.

He slipped into the viewing room and elbowed the detective standing near the glass. "What's he say?"

The older man pulled at his mustache. "Hey, Vaiden. Sumbitch says he was meeting a woman for some rough sex. Made arrangements on the internet to meet her. She requested a rape fantasy and he was gonna be happy to play it out. Can you believe folks?"

Vaiden rubbed his eyes. "And he chloroformed her because?"

"Part of the deal. He claims all the supplies were put in the closet for him and all he had to do was let himself in with the key she left above the door, hide, and wait." The detective coughed into a handkerchief that he stuffed into his pants pocket. "Boys're getting his hard drive now."

The suspect inside held his face in his hands, the tips of his fingers buried in his hairline. His shoulders slumped forward and he rocked back and forth slowly.

The detective slapped Vaiden on the shoulder. "He's all lawyered up right now. Give you a call when we get that computer cracked open."

Keeping his eyes on the shell of a man on the other side of the glass, Vaiden nodded. "Do that. I gotta get out of here." His cell phone rang and he checked the number. It was an officer out in Short Pump on the far west end of Henrico.

They'd found the backpack.

✧

Charlie braced herself on the far right side of the trunk, her knees bent, her back pressed against the ceiling. She held the trunk release with three fingers of her left hand, the tire iron with her right. Her knife she'd stowed back in her pocket for the time being.

Both car doors slammed and she listened to determine the proximity of the occupants. One voice was decidedly female, the other male. They were arguing. The conversation halted as the woman screeched out in frustration and uttered a foul curse.

Keys jangled close to the trunk opening, and Charlie yanked the release handle and sprang upward. Squinting against the sudden sunlight, she swung the tire iron in a wide arc.

One end of the cross-shaped implement thumped into the nearest person, making solid contact with his jaw. He hit the ground hard and Charlie got a good look at his face.

Leonard Freaking Kedansky.

Not the man from the office who'd knocked her out.

She left analysis for later and flung herself from the cramped space toward the woman. They landed together on lumpy grass, Charlie's knees on either side of the woman's hips. She stared down into the face of Alexa Reynolds.

Though Charlie had a grip on Alexa's upper arms, her momentary shock at seeing not one, but two familiar faces gave Alexa the advantage.

The other woman rolled to the side and reared up, raising a bony fist with a snarl. Charlie tucked in her legs and mule-kicked into Alexa's chest, wiping the triumphant grin from her face.

"I've been wanting to do this for a while now," Charlie said as she leapt to her feet and backed Alexa toward the car.

Both women went for the tire iron on the ground. Alexa reached it first, hefting the metal in her fist. She stepped toward Charlie and swiped the tool awkwardly through the air. Charlie seized the opportunity and twisted, sending a roundhouse kick to Alexa's upper body.

Limbs and light auburn hair flew up as Alexa fell backward into the trunk. She coughed for air and Charlie acted quickly, before Alexa got her wind back. She nudged Alexa's feet inside and slammed the lid of the trunk down.

Leonard, lying close to her legs, stirred and grabbed her ankles. Charlie lost her balance and one palm slapped the trunk as she caught herself. Her thumb connected with the keys that still hung from the lock. She snatched the keys and threw them down the road past Leonard's head as she kicked her ankle free of his grasp. He lumbered to his feet, clutching his jaw, which was already turning purple.

Charlie spun on her heel and ran, away from the car, away from Leonard and Alexa. How the hell did they even know each other?

Gently sloping hills surrounded her, far-off fences etched out property lines. She was headed away from the dirt road, but she didn't care. Leonard's uneven footfalls stopped behind her and she turned her head without slowing her pace. He'd abandoned the chase, and was hollering into the trunk.

Charlie paused to catch her breath, unsatisfied with her mere half-mile distance. She had to get farther away, but she had to think first. Running like a crazy woman into the hills and trees would not save her life. Using her brain would.

Leonard walked a circle near the rear of the car, his head low to the ground. The keys. He was looking for the keys.

He noticed her watching and pointed at her. "You can't get away, Charlie! There's nobody out here to help you! Nobody knows where you are!"

"You watch me," she muttered and then jogged over the nearest rise. Through a small copse of trees she could see another skinny dirt road and she ran toward it.

Knowing she couldn't outrun Leonard once he found the keys, she only followed the road a short distance to a grouping of cedar trees. She crouched in the shade, using the branches for cover.

They must have driven her to Goochland County, just over the line from Henrico. That would explain the long drive down the straight road. Only Broad Street kept that arrow path. And in Goochland, most of the countryside held horse farms. If she could find her way to a farmhouse or a barn she might be able to call for help.

She scouted the horizon for signs of habitation. Nothing. She checked the sun and decided to run north. Even if she didn't hit a house, she'd eventually get back to Broad Street—or Route 250, as it was known in Goochland. From there she might be able to flag down a passing vehicle.

"Where the hell are you, Vaiden?"

✧

"Where the hell are you, Charlie?" Vaiden mumbled. Through his darkest sunglasses, he watched Trevor Harrison, the crime scene investigator assigned to the case, work his magic on the backpack purse. His breath stopped while he waited for Trevor to drip a chemical onto a swab he'd run across the pack.

"The substance on the torn opening is negative for blood, Vaiden." Trevor's mouth stayed in a grim line. "But these old stains on the straps, I don't think I should bother testing them. Didn't you say she had this bag for a while?"

"Yeah. And she was hurt in Peru a few weeks back." Vaiden examined the straps without touching them. "This thing's been through as much as she has."

He tugged on a glove from Trevor's kit and used tweezers to extract the pill sized tracking device that had wedged itself in the bottom lining. At least the thing had got him this far. He bagged the device and removed the glove.

The pack had been dumped at the edge of the rear parking lot of the newest mall in the county. The trees backed up to Interstate 64 on one side, and stopped abruptly at the red mud construction area.

Vaiden read the names of the businesses on the nearest outside wall. He'd sent officers to ask employees if they'd seen any cars back near the woods, but so far no one had radioed with news. It was a long shot and he knew it.

The scent of cigarette smoke wafted past him. A quick inventory of the men working the scene showed no smokers. He scanned the parking lot in the direction the wind came from. A thin squiggle of smoke rose from a dumpster at the edge of the construction site. Curious, he approached the dumpster cautiously.

The smoke didn't rise from the deep blue dumpster itself, but from a fragile figure huddled on the opposite side. The small long-haired girl faced away from Vaiden. He cleared his throat.

She started and threw the butt to the pavement, hiding it beneath her shoe before turning around. She clearly hadn't been expecting Vaiden, and her chagrin wiped from her face instantly. "I'm on a break. Buzz off." She withdrew a red and white pack of cigarettes from her pocket and slapped it against her palm.

Taken aback, Vaiden puzzled over her response. He slipped his black sunglasses from his face. "Excuse me, I'm a detective with the Richmond Police Department. You say you're on a break. You work here?" He gestured toward the mall.

The girl, who couldn't, in his estimation, be a day older than sixteen, crossed her arms and pursed her lips around the filter she'd inserted between them. She took the cigarette out of her mouth and pointed it at him. "You got ID?"

Thinking he should ask the waif if *she* had ID proving she was old enough to smoke, Vaiden backed up a step. He showed her his identification in one hand, and waved his other hand toward the small group of officers not a quarter mile away.

The girl shuffled forward and peered around the dumpster. "Well, ain't that something." She produced a square silver lighter and rolled the flint with her thumb, lighting the cigarette. She coughed after the first inhale. With a look that dared him to comment, she gripped the cigarette awkwardly and held it to her side.

Vaiden waited. She didn't disappoint.

"Look, all the smokers get twice as many breaks as the rest of us, so I told them I smoked. Okay? Is it a crime?"

"Depends. How old are you?"

She squinched her face. "You wanna know about them

folks who were over there a while ago?"

Vaiden crossed his arms. "Why d'you say that?"

"When I was out here earlier there was a couple fighting about something. I just stayed right here"—she indicated the spot he'd found her—"and had my little break."

"Fighting? In what manner?"

She laughed. Fifteen. Fifteen on her oldest day.

"I dunno. He was mostly quiet. His girlfriend though, whoo, she was laying into him. Banging on the car with her fists and stuff. No man with a backbone woulda put up with the way she was talking to him. Guess that's why he yanked her bag outta her hands and threw it."

She'd seen them. "The woman, what did she look like? Brown hair? About this tall?" He raised a hand to the level of Charlie's height.

The girl shook her head. "No, I couldn't really see them too good, but her hair was more on the reddish side. Too pure to be real."

"What?"

She widened her arms to show him what he'd thought was a jacket was actually a black smock. "I wash hair. I would know."

Not her? His mind reeled. Not Charlie? The two theories about who could have taken her suddenly crashed together in his head. A male and a female, with Charlie's backpack. He smiled at the girl. She'd seen the car. "Come with me."

She resisted his pull on her elbow. "I gotta get back in to work. I can't be out here all day. I'll get fired." Her protest didn't reach her eyes.

Vaiden kept a firm grip as he led her back to the other policemen. "I'll let your boss know you're helping us. I need you to look at some pictures."

She grinned and tossed her cigarette to the ground, stomping it out as an afterthought. "Good. Long as I'm still on the clock, I'll tell you the whole story. Did you find their dog?"

Vaiden stopped. "Dog?"

The girl's head bobbed up and down. "Yeah. When they tore off there was a fluffy black dog standing there. He was all whining and barking. But when I started to come see if he had a collar he ran off toward Broad Street." She sucked in her breath through her teeth. "Hope he didn't get hit by a car."

Chapter Eighteen

Once she cleared the top of the second hill, Charlie spotted a dirt road. Ignoring the stitch in her side, she pushed through the pain and ran toward the road. A black-stained wooden fence lined one side—a good sign. Though the farms in Goochland could be huge, she hoped the ill-kept road would take her to a residence with haste.

A quarter of a mile down the rutted drive, a barn came into view. Very large and impressive, the structure could use a coat or two of paint. Even from the road the weather-beaten boards said this operation didn't make much money. But why, then, she wondered, were the rails of the fence so well sealed?

As she climbed the fence and forced her feet forward, Charlie smelled fresh manure. She half-walked, half-ran, hopping over the various piles of dung. The grass was well-eaten the closer she got to the barn, and stood barely an inch tall.

She stopped at the front corner of the building and bent at the waist, pressing her fingers against the sharp pain beneath her ribs. She made a mental note to take up long distance jogging. Maybe marathon running.

From her position, she could just make out a farmhouse on the horizon. She groaned. It was at least another mile away. She shut her eyes and listened for Leonard's car. Nothing yet.

He hadn't found the keys.

Her eyes popped open and she gasped. If he'd come after her on foot...

She peered around the corner of the barn. No one had followed her.

The low nicker of a horse and a responding whinny, both from inside the barn, brought her focus back on how she was going to get from Point A to Point B.

The wooden board holding the doors closed slid smoothly through the squarish bracket. Charlie craned her neck to see into the four stables. "Don't be a nag, don't be a nag..."

A donkey shoved his gray face over his stall door and gave the wood a kick. She pictured herself riding the short animal across the fields and chuckled. Some getaway that'd be. Leonard would laugh so hard, he'd probably fall over and incapacitate himself.

The calls she'd heard were not those of a donkey, so she didn't despair. She grabbed a bridle hanging on the next stall door and clicked her tongue. A Roman-nosed mare gaped at her from the shadowed rear of the compartment. The chestnut stood almost seventeen hands high and wore a white blaze from eyes to nostrils. The jingle of the bit in the bridle brought her forward.

Charlie wedged her toes in the slats of the stable's gated door and balanced while she slipped the bridle over the horse's ears. She connected the tiny buckles, then opened the door and led the horse out.

A small English saddle sat on a perch in the rear of the barn. She doubted it belonged to the big mare. More likely, it was for the petite horse that blew thickly from the stall next to the donkey. There was no time for a saddle anyway, and she didn't know squat about riding English.

She'd have to stand on something to mount. Six large empty wooden crates stacked against the wall caught her eye. She shifted one. Empty. Perfect. She dragged it out a bit and led the mare over to it. She swung onto the chestnut's back, winding her hands in the mane near the withers with the leather reins wrapped around her fingers.

Charlie nudged her with her ankles. The big horse sidestepped and then walked into the sunshine. Charlie shielded her eyes and took a gander behind the barn. The hum of an engine grew louder in the near distance. She couldn't know if it was Leonard and Alexa, or someone else entirely, but whoever the driver, the person was moving fast.

She kicked the horse into a canter and held on as they began to cross the field.

✧

The girl hadn't been much help in identifying the make or model of the car. She'd known it was medium blue, had either lots of rust or red mud on the lower half and a silver trim down the side. She thought it had four doors, rather than two, but couldn't be positive.

To keep from getting angry with her, Vaiden reminded himself that the girl had given them a hell of a lot more information than they'd had without her.

He alerted Dispatch and had them contact the sheriff in Goochland to be on the lookout for a car by that description. If the car had turned west on Broad Street, there was no place else to go. Route 155 hadn't been completed, so the couple couldn't have taken the future shortcut to Powhatan County and Midlothian.

Vaiden climbed into a car with a patrolman. They left the mall, traveling west. He leaned low, eying every car, hoping against hope that he'd spot the vehicle that would lead him to Charlie.

Immediately beyond the 155 interchange, houses became far apart, businesses almost nonexistent. A few miles later they crossed the county line. Shortly past the only strip mall in the vast low hills, the area stretched out into alternate sections of woods and hills. Always along the straight road.

A herd of Black Angus cattle pulled his attention for a moment. He'd thought they were something else. They brought to mind another creature.

That girl in the mall parking lot had seen the dog.

Vaiden wasn't one to buy into superstition or spooks, but there had been too many coincidences in the appearance of that black dog since he'd met Charlie. He didn't know if it haunted her or guarded her. Either way, wherever that dog had gone, that's where he wanted to be too. If that dog had headed west, then he damn well knew Charlie'd been taken west.

✧

Charlie debated trying to ride the horse toward the main highway by cutting through the trees off to the right. The steady approach of the engine whine discouraged that thought.

She wheeled the horse toward the farmhouse and dug her heels into the horse's sides. The big muscles beneath her gathered and rolled. She found the rhythm and rocked with the mare, thinking to herself that she should ride more often.

Over the noise of the wind in her ears, a car skidded to a stop on the dirt road behind the barn. Charlie twisted and raised her right elbow to look beneath and behind, observing the blue auto idling on the other side of the fence. She could make out only one figure in the car. It was not Alexa.

The horse stumbled and Charlie tensed, clenching her legs around the animal's body to keep her balance. She could hear the car moving again, spinning in the rocks and dirt, and then a loud crack like a rifle firing—or wood splitting.

She ventured another peek. The car had smashed through the fence and was now barreling across the field toward her.

She kicked the mare's sides. The mare didn't have much speed in her, but she did slide into a smooth gallop.

Another loud noise and something whizzed past Charlie's head. She started in shock.

He was shooting at her?

A second projectile flew past her, the sound like a Japanese hornet as it just passed her ear. Instinctively she lowered herself, flattening on the horse's back, her short breaths taking in the scent of horse sweat. The mare, too, detected something amiss and pressed just that much quicker.

She led the horse on a zigzagged path, not so much to elude the car, but to avoid giving Leonard a clear target.

Just a little farther to the farmhouse. Now that she'd cleared the last hill, she could make out two other buildings near the main structure. One was small like the shacks built over wells; the other was a larger shed.

The roar of the car engine drew her eyes back again. The sedan bounced roughly on the uneven terrain, the front bumper smacking into the ground off and on. If he didn't lose an oil pan on a rock, he'd surely lose his shocks from the rough treatment of the tires.

Neither of these would keep him from catching up to her.

Leonard leaned his arm out of the window again and Charlie turned forward, pressing low against the horse's neck. She needed to get closer to the shed, the nearest building, to protect the mare. The even-tempered beast did not deserve to get shot.

A third shot zinged past and Charlie tugged on the reins enough to decelerate the horse. She swung her leg over the horse's back and dropped to the ground from as low a position as possible, rolling across the tufts of grass to slow herself.

She ignored the ache in her shoulder where she'd taken the brunt of the fall and sprang to her feet. The mare veered far to the left, frightened by the oncoming car. Charlie ran in the opposite direction, toward the shed.

From the back door of the farmhouse, a man with a shaggy growth of beard stormed outside in mid-holler. His arms waved toward the car, and toward Charlie.

She couldn't hear him over the noise of the blood pounding in her ears. The car swerved in front of her and skidded to a stop.

✧

"Brooks, right?" The silence in the car, broken only by sputtered announcements on the radio, made Vaiden's nerves tight. He scanned the road.

"Bug."

"What?" Vaiden glanced at the officer driving the car.

"They call me Bug, sir." The officer, well over six feet tall, solidly built, smiled crookedly at him.

They'd been driving for roughly fifteen minutes, not traveling too fast. Vaiden was careful to survey in every direction. He had to find Charlie before Leonard Kedansky and

Alexa Reynolds hurt her. If anything happened to her… He never should have gone along with Jarod's stupid idea.

He took a deep breath.

Charlie was a tough woman. A regular Indiana Joan. But she was *his* woman, and he couldn't bear the thought of being without her, being unable to protect her.

What would she do, faced with someone truly filled with evil? Someone like Orion who killed and then destroyed?

A dark shape dashed into the road not thirty yards ahead.

"Look out!" Vaiden shoved his hand onto the dashboard as Bug slammed on the brakes. His arms locked and he had to make an effort to bring himself back to a comfortable sitting position.

In the middle of Route 250 stood the black dog. Rigid on all fours, paying no attention to the patrol car, and facing a dirt road.

Bug beeped the horn, then flicked the siren on and off. The dog didn't flinch.

Vaiden stared transfixed at the creature. How could it be the same animal? Moving around the city was one thing, but beating them here… His breath hitched.

"Turn down this road."

Bug, who'd rolled down his window and leaned out, pulled his head back inside. His gaze flicked between Vaiden and the immobile dog. He licked his layered teeth and shrugged. "You're the boss."

Vaiden exhaled thickly, glad Bug hadn't questioned him. He lowered his own window as they passed the dog. The animal snuffled and padded across the pavement after them.

The radio crackled and Bug picked up the mike. The dispatcher told them a car matching the description had been seen on the very road they'd just turned down. Bug accelerated after replacing the mike.

"Do I want to know how you knew to select this road?"

Vaiden chuckled. "No, man, I don't think you do."

"Well, all right then." Bug seemed satisfied with the answer.

A mile down the dirt road, a tire iron lay in their path. Then just a little farther, they noticed evidence of tires heading into the grass on the shoulder. Bug idled the car. Vaiden jumped out and examined the ground.

The driver's door closed and Bug squatted on the ground beside Vaiden. "See this?" Bug rolled a red fragment between his giant fingers.

"Broken tail light, maybe." Vaiden frowned. The bent grass continued back to the road. The car hadn't been disabled. He tried to imagine what could have made so much dust rise and land on the green blades. If Charlie and the suspects had stopped here, there'd been a struggle.

Bug stood and dropped a hand on his shoulder. "Up there."

Vaiden followed Bug's line of vision. Sure enough a thin line of bent grass led up the small hill. He smiled. "She got away."

The echo of gunfire drew both men's eyes toward each other. They hustled back into the car and Bug raced the engine up the hill and around the curve.

Vaiden's heart pounded in his chest. Charlie didn't carry a gun.

✧

Charlie balanced on the pads of her feet, uncertain which way she should run. She couldn't make it to the shed, that was certain. If she ran to the farmhouse, the man standing on the concrete steps with his hands on his hips in outrage might not be of help, and he might get hurt if he tried. Running to the well-house seemed a poor choice, given the structure's size.

Leonard decided for her when he opened the door and climbed out of the car. The pistol remained in his right hand, but his arm stayed down by his side.

A woman could be heard inside the trunk, spilling curses and threats. Charlie grinned. Leonard had found the keys, but hadn't let Alexa out yet. Interesting. At least it evened the odds for Charlie. Except for the damned gun.

The screen door on the farmhouse thwacked and Leonard twitched. He lifted the gun toward the house and fired twice, but the bearded man had gone inside.

Charlie seized the opportunity and ran behind the car toward the shed.

"Damn it!" No gunfire accompanied Leonard's outburst.

She looked over her shoulder. He threw the weapon into the car before he came after her.

A scattering of garden tools lay next to the shed wall, as though knocked over and forgotten. Charlie stepped deliberately on the metal end of a rake and popped the implement handle upward into her hands.

She spun around, wielding the rake, and conked Leonard on the head with it. He fell to his knees, clutching his forehead, a trickle of blood seeping between his fingers.

Charlie frowned. She didn't like hurting people. Didn't even like hurting animals they'd killed for food while on remote digs. But sometimes it had to be done. Like now. Besides, the whiney way Leonard was groaning, he'd be fine with a few stitches.

She jogged tiredly toward the farmhouse, her legs moving

like they were weighted. Just as she passed the abandoned car, she heard the rear passenger door open.

She had no time to wonder how Alexa had freed herself from the trunk. Thin thighs landed on her back and wrapped around her ribs, while bony fingers clawed at her hair.

"You hag! You killed Lenny! You killed my brother!" Alexa dug into Charlie like an ill-fitting metal-reinforced backpack.

Taking hold of the hands in her hair, Charlie heaved forward, flipping the smaller woman onto the ground in front of her. She bent her knees and waited for Alexa to try again.

The glint of hate in the faux strawberry-blond's eyes bewildered Charlie. What had she done to these people to engender such dislike? For years all she'd heard from Leonard was praise and admiration for her father. Since Alexa had come to work at the real estate agency, she'd been nothing but helpful, though by some standards a bit cool. But Charlie had never thought ill of the woman for it. A business was no place for friendships or more than casual conversations.

"What do you want from me, Alexa? Why are you doing this?" Her voice rasped.

"It's all because of you," the woman grated out as she rushed at Charlie.

Stepping to the side, Charlie angered Alexa by making her miss her target. She couldn't prevent the assault the second time, and she and Alexa hit the ground together, struggling for the upper hand. Charlie knew if she could pin the petite female with her legs, she could hold her still. Long as dear Lenny stayed put, anyway.

After a few strong shoves, Charlie had done just that, and sat on Alexa's stomach, fighting to hold the wiry arms down.

A sudden shower of ice-cold water surprised her into letting go of Alexa's hands. The woman slid from beneath her, but rather than attacking Charlie, she ran toward the source of the hydro-assault.

The bearded man had emerged from his house and stood holding a green hose, his thumb half over the stream of water. He continued spraying Alexa as she neared. Each time she started her approach, he squirted her in the face again. Soon Alexa danced about him like a drenched cat, as though determined to make him stop and make him pay.

Charlie hauled herself up and ducked into the shed. Several long loops of bailer twine hung on a spike on one wall. She snatched four of the sections of twine and hurried to aid the bearded man. Together they managed to tie Alexa's hands. He surprised Charlie by also binding Alexa's feet and then hooking the two sets of bound appendages together.

He nodded at Charlie. "Hog-tied." Only then did he bend toward the spigot hidden behind the steps and turn off the water supply. "Where's the other one?" He drew a knife from his pocket and split the twine circle into a straight line.

Charlie pointed to the area between the shed and the well-housing. "Thank you for helping me."

"Name's Griffin. You're next if you start wigging out like these two. You planning to?" From his stern expression, she knew he meant it.

"No, sir, Mr. Griffin."

"Just Griffin."

They reached Leonard, who was still holding his head. Griffin dug into his bottomless pockets and handed Charlie a handkerchief. She eyed it dubiously.

"Pressure. Stop the blood." He jabbed a finger toward Leonard's forehead as he jerked the bloodstained fingers from the injured man's face and yanked them behind his back. Griffin scowled at Leonard's right hand. "Who the hell are you, boy?"

"What is it?" Charlie started behind Leonard to observe whatever Griffin had found disturbing.

The older man held up a meaty hand to stop her. "You just take care of his injury. I'll take care of this." The bearded man's mouth set in a grim line as he cinched the rope tighter.

Seeing that Griffin was tying Leonard's hands, Charlie obeyed. The cut wasn't even that deep. Just a split where the wooden handle had struck him. Still, she pressed the cloth to Leonard's wound. He kept his eyes downcast, but the line of his mouth was hard. And he was whispering.

✧

At a fork in the road, Bug cut the engine and they listened. Nothing.

Then, a wailing siren increased in volume behind them. Vaiden turned in his seat. A county police car.

The brown sedan whooshed past them in a flurry of dust and gravel, one grizzled hand appearing outside the driver's window and waving them to follow.

Vaiden flexed his fingers, wishing he'd driven rather than riding with someone else. He hated feeling out of control; he didn't like relying on others. He checked his weapon and leaned against the door, trying to see over the cloud of dust left by the county car.

Soon they drove past a dark fence, freshly broken across all three rails long before they reached the turnoff to the meandering driveway. What did these people do when it snowed?

Both cars stopped near a two-story farmhouse with a slate

roof. The sheriff signaled for Vaiden and Bug to wait in their car while he investigated.

Vaiden cocked an eyebrow and opened his door. There was no power on earth that could have made him wait right then. Not when Charlie's life was at stake.

He came around the front of the car, where a man about sixty, sixty-five, perched on an upside down bucket, a shotgun balanced on his knees. On the ground at his feet sat Leonard Kedansky, bound in back. The bared legs trussed to the hands with manicured nails on the other prisoner probably belonged to Alexa Reynolds, but since she was lying angled away from him, he couldn't be sure.

He glanced inside the dark blue car left conspicuously in the yard. Open doors, open trunk. No Charlie.

His saw then the bloody white cloth on the ground near Leonard and started forward.

"Easy there. You're looking for the girl?" The man's rough voice belied his smiling face. "She's round there. Getting sick."

Feeling as though his heart had shattered and burst, Vaiden ran to the back of the shed. Charlie was bent over, one hand on the outside wall of the shed, one braced on her left knee. He breathed for the first time in hours.

She coughed, pushed away from the wall, and straightened. She spied Vaiden from the corner of her eye and smiled, not turning toward him. "'Bout time you showed up." Her voice was ragged.

He laughed, sure now that she was okay. Pale, but okay. And throwing up was not uncommon when exposed to chloroform. He knew that.

Agonizing because he wanted to hold her, he waited for Charlie to come to him.

She yanked a handful of leaves from the ground and blew on them, then stuffed them into her mouth and chewed slowly. As she approached, he smelled peppermint. The things she knew! The woman constantly amazed him.

She deftly removed the leaves and tossed them to the ground before grabbing him around the neck, landing hard against his chest. He circled her with his arms and held her close, breathing into her neck. She was alive, and he could hold the other two on kidnapping charges if on nothing else. All would soon be right with the world.

He should have known it wouldn't be that easy.

Chapter Nineteen

Charlie stared out of the window of Vaiden's car. Every cell in her body was on alert with him so close to her. She'd been hard pressed not to embarrass him at Griffin's farm by refusing to let go of him.

If she'd been afraid to admit it before, she knew it now. She loved him. Of all the undone things in her life that she'd pondered while in the trunk waiting for the car to stop, telling Vaiden how she felt about him was the biggest. She wanted to be with him, really with him. There had to be a way. It was *her* life, surely she could control *something* in her own life?

She hadn't felt out of control at any time during her abduction, but when Vaiden had finally arrived the seriousness of her situation had slammed into her.

Now that she was out danger, her physical aches also plagued her. Her right thigh panged, along with the knee on the same leg. And every muscle had been taxed, not only by exertion, but also by adrenaline coursing through her.

She scrunched back into the leather seat and pulled her shoulder blades forward, arching her back. Her head rolled lazily from left to right and back again with quiet popping noises.

Vaiden's fingers crept over to her left hand and he tugged her pinky. The simple gesture touched her and she blinked rapidly.

"You sure you don't need to see a doctor for anything?"

She crooked her pinky around his index finger and smiled at him. "I'm fine. Now."

Truth was, she needed *him.* Needed something real, something safe.

And only Rob Vaiden was going to do. She knew that now. There would never be another man for her. She didn't know when it had happened, but her heart had become hopelessly entangled when it came to Vaiden.

The drive back to his house went quickly and soon they stood in the entryway. Charlie leaned back against him. His arms came around her and he breathed onto her neck. His heat surged through her skin and into her icy veins.

She turned in his arms and rose onto her tiptoes. He angled his mouth toward hers...and her stomach growled.

She laughed first, and he dropped his forehead onto hers and kissed the tip of her nose. "How 'bout you get cleaned up, and I'll fix you something to eat?"

Closing her eyes, she inhaled his male scent while his body enveloped hers again. In his arms she was small and cherished and protected. Her stomach growled again. And hungry.

Reluctantly she moved toward the stairs, her knee protesting each step. A long soak would do her good. Then food, then Vaiden.

✧

Charlie raised her heavy lids and shivered in the tepid water. She craned her neck to see if Vaiden had a clock in the bathroom. How long had she been sleeping?

She dipped her face into the water one last time and then climbed out of the huge tub. Her hand landed on the towel on the top of the stack. It was warm. She smiled.

Ten minutes later she descended the stairs wearing one of Vaiden's dress shirts and nothing else. But he didn't need to know that. Yet.

She'd twisted her hair and pinned it in a chignon, and now she patted the still damp coiffure. The smell of Chinese food lured her into the kitchen.

"Go. Sit." Vaiden shooed her out of the room and over to the couch.

She sat and he joined her, a spotless cookie sheet holding several takeout containers balanced on his arm. He grinned, his brown eyes slitted in mischief.

What was he up to?

Charlie tucked her legs beneath her and leaned on the arm of the couch. He winked and her heart fluttered.

Vaiden placed the metal sheet on the coffee table and held up one finger. From his shirt pocket he withdrew a pair of chopsticks.

Charlie tried not to smirk as he opened each of the containers. Finding the one he wanted, he dipped the chopsticks inside and picked up a morsel of chicken.

She tilted her head. So he knew how to use chopsticks. Interesting. She rubbed her hands against the outside of her thighs. "You got a pair of those for me?"

Vaiden doused the chicken in a small plastic bowl of sweet and sour sauce. Sloping toward her, he brandished the near dripping chicken in front of her lips. "Open for me."

Her left eyebrow jerked. He wanted to play. Very interesting.

Charlie licked the sauce from the bottom of the chicken with the tip of her tongue and closed her eyes. His lips covered hers and she briefly wondered where the chicken had gotten to before giving in to the wave of desire that descended upon her with shocking force. She was hungry, but her hunger for this man had gone beyond any simple need for nourishment.

Vaiden's palm drifted up her leg beneath the too-large shirt, but as he neared where her panties should have been, he stopped and pulled back from the kiss.

"No. You gotta eat. You haven't had anything since..."

She shoved her fingers over her eyebrows. "I had tea this morning. And fudge."

Did she just snort at him? He glared at her. "Then you definitely need something." He retrieved his chopsticks and this time fed her the chicken. She tried several times to tempt him from his mission, but only earned a laughing glower and more food.

As half the chicken had already disappeared, she put a hand on his wrist. "I'm not eating alone."

Vaiden checked his watch. "I can't stay. They'll be done booking Leonard and Alexa, and I want to be there for the interview process."

Charlie fastened onto his wrist. "Vaiden, close the boxes."

His brow wrinkled. "But you need to eat more."

"Stop worrying about my stomach." She slipped the chopsticks from his hand and set them deliberately on the table. Then, still holding his wrist, she seized his tie and drew him toward herself.

As he moved over her, she swung her legs onto the couch, the two of them ending in a tangle of limbs.

"I need *you*. Not food." She spoke very close to his mouth.

A wiggle of insecurity made her worry that he might dislike her boldness. The two seconds he paused were an eternity of panic and self-doubt for her. But then a slow smile spread across his face and his eyes darkened.

“Then by all means, have your way with me, Dr. Blair.”

Taking her bottom lip between her teeth, Charlie snaked his tie loose and tossed it over her head. Then she set to work on the buttons of his shirt. Vaiden held himself steady as she caressed his chest with her hands.

She brushed a fingertip over his taut nipples and was pleased to hear him inhale sharply. She tried to pull his shirttails from his pants, but they were lying too awkwardly. “Take this off.”

“You, too.” He stood, dropped the shirt on a nearby chair, and turned toward the fireplace. While he switched on the gas logs with a remote, Charlie shrugged out of the shirt and lifted her chin.

When he turned to her, his jaw clenched and his muscles tensed. Her expression never wavered and she let the earth-shattering love she was too afraid to admit even to herself show in her eyes.

He shoved the coffee table out of the way with his foot and crossed to pull her into his arms.

Her cool breasts pressed into his hot chest and the sensation shot to her toes and back again. She shivered, but not with cold.

His mouth covered hers, quenching the thirst she had for his kiss. His lips, though forceful, held tenderness. Tears wet her lashes.

His mouth drifted across her jaw line to her neck and Charlie let her head fall back. The combination of his wet tongue and warm breath on her skin stoked the flames within her.

She clutched the sides of his head, guiding him. Vaiden lowered himself to his knees. After sending her a heated gaze, he captured one nipple in his mouth, circling the tip with his tongue.

Even as her eyes shut, she could feel the searing warmth from his eyes upon her. His kiss moved lower still and she sucked in her breath.

Vaiden eased her to the floor and stroked her body with his long fingers. He'd shed the rest of his clothes, but she had no idea when he'd done so. Her fevered response to his touch had reduced her to pliancy. Her limbs grew heavy. Perspiration coated their bodies and wet the hair at his temples.

She pulled him down, dragging her mouth to his in a languid kiss. Her desire had grown hectic and passionate, but her body was filled already with a burgeoning satisfaction. She loved him. He might not want to keep her, and perhaps she couldn't be kept. The future was uncertain. But right now Vaiden—thoughts of him—his scent—his touch—consumed her.

She reached for him, let her fingers glide up and down on the blazing-hot satin skin. His eyes rolled back a bit, then widened. She smiled, enjoying her newfound power.

His flesh jumped in her grasp and his hand touched hers. "Cease, woman," he groaned. He brought her hands up next to her head on the floor and held them immobile.

Her hips surged upward and he slid himself inside her. She sighed with pleasure.

Her eyes widened in delight as he moved in and out of her. Her pulse thrummed rapidly, every plunge pushing her closer to the precipice.

She heard her own gasps, her own mewling cries, mixed with his growing vocalizations. When she thought her ecstasy could grow no more powerful, he roared her name and she came with him, clawing his shoulders with her fingernails as she tightened her legs around him.

They lay inert for some time before either could speak. Once voices were found, no words were necessary. Vaiden cradled her in his arms and carried her upstairs to his bed.

✧

Vaiden reluctantly left Charlie sleeping back at his house and headed in to the precinct. He wanted to know what had motivated the suspects to attack Charlie. Was it the gold, or was it more than that? And he needed to know if Kedansky was really Orion.

He observed the interrogation of Alexa Reynolds through a glass partition. Jarod and another police official had interviewed Leonard Kedansky before Vaiden had arrived, but so far all Kedansky would say was one sentence: "It's all her fault."

Kedansky's lawyer was asking for a psychiatric evaluation. Yeah, that was a surprise.

Alexa had declined the presence of a lawyer on the pretense that she'd done nothing wrong, and therefore had nothing to hide. She appeared to be blaming everyone except herself for her misdeeds. Her crocodile tears weren't going to fool anyone, but Jarod handed her a small box of tissues anyway. Vaiden listened as Jarod pressed her for clarification.

Alexa dabbed at her eyes and looked at the tissue. "Getting a job at the real estate office was all Lenny's idea. I never dreamed he would make me falsify those records."

Jarod leaned closer, both fists on the table. "And the embezzling?"

Her composure slipped for a fraction of a second. Vaiden didn't miss it. He doubted Jarod did either.

"Em-embezzling?"

Jarod nodded and stepped away to raise an eyebrow at Vaiden through the glass. "Yeah. We had someone go over the records. You've been skimming, Alexa. You wanna tell us what you did with the money?"

The officer seated at the table across from Alexa pushed a stack of paperwork toward her. She glanced at it, then blinked rapidly. "He... He made me do it. Lenny can be awfully violent when he doesn't get his way."

"Let's switch gears a moment then. If Lenny is the violent one, then why did you assault Charlotte Blair and tie her up at your office?" Jarod crossed his arms and rested his chin on his fist.

A full five seconds later Alexa burst into a fresh round of sobs. "If I hadn't hidden her, Lenny would have killed her for sure."

Vaiden's spine stiffened. That was a new one. Assault to save someone from an assault.

"I wasn't aware Lenny was present." Vaiden admired Jarod's method of sounding sympathetic. He wouldn't have been able to separate himself from this case so well.

"No. He was on the way. And if he'd seen Charlie..." Her nails tapped on the table as if in thought.

"And George Wilson? Why'd you do away with him?"

"George?" Her lips pouted prettily. "I don't know what you're talking about."

"You're saying George wasn't at the office that night?"

Alexa shook her head in bewilderment.

"According to Dr. Blair, you poisoned George Wilson that

same night. She watched him struggle for breath while you looked on."

Her face shuttered and her mouth curved downward. "Charlie was probably hallucinating. A blow to the head can do that to you." Her voice had an edge to it, had lost its breathy tone. Her face shifted into a hatred-filled mask. "If George is missing, maybe Charlie killed him. I certainly didn't."

Had the glass not been between them, Vaiden might have gone after her. How dare she disparage Charlie's name?

Jarod lifted the fingers of one hand, a signal to Vaiden to cool his temper. He knew his partner well enough to know how he must be reacting in the next room. Vaiden cursed.

Alexa turned cold eyes on Jarod. "Has anyone reported George missing? Has he been found anywhere?" She huffed. "No. So, Detective, there's no body, no murder, and no crime." She smiled, her lips brittle.

It was true, no evidence of a body had been found in the burned out building. And it appeared Alexa had reached her limit. She now asked Jarod for a lawyer. Wise move.

Jarod waved an officer inside to escort Alexa to a cell. Before she was taken away, Jarod cleaned his throat and dropped a nugget of information for her to stew on. "George Wilson's wife has reported him missing, Miss Reynolds. But no, we don't have a body. Not yet."

✧

Charlie walked through the doors of the hotel at seven in the morning. Vaiden had left her in the wee hours. She'd sensed his absence, but had been too exhausted to ask where he'd gone. He would return, that was what mattered.

A bellman nodded in greeting and she smiled brightly. She'd come to a decision about her future. A decision to take whatever fate put before her. If she was meant to be with Vaiden—meant to be happy—it would happen. Her own confusion had become too heavy a thing to deal with when he hadn't asked her to stay. Hadn't indicated he wanted her to. It was hard to tell with men. Most of the ones she'd known just took situations for granted. As a woman, she needed to hear the words.

"Dr. Blair. Good morning." The tall man behind the main counter blinked down at her. A crumb lodged in his thick mustache caught Charlie's eye and she tried hard not to stare.

"I'd like to get my things from the safe today, if you don't mind. And I'll be paying my bill."

"Certainly." The mustached man walked into a back room.

Charlie dug her credit card from her pocket. Vaiden had saved her wallet, but the rest of her backpack purse had been kept in the crime lab. She hoped they'd return it soon. She'd had the pack for ages and hated shopping for purses more than anything.

The hotel employee placed a box on the counter in front of her and opened the lid with a flourish. His expression was all cheerfulness and courtesy. "Let's just verify your contents." His eyes lit on the items in the container and he sent her a stern, shocked gaze.

He snapped the metal lid closed and pressed his hand upon it, all pleasantries gone from his manner. He cleared his throat and squished his lips together in an attempt to hide a disapproving frown. "You have something in which to carry this?"

Charlie moved her head slowly from side to side. What was the problem? They were just rocks.

He sniffed deeply, lifting one side of his lip. His eyes searched beneath the counter and then he bent out of sight. He straightened right away, reached into the box with a tissue and hurriedly stuffed something into a paper bag. He handed the bag to her. "Your card, please."

Charlie set the credit card in his outstretched palm and held the bag to her chest. It felt heavy. She shoved it awkwardly under one arm while she signed the credit slip.

As soon as she stepped away from the counter, she unrolled the bag and peered inside. The small leather sack in which she'd stored the stones was there, but she'd be willing to bet her doctorate the stones weren't. For, looming bright as the sun and only half-covered by the small leather scrap of a bag, was the golden rod of Manco Copac. A life-size phallus made of solid gold.

Chapter Twenty

Jarod Ronan strode past the door to the precinct break room, caught Vaiden's eye, and skidded to a stop. He tugged at the front of his short blond hair and walked toward him with his head down.

Vaiden stirred his coffee, removed the plastic spoon, and tossed it into the trash can. Jarod had completed his coursework and finally thrown himself into the case full force. He was brilliant at ferreting out information. Vaiden motioned him to the table and they sat.

Vaiden sipped the lukewarm brew and settled back into the chair. He frowned, more at Jarod's down-turned mouth than at the sour milk he'd mistakenly added to his beverage. Should've smelled it first. "You got that look."

His partner sucked his breath in through his teeth. "We found George Wilson."

Vaiden knew Jarod. He would say more when he worked out his phrasing. That's just how Jarod operated. No wonder he'd never asked Ruthie on a date. She moved too quickly from table to table for Jarod to spit out the question.

He rubbed his tongue over his molars, trying to remove the too thick coffee taste.

"Wilson turned up in the James River. Preliminary autopsy shows probable poisoning. We're waiting on toxicology results.

But—"

"But based on what Charlie said about his manner of death, you suspect cyanide." Vaiden, distracted, sipped the coffee and quickly spit it back into the cup. *Damn it.*

He'd stood and crossed to the trashcan when Jarod cleared his throat uncomfortably.

"Harrison and his people had to go back into the Blair house."

The coffee splattered the inside of the trashcan. Vaiden used a napkin to clean his hands, turned, and narrowed his eyes. "Because of George Wilson?" He shook his head. He didn't see the connection.

"It wasn't my idea. But since Alexa Reynolds said—"

"Alexa Reynolds is a murdering—" Vaiden pressed his lips closed, inhaled through his nose, and waved a hand at Jarod. "Go on."

"While they were at Charlie's house, they found a tube of lipstick. The base contained potassium cyanide powder." Jarod stared at the knuckle of his fourth finger and scratched it.

Vaiden's breath became shallow. He didn't like the halting way Jarod was speaking. The coffee came crawling back up his throat.

"The lipstick is in the crime lab." Jarod wrapped his right hand around his left fist. "Until the reports come back, we won't know if the cyanide is the same as what killed George Wilson."

Vaiden had never known Jarod to be so reluctant to tell him new details. He clenched his jaw. *Speak. Spit it out.*

"Her prints were on the lipstick case."

"Alexa's." He met Jarod's eyes.

Jarod looked away, shaking his head. "No. Charlie's. Charlie's prints were on the case."

Vaiden shoved his chair back and rose. He had to get out of here. The room was sweltering. He dragged the knot of his tie down an inch.

Jarod followed him out of the room and grabbed his arm. "You've got to take yourself off the case. Officially. You should've done it days ago."

He glanced at the exit sign. "I don't have a choice, do I? Consider me on vacation."

Jarod called his name, but didn't pursue him. Vaiden was glad for that. He wouldn't be good company. His head ached with too many bits of information. And now Charlie had been implicated in the murder of the real estate agent? Preposterous. She had no motive. And he knew in his heart she wasn't capable of it.

How would she have managed to get the lipstick to her house? She'd spent every night with him or at the hotel since the investigation began.

But he hadn't been with her every minute.

He pushed the thought away. The lab would turn up something clearing Charlie. Of that he was certain. But still. He felt a need to find her. To hold her. And maybe...interrogate her a little.

✧

The gold phallus shone despite the dim light in Vaiden's living room. The deep brown wood of the coffee table upon which it lay contrasted with the rough, pocked, metallic surface of the artifact.

Charlie hugged her arms tighter and snapped her knees together. Her perch on the very edge of the sofa became uncomfortable and she scooted backward slightly to get more cushion under her bottom. She'd been staring at the rod for at least an hour.

Several times she'd decided to walk away, to get a drink, or do some other tedious errand, but she was riveted to the spot. How in the hell had that thing gotten in the hotel safe? And where were the Ica stones?

Her eyes no longer focused on the actual shape of the rod. Her vision blurred into the gold, which through her tired eyes almost seemed to breathe. She reached one shaking hand toward the rod.

The doorbell rang and she squeaked, jerking her hand back. She stood and took a step toward the door, then looked back at the gold object. She waved her hands in the air and hopped, not knowing where to hide it, but knowing for sure that no one should see it. The bell sounded a second time and she scooped the rod up, stuffed it into the paper sack, and pushed the whole ensemble beneath the sofa.

After exhaling slowly through her nose to calm herself, she swung the door open.

Griffin, the farmer, held a grease-stained baseball cap between his hands. His shoulders slumped in relief when he saw her.

"Charlie. Can I come in?"

She didn't recall telling Vaiden's address to Griffin, but perhaps *he* had. It wouldn't surprise her.

"Vaiden's not here right now." Once the words tumbled out, she drew her breath sharply—not the wisest thing to tell a man who, though he'd helped subdue Leonard and Alexa, was practically a stranger himself.

"I've come to speak to you, actually. Something that's been bothering me." He craned his neck toward the living room.

She knew she should ask him to come in, but something kept her from doing so. Best to be done with it. “What is it?” She braced one palm on the door, the other on the frame.

The action was not lost on Griffin. He donned his hat, and she thought he was about to leave. But then he spoke again. “You read much of... Are you a religious woman, Charlie?”

No one had ever asked her that question. Since she dug up communities of mostly pre-Christian people for a living, the topic didn’t come up often. She shivered and rubbed her bare forearms again. Behind Griffin, leaves swirled in a small wind.

His eyes burned into her and she returned her gaze to his face. “I believe in a god. I believe there’s a heaven.” She shrugged.

“Hmm.” He drew his lips back over his teeth and spat into the bush next to the house. “I wasn’t going to say anything about it. ’Cause it wasn’t my place. But I figure I’d better tell you. Winnie would want me to.”

“Winnie. Your wife?” She hadn’t seen any evidence of another person at the farm, other than a small plot of two graves she’d stumbled over while waiting for Vaiden. One had a woman’s name inscribed, and with one large marker, and one very small, the granite stones seemed to scream out ‘mother and child’.

Griffin nodded and turned his face to the ground a moment. When he met her eyes again, his own were wet. “That man who was chasing you. He’s evil. I knew it from the moment I saw those seven moles on his palm.”

Seven moles. Leonard had seven moles on the palm of his right hand. The nickname from her father’s journal: Seven-K. The student who’d tried to steal from the Peruvian museum.

“You know who he is, don’t you? What it means?”

She’d seen Griffin’s reaction while tying Leonard. “A sign of the anti-Christ. Yes, I've read some of the apocalypse theories." But how many people were there in the world with moles on their palms? *Seven* moles on their palms. Probably at least a dozen, maybe two.

She smiled at him. "Thank you. For being concerned, I mean. But I'm safe now. He's in jail."

He spit again and tucked the leftover dribble of tobacco juice into the corner of his lip. "His reach extends far. Be careful."

His big bear of a body shuffled quickly back into the overcast afternoon. He climbed into the tall four-by-four and gave her a terse wave.

Charlie closed the door and locked it. This couldn't get any more bizarre.

✧

He wasn't at the precinct, and Vaiden didn't answer his cell when Charlie called. She sat in the driver's seat of her Jeep, a cell phone in her right hand.

She shivered and turned the engine over so she could crank the heat. Her gaze drifted to the world outside the small compartment, and her eyes lit on a newspaper box. Nate. He'd know where to find Vaiden.

A few minutes later, she had Nate on the phone at work, thanks to a very helpful receptionist in the office of the ombudsman.

"Nate Vaiden."

"Nate. It's Charlie. Do you know how I might get in touch with your brother?"

Nate's deep chuckle tickled her ear. "Aren't you staying

with him?"

"It's important. I need to tell him something."

He sighed. "Well, could you please get a little more vague?"

She held her tongue.

"He goes to the park when he wants to think. Deep Run. He's probably there."

Charlie thanked him. "Say, Nate, I don't suppose you could make a few phone calls for me to check something out?"

"Am I getting a story out of it?"

"Maybe."

Paper rattled on the other end of the phone. "Go ahead."

"Peruvian consulate. Ten years ago, March. Attempted robbery of an artifact from the Cuzco Museum of Archaeology."

He scoffed. "You've got to be kidding."

"Would you just try?"

He sighed again, this time more dramatic than sincere. "Can I have a hint what I'm looking for?"

"I want to know if the student's name was Leonard Kedansky. And if it was, what was the artifact he tried to steal."

"You don't ask for much." Nate cleared his throat and lowered his voice. "Tell my brother I have word that Kedansky's mother is getting called in this afternoon."

"His mother?" She didn't recall Vaiden mentioning Kedansky having family.

"Oh. Maybe I shouldn't have said anything." He paused. "What the hell. She lives in Chester. Jarod tried to get some information out of her, but she didn't offer anything up. Maybe you and my brother will have better luck. Especially since Rob's been put off the case."

Off the case? "Does no one tell me anything?" She didn't try to hide the annoyance in her voice.

Nate hissed. "Ouch. Guess maybe you and my brother *do* need to talk."

She chuckled wryly, wondering what else she'd been left out of. "I don't know how much talking we'll be getting done, but there's bound to be some yelling."

✧

Vaiden slid over to the right side of the wooden bench to make room for Charlie. She'd descended the asphalt path that led into the park and stood, hands on hips scanning the area around the lake. As her head turned in his direction, he lifted his hand and waved her over.

She nodded and walked around an elderly couple exercising their Bichon Frisé, then made haste crossing the small humped bridge that connected to the shaded area near the observation deck on the lake.

She didn't greet him, just plopped down beside him and sat with her elbows on her knees, eyeing everything *but* him. That stung, but not as much as what he'd found when he'd gone home to look for her. He'd been shaken to the core. He thought she had been totally honest.

He cleared his throat. "I hear you've been in touch with Nate."

One beat of laughter issued forth from her. "The Brother Emergency Network is in place, hmm?"

After he'd gone to his house to ask her about the lipstick and discovered she'd gone, he'd come to the park to figure a few things out. He'd fallen hard for her. Hard enough that the prospect of her being less than truthful had slammed him in the gut.

Though Nate had indeed warned him with a message on his cell phone that Charlie was on the way, even the anticipation of seeing her made him happy and nervous at once.

He'd tried to make decisions about Charlie, but the hell of it was that his decisions depended on her. It didn't matter that he loved her. He would bet his house that she had nothing to do with George Wilson's murder. But this last stunt... He had to know why she'd done it. Why she'd lied.

She pulled one leg beneath her and sat sideways, facing him. Her lips parted, but she pressed them shut, saying nothing.

"Nate said you had something important to tell me." He swallowed. Would she tell him about the gold?

Her regard moved from him to the water, which was visible through spaces between the guardrails on the deck. Deep in thought, she scratched at a tooth with her fingernail. He wanted to laugh at the unconscious gesture.

"The farmer came to see me."

That wasn't bad as far as revelations went, but it wasn't what he wanted to hear from her. "Griffin. Yeah?"

"He drove all that way just to tell me Leonard has moles on his hand."

"Moles."

She tilted her head and peered at him. "Seven of them."

"Seven." Her father's journal entry. It made sense. "Seven-K. So he was the student your father wrote about?"

"So it would seem. I asked Nate to check it out."

He scowled, and then wiped the flash of anger from his mind. It wasn't strange that he should still feel a twinge of jealousy when she mentioned speaking independently to his brother. Nate had accidentally stolen girls from him before.

But that was neither here nor there. Why wasn't she telling him about the gold?

"Nate said Leonard has a mother out in Chester."

Her eyes poured curious green intensity toward him, her lashes black against her light skin. He took in her tousled hair, her oxford shirt, three buttons open, the way her jeans hugged her sweet thighs. Damn, she was pretty.

"Don't change the subject, Vaiden."

Blood rushed to his face. Had he said that out loud?

Her smile morphed into a grin. "I saw that look." She licked her lips and chuckled at his embarrassment. "Now I know how Little Red Riding Hood felt."

A young couple with a small child passed close by. The child, a boy of toddler age, sent Charlie a big slobbery smile. She widened her smile and waved at the boy, her eyes flicking to the parents only briefly.

The boy's father nodded to Vaiden. The parents each held one of their child's hands, helping him to balance. As they rounded the turn toward the other side of the lake, Vaiden pictured himself and Charlie with their own child someday. About the time he realized he was debating the possible gender of their nonexistent baby, he felt Charlie staring at him curiously.

"Sorry." He ran a hand through his dark hair. "Nate mentioned that you might want to see if Lorinda Kedansky might have some insight."

The instant eagerness on her face amused him. She grabbed his hand and then her smile faltered. She released him, but he took her hand back and squeezed gently. Why was she fighting this?

The small family was now feeding bread to the ducks. A few larger birds, geese by his guess, landed nearby and crowded the ducks away.

Vaiden sighed. “Come on. I’ll drive.”

And maybe on the thirty-minute drive to Chester, she’d explain why the gold artifact she claimed had been stolen was hidden haphazardly beneath his living room sofa.

Chapter Twenty-one

If Charlie held her tongue on the ride to Lorinda Kedansky's house, she had good reason. Earlier she'd visited the university, intending to get her mail and leave before she ran into anyone she knew. She'd become a bit of a campus celebrity—in the infamous category—and didn't want to explain to another human being that *yes*, she was okay, and *no*, she didn't know anything more about Professor Kedansky.

A fat envelope on university stationery had been crammed into her mailbox with various memos and science journals. It was the envelope she dreaded. Perhaps Dean Fisher's request to the board had been approved. Perhaps she'd been fired.

The receptionist had entered before she opened the envelope and surprised her with the news that she'd been granted temporary office space. More, anyway, than a closet. As crowded as the university was, Charlie didn't think twice about accepting the offer. The tiny office in the basement was just fine. And the first thing she'd decorated her purloined desk with had been the unopened envelope.

And then she'd stared at it, a mountain of paper in the center of her empty, cold desk. Hard to believe something so small had the potential to alter her life.

"We're here."

Charlie looked up at Vaiden's words.

"Hovel" came to mind as she examined the exterior of the Kedansky home. Dingy white paint peeled off in thick slices. One of the three second-floor windows was boarded up, one had duct tape across the glass in an 'x', and the shutter of the third hung diagonally by one nail.

Mounds of paper and clothes could be seen through the dirty panes. A sleek gray cat slept in the sunshine in the middle window.

Below, on a small porch in the center, a screen with torn webbing blocked most of her view of the bright purple door. Packages, stacked more than five high on either side, covered the rest of the wavy wood flooring. Voices blasted through the walls of the home.

She positioned herself behind Vaiden on the first step while he rang the doorbell. She wondered if it worked.

Charlie sniffed. Urine. She buried her nose in the back of Vaiden's coat.

He reached around and patted her arm, then drew her forward. "What happened to the woman who charged up to Leonard's door on her own? We're in this together, remember?"

He rang a second time. The voices stopped suddenly and they heard locks unhitching. The door swung back to reveal a plump woman about Charlie's height, with a huge gray poodle on her head. No, Charlie thought, not a poodle. That was actually her hair. She leaned toward the woman to get a better look.

The woman closed one eye and peered right back. "'Bout time you came." She backed away, her lavender silk gown shimmering as she held the door for them to enter. As they passed the packages, Charlie noted the international origination addresses.

Vaiden cautioned Charlie with a glance. "Ma'am, we're—"

"Ms. Kedansky, I work with Leonard." Charlie didn't want to give the woman too much information. She hoped Leonard had neglected to mention her name around his mother. Maybe she would tell them something useful. Then again, maybe she'd throw them out. All they *did* know was that the woman hadn't been willing to talk to the cops before, so why should she now?

The woman wrinkled her round face. "I know that. I'm not stupid." She switched on a light. Diamond earrings twinkled from her lobes. "Tea?"

Charlie gasped at the room revealed by the light and Vaiden accepted the offer of beverages, presumably to cover her outburst.

Ms. Kedansky bustled out of the room.

Charlie whirled on Vaiden. "Do you see this stuff?" The furniture had been through several decades of use, and stuffing hung out of the chair closest to her. But every available flat space housed a fine object of stone or metal. All the items were very rare, and very old. She flexed her fingers, itching to examine them more closely.

Ms. Kedansky backed into the room, carrying a tarnished silver tray. Charlie fought the urge to flip it over and look for a maker's mark.

"Now, Lenny said you'd be by to pick up some things for his buyer. Can I see the list?"

"Ma'am, we're not here for a pickup. We'd like to ask you a few questions." Vaiden took the tray from the woman and placed it on top of the pile of newspapers that littered the coffee table.

Ms. Kedansky turned her frown on Charlie. "You said you work with Lenny."

"I do. At the university."

"Ugh." Ms. Kedansky dropped into a blue easy chair covered with dark pet hair. Charlie glanced around for another cat, but saw only shadows.

"That boy." Ms. Kedansky chuckled and settled into the cushions, her slouching posture doing nothing for the designer dress. The center of her bra stuck out, dingy and white, at the bottom of the low-cut neckline. She fondled the diamonds at her loose-skinned neck and waited with vacant eyes for them to speak.

Charlie eased down onto an ottoman in front of the woman. Vaiden sidled over to her. She felt the heat from his nearby leg and was comforted by his closeness. "Did you know that he's been arrested?"

Ms. Kedansky's eyes shrank back, all trace of the false politeness gone from her countenance. She sneered. "That *stupid* boy. You know, there's no one left to help him. What's he done now?"

Vaiden grazed Charlie's shoulder with his fingers. "He kidnapped a young woman. He's going to prison for a very long time."

Ms. Kedansky hissed and uttered a curse word. She sat forward, her feet thumping to the floor, knees spread, one hand on each thigh. "This crap again." She pointed a stone-laden finger at Charlie. "That boy has done nothing but cause me grief since he was a child."

Charlie patted the woman's arm lightly. "I'm so sorry."

Ms. Kedansky cocked her head, her great carpet of hair sliding sideways. "Lenny had a future. He was going to bring good things to this family. And he had to go and drag that girl off."

She shook her head and Charlie caught a waft of musky perfume. She felt Vaiden tense beside her. This girl who had been taken by Leonard Kedansky—couldn't be her. Not the way Ms. Kedansky had said it.

"You know, my Elwin took the blame. We all thought the family would be better off with Lenny's college education than with Elwin's salary as a carpenter."

The fingertip pressure on Charlie's shoulder deepened. As much as it pained her to hold her tongue, she was determined to let the old lady talk.

"And that idiot, screw-up son of ours, he sends me rocks." She bolted from the chair and grabbed Charlie's arm, pulling her along behind her.

They passed through a door and into a narrow hallway that led to the stairs. Beneath the stairway, she unlocked an odd-shaped closet door. The interior reeked of cold dirt.

Inside rested dozens of so-called rocks. Leonard had apparently been sending his mother artifacts from archaeological digs. But by the addresses on the packages still outside, he hadn't been working alone in his endeavors.

Charlie's head began to ache as she thought of the hours of work it would take to determine where the myriad of objects had originated. It would have to be done. She couldn't bear the thought of potentially important archaeological information languishing in crates in storage someplace, forgotten and covered in modern dust.

Ms. Kedansky took in her shock and nodded. "Um-hmm. Took my Alexa to straighten him out. Now we've finally got things how we like them"—she indicated the flea-market dream-home decor—"and he screws it up."

Charlie tried to give the woman what she hoped was a sympathetic smile. "Does... Does Leonard...Lenny have any other rocks around? Or is this it?"

Lorinda Kedansky shook her hands in the air and opened

her mouth wide. "Oh, no! The rocks aren't the half of it. Come, look at this!"

Charlie had no choice but to follow her crinkling purple bottom across the house to the stairs. The wallpaper was probably original, because in the places where it was peeling, sheetrock showed beneath. It felt rough to the touch.

One foot on the bottom stair, she motioned over her shoulder, to Vaiden, indicating with her eyes that he should look around while she and Leonard's mother were upstairs. He was gritting his teeth. He didn't want her to go without him, but as Charlie expected, his curiosity won and he waved her on.

The hallway upstairs had a nice path down the center. A path lined with baskets of laundry, stacks of *National Geographics*, and old newspapers. A fire hazard if she ever saw one. Near one pile of newspapers sat brown piles of what looked suspiciously like cat excrement. Nice. Must have been there since—she checked the newspaper date—last year. Nice.

She caught up to Ms. Kedansky, who was at the room on the far end of the hall. The one that had the boarded-up windows. The bottom of the door scraped against the hardwood floor as Ms. Kedansky shoved it open. The noise made Charlie's shoulders hunch together.

The room was cloaked in shadows. A horizontal shaft of light halved the space from between the boards on the window to the opposite wall. The popcorn ceiling hung thick with cobwebs. And somehow the air inside was different too.

Positioned near the two-inch-wide opening at the window, a telescope stood braced, generous amounts of duct tape wrapping the joint where the legs met.

"Leonard—Lenny is into astronomy? I didn't know that." Charlie stepped closer to the telescope, noticing the threadbare blankets on the bed.

"Don't touch it. He doesn't have a lot, my stupid boy, but he loves that thing." She scratched the crown of her head. "Likes it just so." She patted the air next to it as though fluffing an invisible cushion. "Strange child. Even as a boy he loved that one thing in the sky." Her hip jutted out to one side. "Now what the hell was it called?"

"Orion?" Vaiden spoke from the doorway, causing Charlie to jump.

Strangely, Ms. Kedansky didn't flinch. Her teeth slid forward, then sucked back into place. "I think you need to leave now."

✧

The sun set as Charlie and Vaiden drove back across the river. Though they'd passed an unmarked police car while leaving the Kedansky house, Vaiden didn't think he had anything to worry about. Leonard's mother had never asked their names, even after she discovered they weren't who she'd been expecting.

He doubted she'd be as open with the men on their way to question her. She seemed like a lady who didn't take well to formalities. He had the feeling that if he'd presented his badge, she'd have thrown them out on the spot.

When they arrived home, Vaiden held the door for Charlie. She paused between him and the door and turned clouded eyes to him. She looked as if she might speak, but then the cloud passed and she smiled and entered ahead of him.

He laid his jacket over the back of a chair and started to follow her into the kitchen. A tone sounded, stopping him. A second beep a few seconds later jarred his brain and he realized his fax machine must have jammed.

"Be there in a minute," he called toward the kitchen.

He strode to his small office and bent down to the fax machine wedged on the floor between a shelf and the desk. He'd run out of tabletop space for the machine, and though he could get faxes on his computer, he supposed he was an old-fashioned guy. He wanted his faxes on paper so he could hold them in his hands.

The fax machine blinked, indicating it had stored a message. Vaiden flipped the handle that adjusted the paper and the fax hummed into working mode. Since the screen told him the fax was three pages, he left the room to find Charlie.

She wasn't in the kitchen. A glass half-filled with iced tea sat on the counter. He ran a finger around the rim. She must be upstairs.

He ascended the first three steps, but heard the fax beep three short times. It was finished. He bounded back down to retrieve the warm pages.

The fax had come from Jarod. No names appeared, and the number had been hidden, but he knew it was Jarod all the same. The lab had run a DNA test against the evidence in the original Orion cases. From the figures, Leonard's DNA matched with the case for every victim.

Even in the one Elwin Kent had been convicted for, the last victim, Kedansky's DNA was also present. Whatever had happened, Leonard had participated. Whether it happened like the mother said—that Leonard had been Orion all along, and his dear old dad merely sabotaged the crime scene to take the scent from his son—that, only a jury would be able to decide.

Vaiden had been about to read the last page of the fax when Charlie slipped her arms around his waist.

"News?" She pressed her cheek against his back. She felt

strangely cool.

"Work."

He turned to face her. She'd showered. Her wet hair framed her face, which was devoid of makeup, save for smudges of eyeliner beneath her thick lashes. Most women looked washed out without makeup. Not Charlie. If anything, she appeared more beautiful.

He shifted the collar of her robe to the side and dipped his mouth to her neck, tasting her smooth skin. Her head angled away, allowing him more access to her throat. He closed his eyes and breathed in her strawberry scent.

Paper crunched when he wrapped his arms around her. The fax. Damn. He'd forgotten it. He stepped back, folded the first two pages, and shoved them into a desk drawer. The third, he lifted to show Charlie. "I need to read this. Give me a minute?"

She nodded, staring hard at the back of the paper, almost like she wanted to read it through the other side. "Want me to order a pizza?"

His eyes took in the deep open vee of the robe. He couldn't detect any sign of clothing beneath. If he hadn't spotted her name on the last page of the fax, he'd have stripped her bare and made love to her on the spot. But he had to know what it said, and how she was involved. As it was, his hand trembled and he licked his suddenly dry lips. "No. We won't have time to eat."

Her lashes lowered and her lips turned up at one side. "I'll meet you upstairs." Just before she left the room, she peered up at him and one eyebrow quirked mischievously. "Don't be long."

Once she'd gone, he released the crushed fax from his grip and smoothed it on the oak desk. He scanned the information, then forced himself to read it again slowly.

The hand-written message, sloppy even for Jarod's usual chicken-scratch, contained assurances that Charlie was no longer a suspect in George Wilson's murder.

Though Charlie's print on the lipstick case and its location in her home still made it suspicious, Alexa Reynolds' DNA had been found on the bit of lipstick in the base of the tube. It wasn't enough to charge Alexa, but it was enough to clear Charlie.

Vaiden grinned as he moved into the hallway. He'd known all along she wasn't capable of such underhandedness. And yet...

His gaze glided over the back of the couch in the living room to his left. Incapable of deception. Except for that damn gold artifact. He'd spied the edge of the paper bag beneath the couch when he'd come looking for her earlier.

He'd thought it was just a scrap of paper and bent to yank it from under the couch. He knew the only way an entire bag could be beneath his couch was if someone had put it there deliberately. And the cleaning woman certainly wouldn't have done something like that. Of course, Charlie was a bit of a slob by his standards, but she usually had the decency to pick up her things.

When he first saw that gold rod, his mind went blank. Once he recovered from finding a generously sized solid-gold penis in his living room, the possibility that Charlie had been lying all along dawned on him like a rainy morning sun.

And despite his giving her several chances to tell him about it today—in the park, on the way to Ms. Kedansky's, on the way home—she hadn't said a word.

He wondered how long she'd had it in her possession. If she'd had it the whole time. If she'd planned to keep it for herself because of some personal issue she had with the dean.

But then, why bring it to *his* house? A cop?

He thought back to the packages at the Kedansky house. Could she be working *with* Leonard on an import scheme?

✧

Charlie fought to keep her lids open. What was taking Vaiden so long? She'd seen the heat in his eyes when his gaze dropped to the neckline of her robe. He wanted her.

Lord knew she wanted him. She needed him to take her mind someplace else. Someplace with no artifacts disappearing and reappearing; no crazy colleagues trying to kill her or being murdered; no decisions to make.

So where the hell was he?

She burrowed deeper into the sheets. The crisp chill of the cotton made her feel cozy and feminine...and sleepy.

His footsteps on the carpet in the hallway roused her. She wasn't sure how long she'd dozed. She smelled the warm air settling down from the vent in the ceiling. He must have turned up the heat.

He came inside the room slowly, not turning on the light. His feet made little sound on the floor. Charlie blinked the sleep out of her eyes. She needed to tell him about the gold. Needed to get it over with. He'd find out sooner or later. Better that he should hear it from her.

Maybe he could help her figure it out.

Lying on her side with one hand beneath her pillow, she observed his silhouette as he crossed the room to undress, keeping his back to her. As he passed, she stretched out one lazy arm and grazed his backside with her fingertips.

He laughed quietly in his throat, then turned and slid

beneath the sheets. The darkness of the room only allowed her to see his outline. She rested her head on his shoulder and shivered as his arm, palm to her lower back, pressed her closer.

Her hand trembled as she placed it on his scalding hot chest. Her tongue darted out and she wet her lips. She should tell him about finding the gold. But if he thought she was crazy—or worse, if he didn't believe her, he might rethink their relationship. Whatever she meant to him.

He might think she'd lied.

She released a ragged breath, near tears in her indecision. She loved Vaiden. Wanted to be with him. But it seemed everything from fate to her choice of career was against them having a happy ending.

Vaiden suddenly whirled toward her, catching her head on the crook of one arm, while the other landed on the opposite side of her body. He hesitated above her as though drinking in her features. But that was silly. It was dark. He couldn't see her any more clearly than she could see him.

She inhaled and parted her lips. This was it. Her chance to tell him. She needed to explain before he kissed her and she lost her senses again.

His breath caressed her throat, sending lazy swirls of heat through her body, and she knew. Her words would have to wait.

His mouth plunged downward, taking her into a fiery kiss. Her hands lingered on his biceps only because the power of his passion stunned her.

He ended the kiss with other, shorter kisses, finally embracing her as his hands drifted lower to stroke her body. His hands shook.

Control slipped from her, but she tried to tell him anyway. "Vaiden, I—There's something you need to know."

His mouth covered hers and he moved over her. "Not now. Later." He spoke against her lips and shivers rippled through her. He eased inside her and she sighed, all thought of the world outside falling away.

They made love, not slowly, not rashly, but in a plea of mutual desperation. Even as she cried out his name, Charlie wondered why Vaiden seemed to feel as lost as she.

✧

Not until the sun's rays broke through the darkness of Vaiden's home did Charlie awaken. They'd made love for hours during the night. They'd spoken, of that she was sure. But she couldn't recall any of the words she'd said. Or those he'd said, for that matter.

But she knew this was her last chance. She planned to bring the gold artifact to the authorities' attention today, and, well, Vaiden, even though he was technically on leave, would be told one way or another. She wanted it to be *her* way.

The heat kicked on and, as the first wave of warmth blew against her, Charlie's palms broke into a sweat. Her mouth filled with saliva. She felt weak, almost as if she was going to—perspiration broke out across her forehead.

She swallowed and caught her breath. As her stomach lurched, she flung the covers back and ran for the bathroom.

She braced one hand on the back of the toilet and tried to swipe her wild hair from her face. She swallowed again, and then took a deep breath, hoping she wasn't going to be sick.

Her belly tightened and she gripped the porcelain as the meager contents of her stomach surged upward. Blood rushed to her face and her eyes watered. A cough cleared her throat, replaced by more saliva rushing to her mouth.

As a second wave of nausea swept through her, a hand touched her back; another hand lifted strands of her hair from her cheek. Cool air evaporated the sheen of wetness from the base of her neck.

Charlie spit delicately and closed her eyes, mortified that Vaiden had seen her get sick yet again. "You shouldn't be in here."

He ignored her protests and her attempts to wave him off. "You okay?"

The feeling of blechiness gone for the moment, she nodded and straightened. Vaiden released her hair and wet a cloth with cold water. He pressed it to her face and with gentle motions, wiped her skin, cooling it and bringing her back into control of herself.

Her nakedness suddenly embarrassed her, and she crossed her arms in front of her chest. After rolling his eyes, Vaiden handed her a towel, which she wrapped herself in while he stood unashamed of his maleness.

Even with her shaking limbs and her embarrassment, she couldn't resist admiring his body. Lean and muscular, his form held coiled energy. In her mind, he looked capable of any physical feat. Such a handsome guy. She'd seen prettier men, of course, but Vaiden was... She shivered, suddenly warm again. Vaiden was *Vaiden*.

"Come lie down." His voice sounded quiet and husky.

Charlie stopped at the sink to quickly brush her teeth and rid herself of the awful taste in her mouth. The nausea had passed as quickly as it had overtaken her. She was used to the occasional stomach trouble from camp food or living off the land none-too-carefully, and she knew that once she'd gotten whatever didn't agree with her out of her system, she'd feel like new.

She tried to think back to what she'd eaten the previous day, wondering what had affected her system. There was the pizza they had eventually ordered, but Vaiden had eaten more than she had and he wasn't feeling ill effects. Perhaps the sandwich she'd grabbed at the convenience store on the way to the park had been sour. Certainly wouldn't be unheard of.

She entered Vaiden's bedroom and found him buttoning his jeans. She smiled. He hardly ever wore jeans.

He stuffed his muscular arms into a tee shirt, but before he could bring it over his head, she stopped him.

Now. Tell him now.

"Vaiden? Could you sit down for a minute?"

He looked at her, his eyes full of concern. He sat on the bed in slow motion. "You're not okay."

His worry brought a smile to her face in spite of the tight ball of fear in her belly.

"No, I'm okay. I am. I had a bad sandwich or something."

He raised an eyebrow and cast a half-frown toward her.

Charlie traded the towel for her robe and sat next to him, bringing one bent knee onto the mattress so she could face him. "As bizarre as the past few weeks have been, with the dean's death, and then the campus policeman...you've believed me about everything." She waited for him to deny it, or to show hesitation in his answer.

He drew back slightly, as if offended she'd think he could doubt her. "Yes."

She licked her lips. "If...if the stones are linked somehow to the events... If they held some sort of power, as crazy as it might be, you're willing to accept the possibility?"

He folded his arms, a wall coming down between them.

"Yes." But he didn't mean it. Did he? She couldn't read his emotions now that he'd taken on that guarded expression.

Though he'd answered her positively, she could tell she'd come close to the line he drew between fiction and plausibility. So she pulled her trump card.

"The stone with the scatter pattern. The one I showed you at the hotel. When I asked you, you said you'd never seen the pattern before."

His brows knitted and she hurried on before he gave up on her.

"*I* have. I've seen that exact pattern." She used her knuckles to lightly brush the scarred skin on his back. "It's exactly like your scars."

She leaned back to see his expression, which he'd angled down. He frowned, disappointment showing on his face. Not the reaction she'd wanted, or even the one she'd expected.

"Wait here." Vaiden exited the room without looking at her.

Charlie put a hand over her mouth to slow her quickening breath. Panic wasn't going to help. Just because he needed a minute to himself didn't mean he'd given up on believing her.

She did as he asked, clenching the sheets in her fists, and he returned shortly with a digital camera.

"Take a picture of the scars."

She gritted her teeth and took the camera from him. Once she photographed his back, she handed him the camera. She couldn't blame him for wanting proof. She would want to see for herself too. It might be easier this way.

Vaiden laced his fingers through one of her hands and pulled her after him and down the stairs. His touch, his warmth connected to her brought hope flooding through her. She wanted to cry with relief. He led her into his office and plugged the camera into the hard drive with a cable.

"I scanned your drawings," he explained as he pulled them up on the screen. "Let's try something."

He extracted the image from the camera and brought it up side by side with her sketch of the carved pattern on the stone.

Vaiden leaned in close, his jaw on his hand. He reached back with his free hand and took her fingers again. "This is insane."

Charlie laughed, nearly giddy. "That's what I thought, too. But then it got even more strange." She rushed to tell him before she lost her nerve. "When I went to collect the remaining stones, Vaiden, they were gone from the hotel safe."

He spun his desk chair around so that he faced her. "Stolen?"

"No." She blinked and breathed deeply. Calm. She had to stay calm so that she would sound truthful. Panic would suggest a lie. Her voice hitched anyway. "Replaced."

His eyes closed and his mouth flattened out. He breathed once through his nose, then open his eyes again. "Explain."

Charlie shook her head and lifted her shoulders. She overlapped her feet and dropped gently to the floor, landing in a cross-legged position. Her ears burned. "I wish I knew how to explain it. I put the stones in the box. The concierge closed the box and took it away to the safe." Her hands reenacted the scene in the air between them as she spoke.

She wedged her fingers into her hair and dragged the strands backward. With no hesitation, she told him about the desk clerk and how he'd reacted on seeing what was in the box. She chuckled. "You should have seen the guy's face. He must've thought I was a very rich pervert." Had she told him that the gold rod was a solid gold phallus? Surely she had. Even though she couldn't hear the words in her memory.

She peeked at him. No trace of amusement showed on his face. Maybe not. "Anyway, now I have the gold, but the stones are AWOL."

She rested her elbows on her knees and braced her chin with her hands. His eyes told her nothing. Her heart ached. His face was shuttered, closed, and she lowered her eyes to hide her own pain. He didn't believe her.

To her surprise, Vaiden inclined toward her, took her hands, and pulled her up onto his lap. "That's wonderful."

She blinked. "It is?"

His hands clasped near her hip and he kissed her. "Um-hmm. You trust me."

She wrinkled her nose. Silly man. "Of course I trust you, Vaiden. Why wouldn't I?"

He grinned, his eyes clear and full of love. Butterflies fluttered in her stomach as she watched his handsome face. This look was for her?

Why was he so darn happy? She was in big trouble unless she could find a way to explain the rod's presence in terms the rest of the scientific community would believe. Not to mention how irate the Peruvian officials would be that she hadn't cleared transport of a valuable artifact from their country. She'd be lucky to escape jail time. It would be a miracle if she wasn't banned from their country.

He laughed then, confusing her further.

She stared at his white smile and sucked her tongue over her own teeth. Her front tooth was just the tiniest bit crooked. She'd never noticed until now that Vaiden's teeth were perfectly straight. She wondered if he'd had braces.

Such a sexy mouth. Breaking her train of thought, he shoved upward out of the chair, bringing her with him and picking her up in his arms. She clung to his neck as he carried her back upstairs to the bedroom.

He placed her on the end of the bed, then grabbed up his forgotten tee shirt and slipped it over his head. Charlie lay back, folding her arms beneath her head. He'd gone from one extreme to the other, and his happiness sent warnings racing up her spine.

She swallowed as he finally walked back to her and kneeled on the floor at her feet, pressing against the bed. She sat up, wondering what he was up to. He braced his hands on either side of her and smiled, the warmth in his eyes sliding into her and over her like warm maple syrup.

He licked his lips and her eyes followed his tongue. She leaned over to kiss him, but he stopped her.

All this was because she'd trusted him? Surely he knew how she felt about him? Of course she trusted him. Or was that what this was about? Had they crossed some sort of milestone line in his eyes? She opened her mouth to speak.

"Wait." He held her hands in his, stroking the back of her uppermost hand with his fingers. "First, there's something I want to say."

Charlie's gut tightened and her heart beat in her ears. She wanted to cry. *No, Vaiden, don't make this harder. Don't tell me you love me.*

"I've been doing a lot of thinking. About us." He inhaled deeply and for just a moment, his eyes widened with what seemed like fear. He smiled again and the fear disappeared, replaced with confidence. "I think we should get married." He snapped his mouth shut and frowned.

His nostrils flared. The heat kicked on again and a dust mote floated past. It was an ordinary moment, but somehow Charlie's world shifted irrevocably.

She knew her face had gone blank. Panic surged through her. Part of her rejoiced that he wanted to be with her. The rest of her wanted to run as fast as she could. He'd never settle for a wife who was gone two thirds of the year. She wouldn't have settled for it either. No matter how much she wanted to.

Oh, God. She loved him.

She wanted this. Wanted him. But—weren't they supposed to date for years and years and figure all this out slowly?

Her gaze flicked to his face. His paling face.

He was waiting for her reaction, his every muscle tense. "I want you to marry me, Charlie." He smiled, a little uncertainty creeping across his face. "Will you be my wife?"

Everything she wanted. Everything she couldn't have. Her eyes stung and she raised her eyebrows to keep from tearing up. She should say something. He was waiting for her answer.

But he knew. Deep down he knew they wouldn't work out. That's why he hadn't said it, hadn't admitted he loved her. He must know that once that was said, things changed. She sighed, blinking slowly. She needed to give him time to change his mind then. Being his, *the idea* of being his, started an ache inside her and she could feel herself wanting to throw caution to the wind and say yes, even though there were so many reasons why she should say no.

"I need to think. I...I gotta get some air, Vaiden."

His lids lowered and he nodded before standing and backing away. The lost look on his face nearly broke her heart right then.

Charlie grabbed a pair of jeans and a shirt. "I'm going to the university. If you need me, that's where I'll be. Okay?"

With a look at Vaiden, who had his back to her now, she left the room. She had to get out of there. Had to clear her mind. She didn't want to lose him, but she knew he couldn't be kept. She'd end up breaking his heart.

Chapter Twenty-two

Vaiden sat, elbows on the kitchen table, his fingers on his forehead, his thumbs pressed into his jaw. He lifted his chin and settled his hands around his nose and mouth. He stared at the centerpiece, a clear vase with a handful of wildflowers stuffed inside. They needed water.

He reran the scene in the bedroom through his head for the tenth time. He still couldn't see where he'd gone wrong. No, he hadn't had a ring to give her. And his delivery might not have been perfect—he'd wanted to phrase the question much more romantically. He'd hurried through it in inexplicable fear. He'd been so sure she'd say *yes*.

Although, he reminded himself, she hadn't exactly said *no* either. But if she had to think about it, that couldn't be a good sign.

The phone on the wall flashed a small red light. He grinned. Only his family called his landline. He wondered which of his siblings had left a message. Maybe...

He darted out of the chair and lifted the phone. He could listen to the message later. Right now he had to call his little sister. Genie would know where he'd blown the proposal. Hadn't she been pretending to get married all her life?

There wasn't a family pet or a stuffed animal that hadn't been down the aisle in their foyer with Genie. In a way, he both admired and pitied the man who'd marry her—the unsuspecting groom would get no choice at all in the type of wedding. She had it all worked out.

She picked up on the second ring, and he quickly recounted the proposal scenario to her.

"That's it?" Her voice held irritation.

Vaiden rubbed his head. "Um. Yeah." What? He'd been on his knee; he'd asked nicely.

Genie's heavy sigh told him he'd done something stupid. He waited for her to collect her thoughts.

"You are so stupid."

Bingo.

"Robbie, did you tell her you love her?"

He thought back. Had he?

"Robbie? You do love her, right?"

"Of course I do." A slow smile creased his face. His chest swelled just thinking about her. "She knows that. She *has* to know that I do."

"Have you told her? Have you actually *said* the words?"

He tilted his head to the side. Had he? "No, but she knows—"

"Robbie, we women need to hear the three dreaded words for it to be real. No wonder she said no."

"She didn't say no." Vaiden glared at nobody. He didn't want to think about that. If Charlie ultimately decided not to marry him... He could already feel crushing sadness at the thought of that possibility.

Genie's yell jerked him back into the present. "Then *tell* her, you moron!"

His heart lifted, and his happiness brightened the whole

room. "You're right. That's gotta be it. I'm going to take care of that right now. Thanks, Genie."

He hung up the phone and ran upstairs to find his shoes. Charlie had said she needed to do some work in her office at the university. He could be there in twenty minutes, if he rushed. His heart beat strongly in his chest. Rushing would not be a problem. Not the way his heart was pounding.

✧

Her elbow rested, angled to the side, propped on her keyboard tray. Her fingers stroked her bottom lip, her nails against her teeth. She stared unwaveringly at the envelope on her desk blotter.

The steady beat of her left hand on the deep-hued wood became too much for her and she reached for the missive. Her fingers curled just before she touched it. She couldn't. Not yet.

She wondered what Vaiden was doing. She shouldn't have run out of the house like a lunatic. She should have explained herself. He might have understood.

She laughed, her voice dry and bitter. How could he? Even she didn't know what to do.

The decision should have been simple. If she could have listened to her heart, she'd have said yes right away. Every part of her said she should marry him. Heaven help her, she loved him. He was all she could want in a man. Kind, protective—she smiled—easy on the eyes. But the uncertain future loomed in her mind and prevented her from leaping.

She leaned back in her chair and admired the newly framed drawings of the stones. A gift from Vaiden. They'd been on the wall when she'd blown into the room today. A lone post-it note stuck to the glass of one frame read only: "For you. V."

Seeing the sketches reminded her of the absence of the stones themselves and her lack of a plausible explanation. She rubbed her neck and stared at the stack of parcels against the far wall. Artifacts, approved for transport by their Peruvian liaison, filled the crates and boxes. She only had a small window of time for examining them in depth before they would be returned to Cuzco.

The crates gave her an idea.

She dug out her tiny address book and found the number for Miguel Hernandez, the man who for the past few years had served as her guide and assistant in Peru. She dialed quickly and waited for the call to go through international channels.

It was still the rainy season, and Hernandez had told her he stayed close to home. She prayed he could help her.

The line crackled. "*Diga.*"

She let out her breath. "*Hola*, Miguel. *Tengo un gran problema. Necesito tu ayuda, si tú puedes.*"

"Charlie! I wondered when we would hear from you. What can I help you with, *mija*?" Miguel's clipped English made the corners of her lips turn up. He'd learned to speak English from a British missionary.

She conveyed the bullet points of her story, ending with a request. "Is there any way, Miguel, that you could have, say, accidentally shipped the rod here to the university after the dig?"

Knowing that her guide would understand what she was asking him to do, she cringed when he paused a little too long. If he agreed to the tiny lie, he'd be saving her a heck of a lot of trouble, but as a result putting himself in the line of fire. They'd worked together for several years. Would he trust her?

"Pero, *mija*, that's exactly what happened. *¿Sí?*"

She sagged in relief. "*Gracias, Miguel. Eres mi mejor amigo. El mejor, todavia.*"

Hernandez laughed into the phone. "But we know this, *sí?*" The static on the line muffled his next comment, but she caught the end of it. He wanted to know when she would be back.

"*No sé.* I don't know if I have a job right now." She eyed the envelope. "I will have the gold shipped back to Peru as soon as possible. *Muchas gracias.*"

"*Hasta luego, mija.*" The phone clicked.

She dialed the number for the official in the Peruvian government who oversaw every major piece of archaeological material found at the university's digs. They were naturally very strict about what could and could not leave the country.

Ten minutes of schmoozing later, she'd saved the university's reputation at the expense of her own. She wouldn't let Hernandez take the blame for the rod's exportation. She claimed she must have accidentally packed it in the shipping boxes herself, but left it off the non-transport inventory list by mistake. Miguel, she told him, had shipped the sealed crate, unaware of the important artifact inside.

The official sounded doubtful, but agreed that the item must be returned immediately.

He would probably be calling her supervisor with a recommendation that they find someone more reliable to oversee the dig next year. She smiled. A burden had lifted from her shoulders.

Might not matter, she thought, as she seized the fat envelope and tore it open before she could change her mind. If she'd been fired, she'd have no way to access the university digs anyway.

She switched on the desk lamp to add to the glow from the overhead light. The legalese of the cover letter struck her first. This was no dismissal.

The print stood out boldly from the white linen paper. She lined her nails up with the text and started reading the terms. A loud three beat knock made her jump and she glanced at the doorway without moving her head. She didn't want to lose her place for a casual hello.

The young man pushed away from the doorframe and swaggered in.

Charlie exhaled in irritation when Erik Walker's lanky body came into view. A venomous dismissal rested on the tip of her tongue, like acid. What the hell was that jerk doing here?

He stopped mid-stride, perhaps seeing the death glare on her face. "Whoa. Look, I just came to apologize." He grinned, a smile full of charm and country. One she was sure worked on thousands of freshman each year as he seduced them out of their hard-kept virginity during parties. His type was a dime a dozen. Too rich, too protected, and too full of his damn self.

If she responded, she'd curse. She held her tongue and let one of her eyebrows raise in question.

"I was wrong to treat you the way I did in Peru. I should have respected your authority. And I definitely shouldn't have—"

"What do you want?" She cut him off, tired of the words that pebbled from his lips like memorized staccato tones. No effort was made to hide the disgust in her voice. "You must want something from me."

His good-old-boy grin slid from his face in an instant. He never said the word for what he wanted to call her, but she read it plainly in his face just the same. "Miz Blair—"

"Dr. Blair."

The muscle in his jaw ticked. Charlie had no idea why she let him get to her. Why she baited him. When it came down to it, she was putting herself in a bad position. She was alone with him in a basement, for Pete's sake. She might be able to defend herself. His nose had been badly broken from the one punch she threw back in Peru. He must have had it worked on since then. He barely had any darkness left beneath his eyes.

She'd been lucky. But sometimes luck failed, she reminded herself. She flexed her fingers while she waited.

Erik made a show of clearing his throat. "*Doctor* Blair. I need you to sign this." He placed a single sheet of paper on her desk, covering the one she was currently reading.

She didn't look at it. "Why don't you just tell me what it says and save me the time?"

His lips worked over his front teeth. He was trying so hard not to say what he wanted. Why? Charlie leaned back in her chair now and waited.

"It says… It's a document for you to sign."

"And?"

"And what? Sign it." He crossed his arms.

Charlie chuckled. She couldn't help herself. "What does it say?"

Erik's composure broke for a few seconds and he half-roared before catching himself. "It just says that you don't hold anything that happened in Peru against me, and that you recommend against my expulsion."

Charlie coughed to cover her laugh. "Tell you what, Mr. Walker. Why don't I think about it? Hmm?"

His eyes watched her hands intently as she folded the document and put it in the top drawer of her desk. "Go on, now. I have work to do."

His eye twitched, but he turned and walked away.

Just as he reached the door, she called out to him. "Oh, and Mr. Walker?" He paused without facing her. "Nice work on the nose."

He pounded the doorframe with one fist and stomped out of her sight.

She released a long breath and glanced back at the papers she'd been about to read before she was interrupted. After smoothing out what appeared to be a brand new contract, she inhaled deeply and began to read once more.

✧

Thank heaven for secretaries, Vaiden thought as he raced down the steps. He'd assumed Charlie would be in the department office. For just a second, he'd been afraid something *else* had happened to her. That woman—she attracted trouble like a magnet. She had neglected to tell him she'd been given her own space.

He hoped the gift he'd sent to her in the department office had made it to the right place. He hoped she liked it. She'd rarely told him with words that something pleased her. She told him with her eyes. So much openness and secrecy combined.

That was his Charlie. Oblivious to the fact that she'd been attacked in the very same building in the recent past, she continued with what she wanted to do. No one would discourage her from what she wanted from life. He hoped she counted him on that list.

When he had entered Charlie's empty office, his stomach had dropped, but the busy brunette typing away at the computer in the main reception area seemed to know exactly who he was looking for.

Without looking up, she'd pointed with one hand while the other still pecked at the keyboard. "Charlie's down in the basement. Can't miss her. She's the only one down there," she'd told him.

With relief, and yes, with trepidation, he took the stairs.

The basement of the building was brighter than the upper floors, but it was lit with the awful fluorescent bulbs that he detested. His family said he was nuts, but he was certain those fluorescent bulbs were responsible for the headaches he got back at the academy. Unlike that new training building, this building was built in the late eighteenth century, and the scent of mildew assailed him.

He peered into the first open door and saw her, bent over her desk, reading a thick, stapled set of papers. His heart leaped in his chest. Just the thought of Charlie—as his wife, having his children—made him swell with pride.

She'd tucked her hair behind her ears and had one hand shoved into the mass. He wondered if their children would have her light hair, or his darker shade. Black would look nice with her striking green eyes, he thought. Not his boring brown ones.

He stood riveted to the spot and smiled at the intense expression on her face. Such concentration. Intelligent, and so damned pretty. His pulse sped. He wanted to put his hands in her hair, kiss her until she locked the door, led him to the desk, and—

Charlie sighed, reached for a pen, and then spotted him. She beamed at him and tucked the pen back into a small cup. "You came."

Embarrassed at how far his mind had wandered while he stared at her, Vaiden angled his head. "I had to. There was something I forgot." He swallowed. He'd only told one other woman that he loved her. And she'd never spoken to him again. And now this one had left him hanging after his marriage proposal. Here he was ready to hand her his heart on a platter. He must be crazy.

Charlie walked around her desk, still holding the papers she'd been studying so intently just behind her. She shifted nervously and licked her lips. Her gaze darted around the room. Everywhere but to him.

He stepped inside, closing the door behind himself, and pointed to the papers. "What's that?"

She glanced at her hand as if she'd forgotten what she held. She shrugged. "They didn't fire me." Her smile faded as she stared at the top paper. She didn't look surprised at the content of the papers, just puzzled.

Vaiden held out his hand. Whatever it said, it was causing Charlie considerable distress and he needed to know what they were dealing with. "May I?"

She pressed the papers to her chest, then exhaled and handed the stack to him. Her eyes stayed on his face as he sat in one of the two chairs that faced her desk. His knee brushed against her legs. Focus. He had to focus.

He read the documents quickly, his breathing growing shallow. This was no disturbing memo or paperwork for class, it was a contract. For another two semesters in Peru.

She was planning to leave him! She'd had a pen in her hand when he came into the room. Had she even considered his proposal? Didn't she love him?

A vein in his forehead throbbed. He gaped up at her, knowing his pain showed in his eyes. "You can't go."

She laughed. Actually laughed. But her face held no humor. For once he couldn't read her emotions. Maybe she didn't love him after all. Could he have been that wrong?

"Give me one good reason, Vaiden." She balanced at the edge of her desk, one hand braced on either side of her.

In one motion, he stood and crushed her mouth with his own. If she wanted a reason, he'd damn well give her one. She belonged to him. He loved her, and even if she couldn't admit it, she loved him. And here, he thought, as desire swept through him, was the proof.

Her arms came around him and she kissed him back, her tongue mating with his. The only sound was their breathing, heavy and desperate, as they struggled to shed clothing and yet not separate.

Her back still to the desk, she shoved his shirt up, then yanked off her own while he heaved his over his head. They devoured each other with their mouths, her tiny gasps enflaming him, the touch of her hands on his skin searing him to his soul.

Two pairs of hands tore at belts and buttons. She tugged her jeans and panties down and then off by using her feet. His own pants only made it as far as his thighs.

Blood pounding, Vaiden lifted her onto the desk and plunged deep inside her, driving hard to mark her as his possession. Her fingers raked his back and she rocked against him, climaxing over and over as she called his name, muffling the sound against his shoulder.

He came into her, wanted to shout to the heavens, but gritted his teeth and reveled instead in the pleasure of her tight body spasming around his.

Gasping for breath and covered in a thin sheen of perspiration, she smiled at him, her eyelids low in sated passion. "That's a damn fine reason."

✧

It was dark when Charlie and Vaiden left the university campus. She didn't mention the contract to him, or say what she planned to do, but she'd brought it with her, shoved into her bag at the last moment. Nor did she respond to his proposal.

They went to bed, made love again, this time much more leisurely. Vaiden wanted to memorize every part of her. Still, they didn't speak about Peru. If he asked and she said she was leaving—if it was certain—he wasn't sure he could take it. It was making him crazy not knowing.

The next morning, after breakfast, she curled up on one side of the couch and sighed loudly. Vaiden put down the cloth he'd been using to wipe the kitchen table and walked into the living room. Enough was enough.

"You planning on signing the contract?" It didn't matter. Not really. He wanted her any way he could have her. But he had to know.

She flexed her toes and swallowed. "I don't know." She tucked her feet beneath her and turned so she could see him. "Everything's changed." She was looking at him like she'd never seen him before. Studying him.

This was it. He had to tell her now. If she threw it in his face, well, he'd just have to deal with it. He stepped to the front of the couch and sat close to her. "Charlie, if you really want to go back to Peru, I won't stop you." He held his breath.

She smiled, but one eyebrow cocked up, and he wished he'd phrased it differently.

"What I mean is, I'll go with you. If you'll have me."

"Vaiden, your job." She raised her shoulders in dismissal.

His forehead throbbed and he rubbed his eyebrows roughly. *Say it before you let common sense take over again.* "I'm willing to leave. To quit. Whatever it takes. We'll make it work." He took her hands. Her fingers were cold, so he slipped them inside his shirt and placed them on his warm stomach.

Her eyes softened. "You'd have to fly."

Easy. "I can take it."

"You'd have to live outside. With tons of bugs and dirt. And no cleaning woman."

She was trying to dissuade him. Couldn't be done. "I can do that."

A line appeared between her brows. "I only go to uninhabitable places because that's the way it has to be. I need to find answers, and that's the way to get them. I don't *enjoy* living in a tent for months at a time. Why would you put yourself through that?"

He smiled. "Because I love you, Charlie. And I don't know what I would do without you." He moved her hands to the side of his face and rubbed them against his stubble. "I want to have a family with you. Grow old with you..."

His voice trailed off. At the mention of the word family, she'd gone pale. Her eyes were no longer on him. No longer bright with happiness. Didn't she want a family? He couldn't remember discussing it with her.

Her lashes flew wide and she snatched her hands back. "I—I need to go out." She dashed toward the stairs.

Vaiden ran after her and stopped her on the landing. His jaw clenched. He had a thousand questions clamoring to be asked. He shut his eyes against them. She was not going to run from him again. Not when he'd bared his soul.

"Charlie..."

Her cinnamon toast breath drifted below his nose and suddenly her warm lips brushed over his mouth. "Relax, Vaiden. I love you right back. I just need to do something."

The corners of her mouth turned up. "And no matter what happens. Whatever the outcome. The answer is yes."

She hopped up the last few steps, leaving him standing frozen. Too stunned and happy, he barely had time to acknowledge the sweet curve of her rear as she swayed out of his vision. Had she just said she loved him? That she'd marry him? His grin widened. He stood a little taller and swaggered down to the kitchen. He was engaged.

He halted mid-step and smacked his hand into his forehead. A ring. What was he, the biggest idiot in the world? Why hadn't Genie reminded him?

He picked up the phone to call his mother and give her the news, but Charlie bounded down the steps and he replaced the phone on its cradle. This was a call best done in private. Who knew what his mother's reaction would be? As he circled around, she launched herself at him, making him stumble back a pace before he righted himself. She was smiling, and that made his insides warm. Wherever she had to go, whatever she had to do, she was his. His. And she loved him. No one could take that away now.

He squeezed her close and inhaled the scent of her hair. Faded strawberries. He took in her jeans, the same ones from yesterday, the grey university sweatshirt, and her not-quite-centered ponytail. "Where are you going in such a hurry?"

She skipped back toward the door. Her face was practically glowing. "A girl's gotta have some secrets."

He burst out laughing as she donned her coat and escaped out the front door. Charlie Blair was full of secrets. And he planned on exploring every one of them.

Chapter Twenty-three

The merchandisers for the pharmacy section of the convenience store must have had quite a laugh when they made the decision to stock condoms right next to pregnancy tests. Charlie wished the store was larger, or the shelves were higher, so she wasn't so obviously standing next to either item.

The lights overhead blinked off once, then kept up a steady flicker. Almost like lightning. Charlie squeezed the bridge of her nose and calmed herself. The jerking light made the letters on the boxes in front of her blurry.

A crash somewhere outside startled her. Her breath hitched and she looked over her shoulder through the large window. A tall truck passed too close to the sidewalk and bounced as a tire smacked up and over the edge, then back down. She shivered, something about the truck was familiar.

Charlie backed up to follow the path of the truck, to perhaps see it better, but the shelf behind her stopped her trek. Hissing from the shelf hooks that poked her, she rolled her eyes at her own idiocy and turned back to the task at hand.

She exhaled slowly and glanced up at the convex mirror in the corner of the ceiling. The cashier's spoon face pointed toward her. *Quit staring!* Charlie's face warmed in embarrassment. But why should she be embarrassed? She was an adult. Adults had sex. Adults faced the consequences.

The bell on the door jangled, signaling someone's entrance, and the cashier turned away. *Finally.*

Charlie sighed and scanned the packages. *As early as three days.* She took the blue and white rectangular box and read the small print on the back. It would do. She just wanted to get out of the store and back to Vaiden.

Her shoulder bumped another customer as she spun to stroll casually to the counter. "Ex...cuse me." Her words ended on a whisper and her pulse kicked into panic speed. She knew this man.

Griffin removed his hat and squished the grimy brim in his hands. "Sorry." He gestured with the hat to what she held. "Congratulations."

She blinked at him, then at the pregnancy test, as though she'd never seen it before. Her fingers tightened on the box. She didn't understand why Griffin had weirded her out. He stood looking perfectly harmless, his wild black hair springing up in every direction.

She was not afraid, exactly, just startled. Okay, and spooked. Definitely spooked.

"You're a long way from home." She forced a smile to her lips, and found it came more easily than she'd thought it would. She relaxed and her heart rate slowed back to normal. There was no reason to panic. There was nothing wrong with buying a pregnancy test.

He pointed through the plate glass window at his four-wheel drive parked at the gas pumps. "Had to do a favor for some family." He edged toward the restroom in the back of the store. "She don't drive much."

He tried the handle, and as he opened the door to the bathroom, he gave her a nod. "Nice seeing you."

Charlie saw in her mind the pair of graves behind Griffin's

house and shivered. Nervously, she chewed her thumbnail, scratched at the rough edge with her fingers, and then shrugged.

She needed to make her purchase and get out before anyone else she knew came along. No one should have the right to know if she was indeed pregnant before she herself knew it.

She trudged to the counter and counted out bills. She dropped the seven cents in change into the need-a-penny cup and picked up the brown paper bag. She'd parked her Jeep on the other side of the pumps, and had to cross in front of Griffin's truck to get there.

Out of curiosity, she glanced at the passenger, intending to wave. Instead her jaw dropped and she had to snap it shut. Lorinda Kedansky, Leonard's mother, sat with her head tipped on the seatback, eyes closed.

The breath whooshed out of Charlie as though she'd been socked in the gut. For a few seconds, she stood frozen in the parking lot. The beep of an impatient driver jerked her back into reality. She doubled her walking speed.

It made no sense. How could that woman be family to Griffin, without him knowing Leonard and Alexa when they were at the farm? Her head started to pound.

She hopped into her Jeep and cranked the engine. She drove only a short distance, and turned in at a fast food restaurant. Too embarrassed to use the test in the same store where she'd bought it, she planned to wait out the three minutes in a nice roomy stall.

Slyly tilting her head to check for feet, Charlie traversed the tile and hid herself inside the last stall. She tore open the package and read the directions.

Five minutes later she leaned against the stall door, staring at a pair of red lines. Holy crap. She *was* pregnant. When

Vaiden had mentioned having a family with her, she'd been struck by the reality of their carelessness. They'd used protection. Well, all but that first time and—her face went hot—in her office.

She'd never been on birth control pills in her life. Never had to, since she'd never before been in an ongoing intimate relationship. She'd slept with a total of two people in her whole experience. She and Harold had never made it past first base, and *they'd* been engaged.

She should have been more aware. There was no denying she'd been irresponsible.

The signs had been there from the start. Getting sick. Feeling tired. The absence of certain monthly occurrences. But she'd thought it was all a result of stress from her current situation.

A baby. She smiled. She supposed she should have been angry or upset with herself. Anything but the sheer joy that filled her.

Vaiden already wanted to marry her. Wanted children. And everything was coming together. Now if she could just finagle her job... She'd come up with an idea that might work, but she needed to make a request to the Board of Visitors. In writing.

A pair of gray-haired ladies entered the bathroom and Charlie shoved the test result into the wastepaper basket and then washed her hands. She hurried out to her Jeep and drove off toward Vaiden. And home.

✧

She might like Charlie, but Vaiden knew his mother was going to have a royal fit when she heard his news. To give himself time to work up just the right way to tell his mother he was getting married to a woman he'd barely known for two months, Vaiden pushed the play button on his answering machine.

No number appeared on the digital caller ID screen. Loud clicks and static took up the first few seconds, and he almost hit "erase", but then his father's voice crackled over the speaker.

"Rob?" His father paused and Vaiden smiled. Like he'd screen his father's call out.

Vaiden strained to hear over the static.

"This isn't a secure line, so I'll be brief. Your mother says you've brought someone to the house. Is it serious?"

Vaiden heard Charlie's Jeep out front and willed his father to speak faster.

"Your mother thinks it's serious. Enough so that she contacted me to be sure I was coming home soon. I think that's saying something, son."

Vaiden shut his eyes. No telling what his father's reaction would be to Charlie.

The front door opened and Charlie hung up her jacket. He lowered the volume on the phone.

"I'll be seeing you soon, son. Both of you." The background noise cleared and the message stopped.

Hoping Charlie hadn't been able to hear any of the details, Vaiden faced her. Her eyes smiled, but her mouth seemed uncertain. He crossed his arms. Now what? Had she heard? Was she bothered by it?

He punched the erase button and, while waiting for the beep confirming the deletion, picked up a fax from the tray near the phone. The document bore news about Charlie's father, and the finality of it hit him in the gut. He tried to cover his reaction by pretending the fax didn't exist. He folded it and jammed it into his jeans pocket. He gave Charlie a charming smile. Or at least he hoped it was charming. Anything to avoid the inevitable. "Where'd you have to go in such a hurry?"

She cast her eyes down and rubbed her fingers. Again he noticed the lack of a ring and he closed his hands into fists. He had to rectify that, and soon.

"Something you said made me think—made me realize—I had to run to the store." She stacked her teeth together and hissed in air. Her eyes darted side to side, and then she pursed her lips. "We're going to have to talk some things out." The corners of her eyes turned down and her eyebrows rose.

Vaiden narrowed his eyes and smiled. "Still planning to marry me?" His heart stopped beating while he waited.

All traces of tension drained from her expression and she stepped into his arms. "Yes. Of course. Just try and stop me." He could feel her cheek round out against his palm as she smiled. His heart began to beat again.

Her head rested against his chest and her arms circled his midsection. "When you said you wanted to have a family with me, what sort of timeline were you considering?" Her voice was muffled by his shirt.

A laugh escaped him. "Timeline?" He'd have kids this very minute if it were possible. But he knew Charlie had her own plans. Her own future mapped out. And once he told her what was on that fax he'd tried so hard to ignore, she'd want to go to Africa. "Sit down, Charlie. I have to tell you something."

She sat like a wooden doll and her skin paled. She almost seemed to expect something awful.

He placed his chair closer to her and took her thin hands into his own. "Do you remember the photograph you saw in the magazine at my parents' house? The woman who you thought resembled your mother?"

Hesitantly, she nodded, confusion shadowing her eyes.

"My father happened to be in that region of Africa, and he checked into it. Charlie, he's pretty certain that it's her."

Her mouth opened and for a minute Vaiden wondered if she'd stopped breathing. Soon he heard her short breaths, but she didn't speak for some time. He waited patiently, memorizing the shape of her lips and the tiny gold flecks in her green eyes.

When she finally formed words, her voice broke. "Why... Why didn't she come home? Why was she dressed as a nun? Why—"

He squeezed her hands. "There's more to the story." The space behind his eyes stung. He hated telling her about her father. She was going to be terribly upset. Sure, she'd thought he was dead for years, but to have it confirmed... He took a deep breath.

"Just as you believed, your father *is* dead." Her puzzled look spurred him on. "My father found his grave in Ghana, near your mother's location. He mentioned her having lost her memory, maybe because of trauma." When he didn't know how to solve a problem, he rambled and he knew it, so he closed his mouth.

Tears glistened in her eyes and his heart twisted. Why'd he have to tell her? He could have left it alone. Why cause her more pain? He decided he would do his best to take her to see them. Whatever she wanted. God, he loved her; he hated the bleak gaze in her eyes.

"My father is really dead. I wondered if someday he'd knock on the door, or show up at a dig..." She blinked and a tear rolled down her cheek. "Now he'll never know his grandchild."

Vaiden focused on the teardrop. She dashed it away, but it

shone on the back of her hand. He drew her from her chair onto his lap and pressed her head to his neck. "I'm sorry."

She was right. His family would get to see their children, but in all likelihood, hers would not. Even if they traveled to Ghana to see Charlie's mother, there was no guarantee she would regain her memory. And if she did...

Something Charlie had said made him pause. She'd said 'grandchild,' as if there already was one in the picture. A tentative elation clouded up from his center. Could she be...? No, she'd have told him. But could she? They had made love without protection thanks to his irresponsibility and lack of control... He felt a goofy smile broaden on his face.

He nudged her with his shoulder until she lifted her head. "Is there something you want to tell me?"

The blush that spread across her glowing cheeks confirmed his assumption. They were going to have a child. Vaiden grinned down at her.

She chewed her bottom lip. "Let's just say, whatever your timetable was, it's just been moved up."

Chapter Twenty-four

Without the invaluable aid of Vaiden's resourceful female relatives, they would never have pulled it off. Charlie, pausing in the doorway to the ballroom, stared at the interior of Vaiden's parents' house. Amazing how bright the dark woods and walls became with the addition of thousands of fresh flowers.

Their Christmas Eve wedding, organized within a mere two weeks, was coming off perfectly. She'd allowed the infamous Aunt Deb to fix her hair, and to the cousins' shock, it turned out quite sophisticated and feminine. Charlie was amazed at the amount of curl the woman managed to coax out of her barely wavy locks.

And Vaiden. Charlie's pulse ticked faster. He stood at the far end of the room, his eyes focused only on her. The mounds of his waving, crooning relatives melted away from her vision. There was only her Vaiden, and he waited for her, and her alone. She'd never seen a more handsome man. Ever.

Halfway through the walk to the improvised altar, her heart twinged and she hesitated. What, after all, had she done to deserve a man like him? Could she make him happy? Would he always love her? The tea roses and greenery in her small bouquet trembled in her grip.

Her emotions must have shown on her face, because Vaiden smiled and held out his hand. Just that simply, all

Charlie's concerns faded. Of course she deserved him. She loved him and she would do her best to show him that for the rest of their lives.

The ceremony seemed to take seconds, and the ballroom was cleared of chairs even more quickly. Charlie, as she slow-danced with Vaiden, couldn't recall anything from the moment she'd taken his hand to the present. She sighed and let her head rest against his shoulder.

"Excuse me, Dr. Blair? I mean, well, I guess it's Dr. Vaiden now, isn't it?"

Charlie straightened. Dr. Vaiden. Wow. That sounded so strange to her ears.

The secretary for the anthropology department grinned at her. "It came. I stopped by campus on my way." She passed Charlie an envelope. "Great party. Congratulations!" She waved and slipped back into the crowd.

Vaiden's eyebrow lifted. "Working at our wedding?"

Charlie squeezed his hands, then released them. "No. Solving problems." She held her breath and tore open the envelope.

Vaiden crossed his arms and waited, a smile twitching at the corner of his mouth.

After a quick glance toward him first, Charlie scanned the text. "Yes." She bounced lightly on her toes, the heels of her shoes clicking on the floor. "They agreed!" She wanted to burst, but thought better of it and squealed instead.

Vaiden's face was a study in patience. He sighed. "Out with it. Where do we have to go? Worse than Peru? More remote? Lay it on me."

Charlie swatted him with the papers. "The university has agreed to let me work here, in Virginia. I'll teach a few classes, and sort out the archaeological damage done by Leonard." She ran a finger down Vaiden's lapel. "And here's the best part. The head of the department has moved up to fill the dean's post." She sobered a moment, and hoped Dean Fisher was at peace.

Vaiden waved a hand in front of her face. "Hello? Where'd you go?"

She blinked. "Oh. Sorry. They want me to take the job of department chair." The idea began to sink in and her eyes brightened.

Vaiden leaned down and kissed her. "This is good, right?"

She wrapped her lace-covered arms around him, the letter still clutched in her hand. "Um-hmm. Very good."

His lashes drifted down. "Have I told you today how beautiful you are?"

A giggle trilled out of her mouth. "Yes, but please continue."

He spun her around and hugged her against his chest, facing outward. One hand drifted across her still flat belly. The warmth from his palm seeped into her skin. "This is it, you know, we're two of the lucky few."

Her chin tipped up and she looked back at him. "Oh? Why's that?"

His deep-voiced chuckle low in his throat vibrated through her. "We get our happy ending."

Her lips parted as she readied to reply, but Vaiden's twin cousins rushed over and threw their arms around her. They wiped at their red-rimmed eyes. Michele had a tissue tucked in the cuff of her sleeve.

Michele went for Vaiden next and Nicole grasped Charlie's arm. "I knew it! I knew you two were in love."

"Yeah, Rob," Michele interrupted, "and Genie said you guys are going to Africa for your honeymoon. What kind of honeymoon is that? Sandstorms and swarms of locusts? Do you *know* what that heat could do to a girl's hair?"

Charlie brushed her face against Vaiden's shoulder to hide the tears that stung her eyes when she thought of her parents—her mother—alone in Africa. She nudged Vaiden to get him to respond to his cousins. She didn't think she could quite find her voice yet.

"We're going on sort of a..." His fingers brushed Charlie's cheek. "A quest. There's something that Charlie—something that *we* need to do."

Michele raised her eyebrows and gave him a dubious look. "And you gotta go to Africa to find it?" She shook her head at Charlie. "You gotta be more careful with your things, girl!"

Charlie sidled closer against Vaiden and he threaded his fingers through hers. She laid her cheek against his arm while he explained their plans and the real reason they were headed to Ghana.

He was hers and he loved her. The thought kept appearing in her mind. Some sort of angel had definitely been on her side. Considering all that had happened in the few months she'd been home, she was lucky to be alive, let alone married and starting a family.

Leonard Kedansky faced life in prison. His sister would serve some time, but had taken a plea bargain. She wondered what would happen to the mother, Lorinda.

"No frowning. You'll wrinkle." Genie stood in front of them, her arms outstretched. "Come here, sister-in-law."

Charlie stepped out of Vaiden's grasp, laughed, and hugged her. She'd just moved back toward Vaiden when she thought she saw a familiar, but unexpected face.

She inhaled sharply, the light scent of the flowers suddenly sharp and pungent. What the hell was he doing here?

Vaiden bent low and followed her line of vision. "Who're you giving the evil eye? Oh, Griffin. Yeah, I asked him if he'd like to come. He did help you out in Goochland, I thought it was the least we could do as a thank you."

Charlie had an ache in her back like one attained from sudden fear or confrontation. She had to know how Griffin knew Lorinda Kedansky. It had been bugging her for weeks. The sight of that old lady slumped in Griffin's truck still made her shudder.

"Excuse me, Vaiden. I think I'll say hello." Charlie swallowed

Vaiden touched her cheek with the back of his hand. "Don't be long. My mother is waving a knife at me. I can only assume that means cake." He made a comedic worried face. "I hope that means cake." With a wink, he placed a firm kiss on her lips. "I love you."

Afraid to take her gaze from Griffin lest he melt into the crowd, Charlie winked at her husband and hurried to meet him.

She met him a few feet from the beverage table, sipping from a glass of what appeared to be milk. His great bushy beard had lost its uneven edges, and there were no baseball caps in sight.

She stopped in front of him and caught his attention. "So glad you could come, Griffin."

His voice, when he spoke, stayed low in tone and volume. "Figured you might wanna know...a few things." He gripped his glass in both hands, the thick, short fingers of his hands laced together around the stem. When he sipped, he curled his lips, presumably to avoid getting milk on his facial hair.

"Like how you know Ms. Kedansky?"

The bearded chin bobbed. "Don' know why they never got married. I always thought they were." He backed toward the foyer and she followed, drawn as if attached by a rope.

He drained the glass and squeezed it onto a small table between two vases of roses. “My wife. Her name was Winifred Kent.”

Names swam in Charlie’s thoughts, cramming together in various pairings. She recalled now the grave she’d seen at Griffin’s farm. The name *Winifred K. Rossiter* flashed in her mind. “So,”—she used a fingernail to scratch the back of her neck—“she was Elwin Kent’s...?”

“Cousin. They were born around the same time, and it was a big joke that their names were so similar.” He rubbed his chin beneath his beard with his knuckles. “I never found it much funny. We hain’t kept in touch with that part of the family. I reckon th’only reason Lorinda called me was she was out of options, what with both her children locked up.” He raised his head and met her eyes. “Family’s family, you know.”

As usual when she spoke with Griffin, her initial fear had dissipated as soon as he spoke. She could feel Vaiden’s eyes on her and checked over her shoulder. He lifted his eyebrows in question. She sent him a pleasant smile to stall him.

When she swiveled her head back to Griffin, he’d moved closer. He touched her stomach with the tips of his fingers, palm down. “Yer boy, he’s going to do amazing things. He’ll be so much boy that he’ll scare the devil out of you, but you keep him close.” His voice faded into a mere rasp. “And you keep him from Lorinda’s son. Some things you can’t change, but you’ve gotta try.”

Charlie’s veins went cold. “Lorinda’s son? You mean Leonard. He’s in jail, Griffin. He’s staying in jail.” She sounded like she was trying to convince herself. Gooseflesh covered her arms and she shivered in spite of her well-rooted bravery.

Griffin’s wild eyebrows lowered and he shrugged.

Vaiden's mother called for attention by dinging a glass with a spoon. Charlie peeked back and saw Margaret Vaiden waving her over from the cake table. Vaiden stood halfway between them, eying her expectantly.

Charlie knew she should excuse herself and go cut the cake, but she had to find out what Griffin had meant. If her son's life would be in danger, she had to know more. Even though she knew Leonard was in jail, Griffin's words had chilled her. Any mother would want to know all she could to protect her child.

Cold air assailed her ankles and she turned with a gasp. The front door clunked closed. She looked around the foyer. No Griffin. Her heart leaped up in a frenzy. He'd gone!

She rushed to the door and flung it open. The blast of wind caused her to shiver. The first flakes of an early snow had started to fall. She searched the front lawn and stairs, but couldn't spot him. His huge truck should have been easy to find in the sea of normal cars parked in front of the house.

Instead, the only sign of life was a gray-haired man in a suit bending down to pet a large black dog as it lumbered down the stairs.

The animal didn't linger near the man, but instead when it reached the bottom of the stairs, stopped and pawed at the ground.

Charlie's head tilted. That Chow face. The same dog that had been standing over Vaiden when he'd been hurt? The one who had led Vaiden to her more than once? That dog had been her shadow for months now.

The gentleman lifted a hand in greeting and squinted at her through the snowflakes. She felt she should know him. Of course, given her current attire, he would know she was the bride. He had the advantage.

Keeping an eye on the dog, she ticked through the faces of the relatives she knew. No, his face was a new one, except, maybe, for those lips.

Vaiden's sudden appearance at her side made her jump, then press closer to him against the cold.

He circled her waist with his arms. "What are you—Dad!" Vaiden moved past her and descended the stairs, embracing his father warmly. The snowfall thickened and the men headed toward the house.

The black dog ran a few yards away from the pair, then turned toward Charlie and whined. He lowered his head and barked low and quiet. Charlie's anxiety abated, and a feeling of peace and security settled over her. As the men blocked her view, she caught a flash of a tail. When she could again see the yard, the dog was gone. Like Griffin.

She shivered deep down to her bones.

Vaiden stomped to dislodge the snow from his shoes before entering the house. He gestured with both hands to his father. "I told you he always makes it home for Christmas. Charlie, this is my father. Dad, my wife, Charlotte Blair Vaiden."

Her eyes moistened and she held out her hand to Vaiden's father, still distracted by the disappearance of the dog. "Sir, pleased to meet you."

Vaiden's father had the same build and bearing as his sons. She had no time to assess his other features as she found herself enveloped in a giant embrace.

"Welcome to the family, Charlie." He held her tightly at arm's length and grinned. "About time one of my boys grew up and got himself married." He patted one of her shoulders and pointed with his other hand toward the sheet of small white flakes that filled the outside. "Was that your dog?"

Charlie shared a look of complicity with Vaiden. "No, sir."

She smiled warmly at her new father-in-law. “That dog, he’s a friend.”

The men flanked her just inside the door. Margaret Vaiden’s shriek of delight alerted her to the woman’s approach and she eased out of the way. She reached back to close the door while the long-separated couple reunited.

Something just at the edge of the doorjamb caught her eye and she stretched sideways to swoop the small object into her fingers.

Cold, hard, round, and black.

Charlie turned the stone in her hands. She didn’t need to look to know it was an Ica stone. More specifically, the one bearing the carving of a dog.

Vaiden crooked his arm for her and she stepped up to slide her fingers against his bicep. She slipped the stone into his pocket, earning a curious glance.

“What was that?”

Had Griffin become her protector by accident? She chose to believe a higher force was at work. Nothing else made sense. Not anymore.

She winked at Vaiden. She would explain it to him later. Right now they had a cake to cut. “Just a gift from our guardian angel.”

About the Author

Catherine Berlin grew up on a farm and has been writing stories and spinning tall tales from the time she could talk. She lives in Virginia with her wonderful husband, two fantastic children, and one very furry dog. In her spare time she teaches Spanish, French, and English, hoards chocolate, and makes googly eyes at her husband. She is also a wannabe athlete, and running is her weapon of choice.

To learn more about Catherine, visit www.CatherineBerlin.com, send her an email at CatherineBerlinAuthor@yahoo.com or join her Yahoo! group to participate in the fun with her and other readers at http://groups.yahoo.com/group/CatherineBerlinRomance.

Doing whatever it takes could get them both killed.

Living Lies

© 2008 Dawn Brown

Twelve years after her sister's disappearance, Haley Carling spends her days trying to hold what's left of her family together, running her late father's shop and caring for her alcoholic mother. Then her sister's remains are uncovered in the basement of their old home, and fingers start pointing. At the Carlings.

Dean Lawson, long the prime suspect in the Carling girl's disappearance, is sure he's got evidence proving who the killer is. He's determined to clear his name, and he won't let anything stand in his way. Not even his lingering attraction to Haley.

Haley is just as determined to protect her family from the former town bad boy's accusations. But now someone is stalking her, and Haley realizes Dean's the only one she can trust.

With a killer closing in, Dean wonders if he's made the biggest mistake of his life…a mistake that could cost Haley her life.

Warning: This title contains a mystery to keep you turning the pages late into the night.

Enjoy the following excerpt from Living Lies...

The Mountainview Motel was neither on a mountain nor did it offer a view of one, as the name implied. Little more than a row of shabby rooms slightly north of town, Haley was surprised the place managed to remain open.

As she drove into the lot, she spotted Dean's car parked in front of one of the rooms and pulled up next to it. What was she doing here, really? Hadn't she had enough drama for one day? Maybe, but she needed to know why he was back. Why now?

With a sigh she opened the door and stepped out into the cold. The walk running the length of the motel had been shoveled, exposing weathered wood planks. She crossed to his door and knocked loudly before she changed her mind.

After a moment, the door swung back and Dean filled the opening. He didn't look at all surprised to see her. Al had probably called to warn him after she'd left.

She could understand how she hadn't recognized him. The boyishness had left his face, making his features sharper, almost predatory and, if at all possible, more attractive. Even his body seemed harder and leaner than she remembered.

Her heart rate quickened, and something fluttered in her stomach. Could he really have killed Michelle?

Killer or not, she would have to say something soon. She couldn't just stand there staring like a twit all day.

"I didn't recognize you earlier," she said. Better than silence, but only marginally.

Dean leaned casually against the frame. "I figured."

"Erin recognized you." She should have stuck with silence.

"What do you want, Haley?" His voice was deep and quiet.

“Why are you here?”

He sighed and moved aside. “Do you want to come in?”

She hesitated. If she went inside that room, would anyone ever see her again? Allister was the only person who knew where she was and she didn’t have a whole lot of faith he’d come to her rescue if she needed him to.

“People know where I am,” she said at last.

Dean smirked, but said nothing as she stepped inside, closing the door behind her.

“Nice place you have here, Matthew Clarke,” she said, taking in the faded beige wallpaper and gold shag carpet. An ugly oil painting of a gnarly sea captain hung over the sagging double bed.

“I wanted to keep a low profile.”

“I thought you would have stayed with Al.”

“Have you seen Al’s apartment?” A faint smile touched his lips. “This place is a palace.”

He had a point. She had seen Al’s apartment once and had gone straight home and showered.

“Sit down,” he offered, gesturing to the only chair in the room. As she pulled it away from the desk, she noticed a thick envelope and file folder with bits of paper curling around the edge stacked neatly in the top corner. She would have loved to go through those pages. To see just what Dean studied on alone in a grubby motel room.

“So,” she said. “Why are you here?”

“Maybe I just wanted to pay my respects.” He sat on the corner of the bed, his eyes bright and his mouth still twisted in that slightly mocking smirk.

“By lurking in the parking lot?”

The grin vanished. “I wasn’t in the parking lot the whole

time. I watched the service from the door. When I saw you get up and start to leave I decided to go."

"You came back for the memorial?"

"Maybe." He shrugged.

"Or maybe you're worried there's something to link you to Michelle after all."

A tiny muscle twitched in his jaw. "Is that what you think?"

I don't know what to think, and you're not giving anything away. "I don't think you came back here just to watch Michelle's memorial from an open door. So why not tell me what you're really doing here?"

"What do you want me to say, Haley? That I did it? That I killed her?"

"Did you?"

"If I did, it wasn't too smart to come looking for me now, was it?" His voice was quiet, but there was an edge, jagged, like a serrated blade.

A tiny ember ignited within her. A slow fury growing hotter and brighter each time he spoke. "Are you threatening me?"

"No," he said on a sigh, suddenly sounding very tired. "No, I'm not."

"Why are you here?" she asked again.

"I'm not ready to tell anyone yet, but when I am, I'll tell you first."

"That's it? That's the best you can do?"

He nodded.

"Well, sorry, not good enough. Tell me why you're back. I'm not going anywhere until you talk."

"Suit yourself." He shrugged. "I was thinking about ordering dinner. Pizza or Chinese?"

"This isn't a joke, Dean. My sister is dead."

"I know. And I will tell you why I've come back, but not yet. I need to be sure of some things first."

"Fine. You have until tomorrow. If I don't get some answers before the end of the day, there isn't a person in this town who won't know you're here."

Haley stood and strode out the door, suppressing a smile at the sight of his stony stare.

As she marched to the wreck parked next to his car, Dean stood in the open doorway, half shocked, half irritated, shaking his head.

She'd threatened him.

It took her three tries to get her heap started, taking a little something away from her dramatic exit. But not much. As he closed the door, he could hardly believe it. Quiet little Haley, who used to watch him with those amazing eyes so long ago, had threatened him. And he didn't doubt for a second that she meant what she said. To think, he actually felt sorry for her for a second there.

He would have to get things done tonight. That was probably better anyway. The sooner he finished, the sooner he could get the hell out of this

LaVergne, TN USA
19 August 2009
155273LV00001B/28/P

9 781605 043081